The Ship of Fools

D0308366

Gregory Norminton

The Ship of Fools

SCEPTRE

First published in Great Britain in 2001 by Hodder and Stoughton
A division of Hodder Headline

A Sceptre Paperback

3 5 7 9 10 8 6 4 2

A CIP catalogue record for this title
is available from the British Library.

ISBN 0 340 82102 7

Typeset by Hewer Text Ltd, Edinburgh
Printed and bound in Great Britain by
Mackays of Chatham plc, Chatham, Kent

Hodder and Stoughton
A division of Hodder Headline
338 Euston Road
London NW1 3BH

To my parents

In that posture, he, after God, saved the said Ark from peril, for with his legs he gave it the brangle, and with his foot turned it whither he pleased, as a ship answereth her rudder . . . Have you understood all this well? Drink then one good draught without water; for if you don't believe it, neither do I.

Rabelais, *Pantagruel*

Contents

General Prologue   1

The Swimmer's Tale   11

The Drinking Woman's Tale   29

The Nun's Tale   105

The Penitent Drunkard's Tale   119

The Fool's Tale   206

The Monk's Tale   219

The Choristers' Tale   247

The Sleeping Drunkard's Tale   263

The Glutton's Tale   270

Epilogue   271

General Prologue

Laden like a bowl of cherries, the ship of fools sits on the lawn of the sea. Although a breeze frets the ship's banner, the sea is green and calm as a garden. The ship is rather a boat, is truly neither, for the mast has yet to renounce its life as a tree. Its lush crest is home to a curious lookout (curious lookout because an owl; curious owl because it possesses both mouth and beak). Much else is awry with that vessel: its rudder is a ladle, a chain of command is lacking and the occupants are ill suited to maritime life. They are (in disorder) three choristers, an immodest bather, a drunkard vomiting, a drunkard snoring, a glutton, a fool, a monk, a woman drinking and a nun, in voice, strumming a lute. Items: flagons of ale or wine, a glass, a begging-bowl, a barrel of booze, a knife, a roast chicken, a dead fish, a ball of dough and a bowl of (you guessed it) cherries. Betokening the sin of lust, or the lust for sin – the two are almost interchangeable.

How long has this motley crew been assembled? All the usual pointers to Time are lacking. The seasons do not change. It is perpetually midday, if we take the light as an indicator. Beyond the clement weather, there is no Weather.

This stasis, this sempiternal sameness, is it not tremendously *dull*? Where do they turn for distraction? What are they doing there?

Sitting, standing, lying, crouching, straining on tiptoe, floating in the water.

Yes, obviously. But what are they *doing* there?

Singing. Disharmoniously. The Choristers belt out a drinking song (something to do with stags, wives and taxidermy), the Monk observes the Hours Canonical (old habits die hard) and the Nun sings the Eucharist. Her voice, which is really rather pleasing, is lost in the cacophony, drowned out by the Monk's reedy dirge and the seal-honking of the Choristers. No matter. These stationary travellers, pilgrims without a destination, are simply passing the time. At least, they are filling the moments. That is, they are trying to. If one focuses on the present, there are pleasures – bibulous, conversational – to be had.

At first sight, it is not a picture of unhappiness.

On the surface, frankly, it looks like quite a party.

Let us begin with the least forthcoming passenger.

The SLEEPING DRUNKARD lies in Elysium. Within the murky scriptorium of his brain the chapters of a different book – a book of dreams – are writing themselves. What flaming tigers does he hunt in those benighted forests? What country, friends, is this, where the fields and spires are Home, and the women find him so very appealing? Or does he dream himself as he really is: crumpled in the bow, gripping a flagon, about to be rudely woken?

Now imagine yourself shaken from sleep. Your gummy eyes open on a bulbous washerwoman's face. Place your nose in proximity to a stranger's armpit: such is the effluvium of the DRINKING WOMAN's breath. Mercilessly she demands the Sleeper's attention, for boozing is no fun without witnesses.

'Dear God in Heaven,' the Sleeper moans, 'send your blessed angels to plug my nose.'

But the Drinking Woman cannot care less for the Almighty. Her devotional instincts are pagan. She is Dionysiac to the nobly rotted core.

'How can I,' she drawls, 'sing praises of some god I've never met? It's only natural I love what I know.'

What, indeed, can compare with the opiate, Love? Once experienced, it lingers for ever in the bloodstream. The fierce pleasures to be had in a man's arms! Her body remembers. But Time, the old killjoy, has worn the Drinking Woman down to unsought chastity. She staggers, fat limbed and thick headed, the ruin of some gaudy bacchanal. The flush of youth has gone from those cheeks; in its place, the veiny erubescence of a thousand libations. She paws the Sleeper's shoulder and lifts her flagon in a toast. 'Good health, my dopey!' And empties the vessel in one defiant swig.

The CHORISTERS, for all their noise, have little to define them. They could be labourers, landlords, litigants;

butchers, brewers; pages or executioners. This is not to say that they are essentially the *same* – simply that, on the surface, there is little to tell them apart. Not one, if pushed to it, could recall a time when he was not accompanied by the others. Which is not to suggest that there exists between them a selfless common-wealth. If they were (for the sake of illustration) a three-headed monster, each head would fight for food that was destined for one and the same stomach. Like murderous siblings, each secretly longs to be rid of the others; yet any violence between them would be like severing one's own limbs. This keeps them from falling to bloody action.

Of the GLUTTON nothing can be observed beyond his preoccupation with stuffing his belly. He is tantalised by a roast chicken which, for some reason, is strapped to the leafy spray of the mast. How it glistens and gleams! By standing on the lower branches he can reach it easily with his carving knife. And yet, at every attempt to nick a sliver of its flesh, the bird's rectum shrieks the foulest invective. The blade trembles and the Glutton lowers his knife; for a carcass that knows such dirty words can hardly be appetising.

Indifferent to his neighbour's hunger, a jester crouches in the rigging. A slight, scrawny figure, this licensed FOOL sips from a cup and turns his back on the others. The expression on his face is one of almost serene nonchalance; horses and donkeys nodding into their troughs look no more perplexed by the world than does our tassle-arsed friend. We should note, in his left hand, a moronic sceptre – a baton topped with a mask. It might almost be a mirror, though an unflattering one. For unlike the Fool's face, which it mocks, the mask grins with obdurate mischief.

What does one say of a man who *professes* folly? Who wears his foolishness on his skin and keeps his wisdom to himself? Is the mask's hilarity a clue to his concealed nature? Or should we trust the surface, and accept that only a man with ass's ears can enjoy self-possession? The Fool is a sage, his mask a fairground mirror held up to Nature.

At the Fool's feet kneels the PENITENT DRUNKARD. He is not a popular man. Vomiting, after all, inspires unwanted empathy; we shun its gagging contagion. And the Penitent Drunkard is desperately unwell. His guts are in turmoil; they must be worming and heaving inside him, making him wheeze and retch overboard. It cannot be sea sickness, for reasons already given. Nor travel sickness, since the boat is going nowhere. It must be the drink. Yes, that's it: the Penitent Drunkard has reached midnight in alcohol's Faustian bargain. Even his hair is sick, matted and oily. Gripping the rigging with white knuckles he manages, from somewhere, to rustle up another helping.

Whatever it is that's poisoning him, it remains in need of purging.

The NUN's song offers welcome distraction from the Drunkard's puking. Her bright blue vibrato seems too sensuous for plainsong. And where did she learn to play the lute? Her fingers improvise intricate variations, embellishments which coil through her song like the scrolling eglantine in a Book of Hours.

The Nun is untroubled by the Choristers' caterwauling. She knows that God's Ear is always open, dividing the song from the strain. Perhaps it is for God's favour that she, in speech, puts on displays of fervour? Years of mortification have dulled her flesh; yes, yes. She is a paragon of virtue. No one in need of redemption will be turned from her hypothetical door. Her figure-of-speech charity knows no bounds. Although she prays for the carnal laity, she does not hold out much hope for its salvation.

Our second votarist, the MONK, is a man of great learning. The author of thirteen theological tracts is, by his own admission, a cerebral Atlas, sustaining the Heavens by mental heft. Although a keen neologist, he also serves as sanctuary for obscure and arcane words. Like an academic St Francis, he protects frail and endangered language, giving glottal Greekisms a place of safety in his mind. Astronomer, chemist, fabulist and physician, no School of Thought is closed to him. His mind is antiheliotropic, straining not for the sunlight but for the shadowy recesses of understanding. Currently he is preoccupied with a desire to enclose the human condition within mathematical formulae.

Already he has found the Scatological Parabola. (As one grows from wet-bed to bed-pot, the parabola reaches its apogee, only to fall off in clumsy, accident-prone old age.) Other graphs include a Rhombus of Appetite, Octahedrons of Doubt and Faith, and an Acute Ellipse of Speech. His Sexual Trapezoid remains purely theoretical.

Perhaps the Monk might approve of the last actor in this strange eventless Comedy? The SWIMMER is an avowed foe to material vanity. Having renounced worldly ways, he occupies himself with Speculation.

'All the world clings to *matter*,' he believes. 'Whereas I am not too proud to go naked as a worm. The measure of a man lies not in the cut of his cloth.'

Pleased with his bold assertions, the Swimmer lacks the authority of a thousand books to substantiate them; yet to hear him soliloquise on any subject is, he believes, an almost physical pleasure.

The Swimmer holds that nothing is worse than surrender to the Two Universal Laws – Gravity and Boredom. (Gravity is a surfeit of fear and melancholy; Boredom is the centrifugal force of the cosmos.) Delighted to encounter so many strangers in one bark, he attempts again and again to attract their attention. How his lungs burn, how his heart aches to share his wisdom with them. Out of politeness he will not interrupt their singing. He bides his time, knowing that all things come to silence.

As indeed they do. Its noise subsiding, the crew sinks

back to inaction. There is no sound but the flapping of the banner above their heads. Picking his moment like a berry in brambles, the Swimmer coughs into his fist. And the ragbag crew, leaning over the side, sees the fellow for the first time . . .

The Swimmer's Prologue

'Ladies and gentlemen. I cling to your boat not as a parasite but keen to be of service. (Might you toss me a few of those juicy-looking cherries? Much obliged.)'

The crew watches this naked apparition. He pops cherries into his mouth with hollow intakes of air, munches the flesh secretly, then pulls out the beheaded stem. The Swimmer tongues the naked pips through his lips: plup – plip – plop, they say as they fall into the water. The Swimmer knows how to toy with an audience.

'Your singing has stopped,' he says finally. 'But the fight continues.'

Monk. What fight is that?

Swimmer. Against the enemy.

Nun. Satan?

Swimmer. Boredom. We do not, after all, appear to be going anywhere fast.

This sort of plain speaking meets with black looks. The Swimmer hastens on. 'All my life I've loved stories,' he says. 'Not just the unravelling of a plot, or the kiss of a happy ending. It is the telling itself, the drive and rhythms, that sustains my attention.'

This is not winning the Swimmer friends. His audience finds much of interest in the dregs of its goblets.

Swimmer (*shouts*). Knights and damsels! Fateful quests for illusive Grails!

Fool. Gezundheit.

Swimmer. But I grew tired of the high Romances. Enough of chivalry – how does it square with *your* experience of the gentry?

The Swimmer, enjoying a little attention, pursues his theme. 'Don't you fancy a change from worn-out fancies and devices?'

Choristers. Go on, then, mate – you do better.

(*Fool*. It's hard to invent outside your time.)

Swimmer. By all means. If I might have a sip of ale, I accept the challenge.

There is, on board, no great enthusiasm to part with drink. But fear of silence impels a cup into the Swimmer's hand. When he has drained it, he clears his throat and begins.

The Swimmer's Tale

Heaven's eye was at its blazing height when the boat cast off for Lapo. The island, foreshortened by the glare, sat transfixed on the water, her tall cypresses barely cooling the stultified cattle. Dazzled by the sun, which the lake reflected in a million mirrors, three young men pulled their shirts over their heads, each to his own shade.

Hot-skulled, they rowed in silence.

Cesare wondered, as his oar-locks clicked, if they were not alone on the surface of Creation. For there was no activity on either shore. Earth's crowded towns, its towers and tongues and castles, had dissolved, not into darkness but in blinding light. Baldassare, for his part, imagined himself underwater, floating coolly in the kelp and looking up, as fish must, at a sun of travelling coils. Only Alfonso concerned himself with their progress, cricking his neck in search of a place to land.

It was Alfonso who had endorsed Baldassare's proposal of an outing, which Cesare had planted in Baldassare's brain, after a suggestion from Alfonso.

'It will have to be on Sunday,' Alfonso had advised. 'And noon the hour, when our mentors will be napping.' For the waters they would have to cross were forbidden to them, maligned by rumours of fearful currents.

'Clearly balls,' said Cesare. 'That's just a story they tell to stop us having fun.'

He was right in one respect: apprentices are not taken on to enjoy themselves. Nor did they. For Cesare, like his friends Alfonso and Baldassare, shouldered the burden of undelivered promise. It pursued him like an odour, obtrusive with men and women alike. Unhappily trammelled, as he saw it, by duties not of his choosing, he dreamed of a life more glorious than shaving old men or cutting for kidney stones.

'I think I'll be a pirate,' he would blurt, his speech slurred on adulterated wine. 'Or cross the ocean as a conquistador. I'll discover the Dorado and come back and buy the whole village.' This was a gentle fantasy: three more glasses and the Pope would be his footstool. 'You mark my words. Cesare will see much of the world, and the world will see much of Cesare.'

Together the friends had plotted their adventure. Standing on the shore at the foot of the village, they had pined for their *terra nova*: Lapo, the cypress isle, where Venus's temple stood in ancient times. Cesare had licked his lips as though at a land to conquer. Alfonso praised, as best he could, the Arcadian prospect. Baldassare claimed to catch the fragrances that wafted across the lake.

For Baldassare was a sensualist. He had encountered the term in his service as eyes to a blind scholar. 'Sensualist,' the cleric explained, his face as sour as a lemon-sucker's, 'a man that lives by, or for, the senses. With emphasis on the tongue, lips, fingertips and – . Beginning with a taste for cake, or over-frequent bathing, the sensualist immures himself in the body. Agape, the sacred love for one's fellows, yields to Eros and honeyed ruination.'

Baldassare had needed no convincing. In between his reading duties, he would stroke a velvet hem, or plunge his nose into the delicate gills of mushrooms. At supper, alone in his room, Baldassare sucked his food into savorous pap, allowing it lasciviously to dissolve in his mouth. Of other senses that he engaged, one way or another, he never spoke, neither to Alfonso nor to unflappable Cesare.

Last in the boat – that is, farthest from the coveted shore – sat Alfonso. Moodily he suffered Baldassare's knees in his back as he trawled his head for words to fit the scene. You guessed it: Alfonso was a poet. '*Poeta*', he had declared himself to his friends, though Cesare, chewing salami, had heard 'potter' and secretly deplored the lack of ambition. Wanting artistic patronage, Alfonso served time as a schoolmaster, dulling by rote the village children. Daily chores exhausted him. He read attentively but his exemplars could agree on nothing. He copied Art at Nature's expense; he copied Nature without much Art. For the lack of an earthly or Heavenly muse, the mind-sprouted laurels wilted on his brow.

So now the apprentices, having rustled a boat in the midday heat, were set upon their story. Not a sound fluttered from rooftop or campanile. The land simmered like a liquid on the boil. Buzzards circled, as though afraid to touch the scalding earth.

'Well, it's true,' Cesare exclaimed suddenly. 'There really *are* strong currents in the lake.'

Shaken from cloudy preoccupation, Alfonso became aware of the claim of the oars on his arms, of the swell against the boat, which he felt, through the wood, in the soles of his feet. The shore of Lapo, its yellow sands chalky in the glare, seemed far off. It was as if their boat were magnetised, with the mainland the amorous pole, for their efforts left them merely stationary.

'Put your backs into it, lads. We're snagged for a bit. Perhaps three yards and we'll be clear.'

No sooner had Cesare spoken, and the friends redoubled their efforts, than the current, an aqueous zephyr, changed direction. Now it assisted them in their progress, and each boy exulted at their combined potency.

It was Cesare who, flushed with his command, spoke first. He could contain his secret no longer:

Somnium Cesari

'Alfonso. Baldassare. We've shared everything, haven't we, since our scab-picking days? Trinkets. Daydreams. Measles. We cannot lie to each other, and withholding our adventures is just a softer kind of lying. So you should know: I've fallen in love.

'She woke me where I lay sleeping, out of the setting sun,

*under the cork oak in Guido's field. I felt her cool lips touch
mine, and her breath enter my body. I opened my eyes on hers,
that were fawn-brown like a wild thing's and intent.*

'Her name was Fiammeta. Her parents must have been seers
to christen her so aptly. For her hair was red like autumn fern
that the low sun catches. It sat in a shock of flame on her head,
which haloed with the sunset when she kissed me.

'Leading me through Guido's field, she took me to her home.
It was a comfortable furnished house, with wooden toys in the
garden. (She did not take me inside. Through an open window I
glimpsed a bed where Fiammeta's three young brothers slept.)
We came to a bower, where we sat, secluded by a cypress hedge
from prying neighbours. As the sun took its eye off us, the air
chilled. She rested her brow against my neck and I could feel my
pulse on the bone of her skull.

'Should I choose her, she said after thrilling silence, she would
be the traveller's perfect consort – the fixed point to my roving
compass, the ground to which I would return, bloodied from
my conquests. What more did an explorer need, she asked, than
a hearth to return to after long labours? Fiammeta would be my
private world, the obverse to my public self.

'Oh, my friends, she was full figured and fertile. I kissed her
between her breasts; I put my hand on a child-bearing belly and
felt the power in her womb, swelling under my licensed touch.
We parted on my promise to meet her again – when I'll anchor
in the bay of her thighs . . .'*

Still rowing, the listeners sweated. They peeped at the
flashing water from beneath their shirt-veils. They
listened to the plunk of their blades in the water. Cesare
dared not puncture the silence, which every second
became more terrible to him. How would Baldassare
respond to his new allegiance? Or Alfonso critique his

attempt at high oration? Against expectations, the young poet laughed:

Somnium Alfonsis

'You tell us, Cesare, you've met the lady of your dreams. Well, so have I. Your paramour kissed you before you spied her? So did mine. And yet, where yours is fierily buxom, my love is as pure as fresh-fallen snow. No list of Good Women could be complete without her. Fair Thisbe, spurned Dido – er, the Roman one that got raped – are templates, of journeyman craft, to my beloved. Dante had his Beatrice, youngest of Love's angels. So in her I've found my Muse, the spring and subject of my canzone.

'It was dusk, sundown, eventide, after a day hot like today. I had fallen asleep, I confess, reading the Vita nuova in my empty classroom. Fatigued by teaching, I did not hear her enter. When with her lips and sweet breath she woke me, my vital spirit trembled. Her mouth was coral red, her hair fell in golden curls from her headdress, and the blush on her cheeks faded to faintness along her neck.

'Taking my hand in hers – the nails were as nacre and her teeth as pearls – my Lady led me from the classroom. As we travelled through streets where dogs still panted, I admired her gown, its fur-lined sleeves, and the lavish layering of her headdress. She was as light on the ground as blown gold leaf.

'I barely recollect the route to her villa. Tall cypresses, trimmed into heraldic shapes, signalled our arrival. Whereupon she led me, through a maze of box, into a formal garden. At its centre a marble table stood, draped in laburnum. Arranged upon its surface sat silver plate and a Venetian mirror. There were oranges and gaudy parrot feathers, and a statue of three gilded youths frozen in leave-taking.

'*We sat, I tell you, in that fragrant bower, our hands inter-twined, and she told me of my future life, how in exchange for a poet's dedication she would yield up her riches. She adored me as some mortals are adored by the gods. On her flawless breast I fixed a necklace of pearls. And Love was Mistress of my heart . . .*'

Now Cesare, a little of his thunder stolen, congratulated Alfonso on his happiness. Reaching past Baldassare, he slapped Alfonso too vigorously on the back. Alfonso, in riposte, flicked water at Cesare, striking Baldassare full in the face and jogging the boat ninety degrees off course.

They had to fight to manoeuvre against the change-able current.

'What's her name, your amorata?' Cesare asked in a high-pitched voice.

Alfonso sucked on the question, his head in the heat beginning to throb. He had forgotten to ask.

Baldassare, all this while, had held his tongue. It was impossible for Alfonso – with his back to him – or for Cesare – to whom his back was turned – to read the anguish on Baldassare's face. When he spoke, then, Alfonso and Cesare paid only vague attention. Initially, at least:

Somnium Baldassaris

'*I was in the dark. I was walking at night in a forest of yews. I could not see through the dry twist of branches that closed overhead, forming a tunnel. My fingertips told me nothing.*

My nose and ears were deserts. My eyes clung to a narrow light in the distance. I realised that the light was growing – that's how I knew I was walking, though I couldn't feel my legs – because the forest was falling behind me, its great weight of silence gathering.

'Then, with my senses still sleeping, I was standing in the cool of the dawn. In a clearing of dry rock, I met her. She sat beneath a juniper tree. She wore a white gown and headdress. In her lap lay three effigies, male senseless dolls, each with a tuft of hair fastened to its crown. I could not describe her to you – only that her face had awaited me since my birth, that I saw it for the first time and had known it always.

'She climbed a stair that grew from the rock, and I understood that I was to follow. Then she spoke to me without words, as sometimes happens in dreams. I asked her name. She replied, since I placed store by such things, that I might call her Ombretta. In a parched Garden she wore white and blue, and her face was shaded by a dark cypress. The dry earth at my feet welled up and sprang water. Flowers uncurled and leapt: gentians, forget-me-nots, yellow-tongued irises. As the ground came to life my innards thawed. It was like breathlessness, a gaping hole in the heart. What is this feeling of desolation that accompanies love? At the very instant of its birth we feel its death in the offing. I prayed that she might prove eternal, my bella donna. That I might walk from work one day and find her incarnate, plucked palpable from the shadows.

'She stood, with her fingers about the pole at the base of a second stair. I could not raise my head to follow. I was dumb and deaf. But her kiss brought my senses back to life. I heard the chorus of morning birds and saw bright Spring colours. I was whole at last – inspired – and awoke in the shout of the day.'

'You mustn't mock me,' said Baldassare immediately. 'Dreams *can* foretell, you've only to read Scripture to see it. All right, so your women are flesh and blood. But there was *weight* to my vision, I tell you. So, Cesare (I can feel your eyes on my neck), allow me my dream. And you, Alfonso, with your living muse, don't hate my silly ramblings.'

In fact, neither Alfonso nor Cesare seemed inclined to pass comment. Baldassare felt the loading of Cesare's silence, he saw the muscles strain in Alfonso's shoulders. Licking his lips, Baldassare found them chapped and bubbled by the sun. 'I've a further admission,' he said. 'When I proposed this outing to Lapo as a protest against our condition, my true motives lay elsewhere.' The words stuck like fishbones in his gullet. 'Ombretta told me to come to Lapo. That she would await me in the ruins of the temple. Don't you see, I must be *sure*. With all that's in play, how could I not take the chance?' Baldassare stopped to squeeze a ball of tension down his throat. 'But that omission, on my part, is not the worst of it. Heeding talk of these currents you dismissed, Cesare, I guessed I would not be strong enough to make the crossing *alone*. I needed our *combined* strength to reach my goal, and would have dropped your company as soon as we arrived.'

Nothing could have prepared Baldassare for the effect of his confession. Cesare threw down his oars and jumped to his feet in foul-mouthed protestation. Alfonso turned on his seat in remonstration. How could Baldassare have done such a thing? Abused their love? And in such fashion? Devil! Fraudster! *Traditore*!

Baldassare, shocked by his friends' outrage, sheltered his head beneath his arms, as though for protection against coming blows. His oars, unmanned, slipped from their locks into the water – closely followed by the oars of his accusers.

Surely, I see you thinking, this scene is out of proportion to the offence? Baldassare's sin is venial, at worst. Ah, but the fury of Alfonso and Cesare is less one of righteousness slighted than of mendacity exposed. Alfonso will never confess to the same intentions as Baldassare. Nor will Cesare, whose Fiammeta inflamed him beyond reason. So Baldassare, blushing with shame beneath his shirt, need not have loathed himself so mercilessly. His indignant friends were likewise guilty, defending themselves, by assault, from the shame of their own impenitence.

'You risked all our lives for a *dream*?' Cesare shrieked, wading deeper into the dark waters of his pretence. 'Our friendship chucked away for an imaginary bint?'

Alfonso, without filtering the command through his conscious mind, found himself extending his right arm above Baldassare's head into the soft of Cesare's belly. Cesare sat down, winded; a sheet of water dragged, with his momentum, into the boat. Alfonso, astounded at his own violence, braced himself for a counter-strike. Baldassare emerged from his elbow carapace, baffled by the hiatus.

'What did you do *that* for?' wheezed Cesare.

Alfonso, finding in himself no answer, evasively

reached for his oars. Baldassare did likewise. Alfonso saw the twitching in Baldassare's cheek. Baldassare turned and saw himself reflected in Alfonso's panic. He looked at his oars in the blinking water – not just his own, which were painted blue on the blades, but also the red-bladed oars of Cesare and the silver-striped oars of Alfonso.

The boat lurched and began to spin. 'I'll probably spit blood tonight,' said Cesare, bent over his pain. Then he too saw his oar-locks empty . . .

Terror sprang through them like flight in a flock of birds. Thoughtlessly they stood up, stumbled, sat down again. The boat was in the grip of an implacable will. It shook them like a spinning-top, heaving their hearts into their mouths, before revealing itself to them in all its awful splendour. 'A whirlpool!' Cesare cried, and he dived into the bow to use his hands as paddles. Alfonso did likewise at the stern, undoing all Cesare's efforts. Baldassare, clasping his trembling hands in prayer, saw himself for an instant from the sun's vantage: a tiny speck in the hot landscape, an atom of turmoil in the still expanse.

'God help us! We're sinking!'

The fragile boat creaked and spluttered, gorging itself on water. Cesare abandoned paddling and took up bailing instead. Baldassare cried to the mainland for help. Alfonso, his head spinning with the movement and the sun, vomited into the water, and watched the green spiral expand around them.

For several minutes the boat agonised. A mainlander

– had there been one attending – would have heard it give up the ghost: a crack, from that distance, like a snapped pistachio nut. This imagined witness would then have seen the frightened crew lurch into the water and struggle briefly, as flies in a pond.

Alfonso splashed first, Baldassare following, and Cesare bringing up the rear. Though he guessed he was probably about to die, Baldassare could only think, as he fell, that their scorched bodies would make the water hiss on impact, like horseshoes plunged glowing into the bucket.

After some thrashing and much quenching of thirst, the three boys gulped and sank. Not one of them could swim.

They say that a man will surface three times before drowning, and that on the third gasp the entirety of his life flashes in dumb-show through his mind. It follows from this that an old man, full of years that must cede space to water, takes considerably longer than infants – whose store of memories is almost empty – to sink. Cesare, Baldassare and Alfonso, though no longer children, had few recollections to keep them afloat. Each fastened to a vision of his lady: Alfonso as she appeared in his sleep, Baldassare to Ombretta, and Cesare to his Fiammeta. Alfonso recognised, as his eyes opened on torrents, the depth of his self-deception: Baldassare's confession had so menaced his illusion that he had turned brutal against it. Glimpsing Cesare in the gyre, Alfonso wondered whether he had kept the same secret.

Cesare, upside down, sought Alfonso and pondered the same question.

This was on their second descent. As a man the boys surfaced a third time. Kicking and struggling, they reached for air as at a falling rope. Between the planes of sky, sand and lake, in the seconds before the water claimed them, they saw the Lady. Her lips were red, her hair was gold. Her vestal gown, of antique form, was white, and white too, almost as pale as her garment, was her face. In her arms she rocked three dolls, which she cast into the lake.

The boys went abruptly under. Each one felt like a pot on a wheel, stretched too far and thin. Distending, he collapsed upon himself, as though a powerful hand pushed him into the pit of his own stomach. Somehow Baldassare's left hand found Alfonso's right leg; Alfonso with his right hand found Cesare's left; with his other hand Cesare held the right hand of Baldassare. So they spun – linked in a chain, either of help or hindrance – until the too-bright world – with its implacable star – turned black.

They were washed up as flotsam on a sandy bank, in the tangled roots of a parasol pine. Prodding themselves, they felt for their heartbeats.

'Alfonso,' croaked Cesare, 'Baldassare, are you all right?'

The others blinked and nodded.

'Some benevolent current,' said Baldassare.

'Must have caught us,' said Alfonso, 'and washed us on the—'

They cast about for their bearings. Propped on their elbows, with their heads cleaned out, they looked at the distant prospect of Lapo.

The sun sank below the tired hills, promising respite. Swallows flew, flung like seed across the lake. After a wordless hour the boys heard, floating through the shadows, the angelus bell, and arose to join their masters.

Many years later these events seem quite unreal to Alfonso. Successful merchants shun the fantastical: hard facts are their currency. So Alfonso's recollections of an erotic dream, of mutual deception and near-drowning were merely the effusions of a sun-stricken brain. Sitting in the handsome courtyard of his seaside villa, a stone's throw from rooms replete with worldly goods, he gazes back on his former self with tender contempt. Now, for poetry, he looks no farther than the irregular line endings of an accounts ledger. It had not, after all, made him happy. The life of study that the craft would have demanded of him would, in the end, have killed the very thing he thought he'd sought to celebrate. Alfonso the poet would have dried up, writing out of an empty self, as the body in hunger feeds off its reserves. Instead, with his submissive wife and his silver, he has found his way successfully to a life without vocation.

Baldassare, over time, has turned godly. In a monastery near Verona he applies himself to prayer, lowering his nose into a psalter and digesting its eternal nutriments. Unlike Alfonso, he does not dismiss the Lapo business. On the contrary, upon its foundations he has built his life of Observance. To atone for his betrayal – of which he believes himself uniquely guilty – Baldassare mortifies, with a lice-crawling hairshirt, the body that had almost lost him. Many times a day he sings '*Salva nos stella maris*' and kisses the Virgin's alabaster toes. Sometimes, in his sleep, the White Lady is a temptress casting his soul on seething waters. At other times she is the symbol of beneficent love, receiving his tremulous spirit amid the weeping rocks. Though never less than strenuously honest, Baldassare will not share these dreams with his brother confessor. He cradles them to himself, as uniquely his own as his body's odours.

Finally Cesare – long since dispensed with as bluff confidant – leads no great expeditions. New routes to the spices he leaves to less settled and hungrier men. For Cesare was chastened by his adventure, acquiring from it a sound distrust of boats. Now he rarely leaves his barber-surgeon's shop, where his three sons are in training one day to succeed him. Cesare's youthful escapade – though stretched, over the years, into a yarn for lathered customers – taught him to settle for his lot. Dreamed Fiammeta's promise of domestic bliss, realised in the plump figure of a gap-toothed housewife, ensures him hot dinners and darned stockings. Quiet and comfort, sharpened by the apprehension of travel, have left Cesare a modest patriarch.

All three friends (though each no longer knows of the others' whereabouts) have come in time to their senses.

Are they happy?

They are still alive: the question does not apply.

Explicit liber adolescens

Having finished, the Swimmer is only just beginning. The tale was a prologue to his extrapolations.

Swimmer. Now I shall explain to you the meaning of it all . . .

But he gets no farther. The Fool swings down from the rigging and fairly lobs his cup at the fellow. 'What a great idea,' he cries, 'to entertain us while we wait.'

The Swimmer parts his lips to acknowledge the compliment.

Fool. You must be parched after all that talking. Have a drink on me.

Swimmer. But I should like to continue—

Fool. ANYONE ELSE GOT A STORY? A ballad perhaps? Old wives' tales?

The Fool is relieved to hear the Drinking Woman rise. 'Old wife yourself,' she says, 'tinkle-toes.'

Swimmer. Wait – stop – puh!

Drinking Woman. I've got something. It's not so restrained as clever-clogs here but a deal more fun.

Swimmer. Just a moment, I've not finished.

Choristers (*to Drinking Woman*). Oh come quickly yes let's have it!

With improbable enthusiasm the crew surrounds the

Drinking Woman, presenting the Swimmer with a view of backsides.

'It's a story I learned years ago,' the Drinking Woman says, 'when I was a child. And then later, in more detail, when I got the curse. Both versions came from our village midwife, Mistress Fibula, who had a gob crowded, if you see what I mean, with gossip and legends. Of course, I have no learning. Fancy turns and phrases are beyond my ken, though I had a scholar once and maybe some of his talk rubbed off on me. Still – to the best of my knowledge – you'll get the low-down as Mistress Fibula gave it. I shall leave out none of her colouring, nor those incidents that convince me of the truth of the story.

'But listen to me: what a *preface*. Without more bull, let me begin.'

The Drinking Woman's Tale

The Grand & Inestimable Deeds & Talents of *Belcula*, Milkmaid, with her unmanned companion *Dutchcap*, formerly composed by *Mistress Fibula*, & Here Recounted from Memory

BOOK ONE

Of Belcula's birth

Atop a haywain one morning, Hildegard von Spewer, maddened by sap and cuckoos, raises her arse to greet the sun; whose celestial fire is eclipsed by Martin the farmboy. Finding herself knocked up out of wedlock, desperate Hildegard (only daughter of Oswolt von Spewer, merchant) takes herbs in hope of miscarriage. Cramps, explosive bowels and gruesome piss follow, the poisons putting off new advances from Martin but failing to penetrate Hildegard's womb. Only the girl's astounding fatness allows her to hide, within its folds, the swelling mark of her shame.

Months pass until, one winter's night, Hildegard delivers herself of a girl; this not in childbed but in a ditch. Panting and torn, Hildegard lumbers bow legged from the scene, bracing herself for the sound of mewling. Down in the ice a heart the size of a crab-apple shudders and thuds. For want of a finger, tiny hands grip an umbilical shred. Suddenly, lustily, the baby twitches: gunk flobs from her lungs, she coughs mucus and starts to bawl. *Weeg weeg!* It's enough to make one's blood curdle. *Waak waak!* In the village of Varenburg, the birth-shrieks fill with apprehension the sleeping farmers, tailors, tinkers, nailers, potters, beggars, scrubbers, thieves. The very Oswolt von Spewer, moaning into his taffeta nightcap, fights a dream, deep within the coffers of his soul, that the first note of his tragedy has sounded.

Of Belcula's infancy, & the manner of her salvation

What hope, you may ask, has a newborn in an icy ditch? By rights the girl should freeze to death, passing into that night where, priests say, floats for ever the unbaptised spirit. Only God, ever vigilant for His strangest works, chooses this moment – when other beasts of the forest nuzzle and ruffle against the chill – for a boar-sow in search of chestnuts to stumble upon the baby and mistake her yexing for a piglet's squeal. The great beast hunkers gently down and takes the infant in its fur. The baby, finding a teat already peeping milk, hugs it tight. And so it is that, clinging to the bristles, she is carried to her first home; where she learns to walk like her siblings on all fours, to snuffle for mushrooms with her snout and feel no shame in her nakedness.

If you wonder at this, think how History has similar

instances to offer; and since Mankind has dominion over the animals, it seems only fair that on occasion the law be reversed – as on days of Misrule, when the dumbest dolt can play the king. Not that our girl is without qualities; for in agility she surpasses her porcine peers, and can throw her turds wheresoever she pleases. In bodily strength (though no match for a boar) she surpasses the human norm, being a very Hercules of the 'Weaker Sex'.

But of these qualities, and the stead in which they will stand her, more later. Let us move swiftly (skipping nine months) to a day's hunting. In years of peace, the Baron Enguerrand de Oorlogspad likes to exercise his mount for more profitable and warlike times. It is his livery – crimson with gold brocade – that adorns the flanks of his horses. Those are his servants that beat the brushwood in hope of his munificence.

On this particular outing, the boar-sow with her runt is resting in bracken when she first gets wind of the hounds. The forest fills with the bugle's clarion, and the boar-child, fearful at her nurse's fear, hides behind those great grey flanks. Spurred by the flairing pack, horses and riders approach. The boar-sow cannot shrink, nor mask her smell. Shrill of horns and crying of hounds madden her. When beaters come too close to her young, she breaks from cover. There are shouts from the men, *Hi! Hi! Hei!*, and dismay in the hooves of their horses. Hounds, seeking the wild boar's throat, are shaken off like burrs. Archers load and loose their bows. Twenty-nine arrows hail before one sticks.

Snagged in the bowels, the sow feels her hindquarters flinch; she flies from the pain yet it pursues her.

For nearly an hour the boar runs and stands, stands and runs. She has arrow shafts for hackles and her snout has filled with blood. At last she is cornered between two fallen trees. A man in scarlet brandishes a sword. It gleams for an instant like a piece of the sun, then beds itself hotly into her side. The sow's heart – which beat once like a forge – shatters; there is foam at her jaws; and her eyes fill with mud, which is the Death of Animals.

After a kill, boys, comes the butchering. First, the beast's head is severed and speared. From throat to crotch the trunk is rent; bowels flurry from the belly, to be broiled on coals and cast to the hounds. Then to a spar, under which strong men labour; the sundered parts are suspended, and so readied for the journey home.

All hope, a second time, seems lost for our child. Cowering, and reeking of wildness, she is found by the red-muzzled hounds. At their keening the hunters halt. Enguerrand de Oorlogspad flicks his glove at a fly, lazily, and lazily nods at the beaters. These, with weary arms, thresh the tremulous ferns, until one spots, through the green spray, a quaking and beshitted girl.

« How she quakes (the beaters murmur). Poor wretch, she must've been stolen. There's no knowing what the brutes won't eat.

—Let us praise God (says the Baron) for sending us to this innocent's aid. »

This popular legend is hardly blemished by the foundling's lack of gratitude. For when bloody hands close about her she snarls and bites, throws off several servants and stuns three affectionate hounds. Only under restraint of ropes is the child returned, amidst *Te Deums*, to the world of men.

Of flaxen hair & a woman's influence

Let us skip an interlude of scrubbing and dressing, of piss-pot lessons and futile enquiries. It is enough to tell that, after three months chained to a wall in the Baron's castle, the unchristened child is given up for an orphan and a creature quite beyond improvement. Bad things turn to worse when Enguerrand de Oorlogspad learns the cost of his benevolence, in terms of servants maimed, nurses brained and soldiers cudgelled.

One evening at banquet with his knights, the Baron loses his rag. « Will no one rid me of this tiresome pest? » he foams. Ambitious heads meet in dark conference. Their mutterings of poison and pillow-stifling so alarm one serving-girl that she resolves to rescue the child from its keepers. All evening her mind is knotted in strategy, and habit alone prevents her spilling sack over chivalrous breeches.

At last, through greasy snores and chicken bones, the serving girl slips. Greyhounds, slack-bellied on their master's scraps, lick her heels and whimper. The serving-girl descends to the dungeons. Patting the sleeping lump of the nurse, she finds on her girdle the key to the cell. The orphan within is fast asleep: too fast to feel herself bound inside a wicker basket and lowered, in flaxen knots of the servant's hair, into the moat. There is no cry of alarm from the basket as it nudges into an off-spilling stream. The servant girl ravels up her locks and, daring at last to breathe, returns to her quarters.

For two hours the basket travels, spinning and nodding, through water meadows where woodcock glug, until it comes to rest in the lap of a millpond.

I have heard, my boys, of foxes that will tame themselves for food, and wolves that turn helpmeet in times of great hunger. This is in no way perverse: it is survival, as Nature intends. So our heroine (awaking to changed circumstances) adopts the matronly mound of the miller's wife, whom the dawn brings cooing to the water. With a player's skill the child pouts and gurgles, until she can be resisted no longer, and the miller's wife, hoisting the foundling to her hip, runs clucking back to the mill.

« Willy (she huffs to her breakfasting husband), can we keep her, can we?

—D'you see the size of it, Fanny? We'd be eaten out of house and home.

—But she's *adorable*.

—We don't know whose it is. We don't know where it's been. »

To get her way, the miller's wife produces an ultimatum on terms no doting husband can withstand.

« What (says the miller) – even heavy petting?

—*Even* heavy petting.

34

—Even *heavy* petting?

—Even heavy *petting*. »

So the miller's wife has her way, and the girl-child finds a home.

On etymology, & the exit of old Adam

For the baptism of their faery-child (so strange was her delivery no other explanation pleases), Willy and Fanny Molenaer gather all the worthies of the parish. Roger the boatman is there, with his wife and tender bladder; also Cornelius Fuchs and his hare-lipped children. From farther afield, Frans Wankerts the bird-limer sits with Dirk Diegler; while, snoring and farting at the back, Rumbartus Arst admires the tuberous daughters.

Now the aged priest emerges: it is time to abjure the Devil and his Works. The proud parents stand at the font, beside the godfather-to-be. Young Martin Bolerckx, having recently come into money, is no longer the farmboy he was, and he smirks with new-found status. As for Martin's (god) daughter, disgruntled to be washed and fancy dressed, she whines and squirms in Willy's arms.

« Dearly beloved » intones the priest – then continues in Latin to an illiterate flock. We've all been there, of course, and caught the Nodding Sickness. So let us skip to the moment when the priest takes the child into his arms. This is not something Father Hermann enjoys any longer, what with his tremors and pleuritis, his pyrexia and phimosis, his cirrhosis, his phlebitis and rheumatoid arthritis. Newborns are one thing, all gums and spasm – he can cope with newborns. But this one's a whopper: Father Hermann has sat lighter *choirboys* on his knee, in his time. Still he perseveres, resting the weight on the ledge of marble. The toddler, looking into the font, is gripped by an urgent impulse and – lifting her dress to expose a dimpled bum – makes water in the holy vessel. The church resounds with a feminine tinkle. The Molenaers, perceiving with horror their child's sacrilege, exclaim, in Walloon, *Quel culot t'as!* Which (for some reason known only to the priest) becomes « Belcula ».

So it sticks: Belcula Molenaer. Regenerate and registered in Heaven's ledger.

How siege is laid to a pigsty,
with the ingenious conquest of the same

Imagine, if you will, Belcula's happy childhood. Each day at its dawning is a new world to discover. Poplars sigh; birds sing; the watermill chops and stutters. Belcula shuts her eyes when Fanny comes to wake her, then flings herself into warm, floury arms. Being 'daft' (as the neighbours say), she is excused the chores of school or housework. Mute but for laughter, homely yet drawn to the wild, she is restless, tousled, dirty kneed. She runs everywhere, climbs everything and swims naked in the river.

One May afternoon, shortly after her twelfth birthday, Belcula struts glistening from the water to empty her bowels. As she squats and pushes in the bushes, she sees eyes peeping through the hawthorn. Most of us this situation would, at the very least, constipate; but Belcula, lacking shame, shits on, and finds in the boyish titters a thrill like the shudder of an eel in a poacher's pantaloon. Her turds dropped, Belcula meets the oglers' eyes and begins, very slowly, to gyrate. Her dance is belly proud, wet curled, with loose hands roving. When she has finished she wades back into the water; where she plays like Diana at her bath, or some naiad whose lightest parts are her hams. The boys, with sticky breeches, scatter through the fields.

Now two of these young voyeurs are brothers: Mauritz and Piers. Until this hour, it was their chief delight to catch skylarks and wing them. What camaraderie they found in that mess of feathers! Never (they'd swear over reeking hands) would experience sunder them! Yet as he watches Belcula's dance, each boy feels the dart of Cupid pierce his loins (which are the seat of male emotion). Running home, neither Mauritz nor Piers shares with his brother the wound he has received. Each boy in his sickness tosses and squirms; nightly in bed he does his Lady honour; and when he has finished, he sighs « alas! »

Through three hard years the brothers sweat as their Paramour performs in the woods, by the brook, in the tickling rye. By the age of fifteen, Belcula has ripened into every boy's torment. Hers is not the kind of beauty that poets praise but the kind they *want*. (If only they'd admit it.) Breasts like melons, if you like. A rump, gentlemen, that should have its own moon. *Legs*. (Well, what can be done to legs, which you find so charming?) Belcula's couldn't be lovelier if the King's carpenters had fashioned them, and these are flesh and blood.

Happily, cruelty is not in Belcula's nature. Endowed for pleasure, she's not immune to desire herself. Thus, when a fortified Mauritz (being the bolder of the two) declares his devotion, she accepts the courtesy and jumps his startled bones.

Oh, what joy in that first day-and-night-and-day of lust! Mauritz (in the occasional lulls) dreams he is a ship at sea, punished on mountainous waves; Belcula, dreaming of nothing, tows her lover impatiently back to port.

The idyll does not last long.

One evening a suspicious Piers follows his beaming brother. Shadowing him, he is impelled behind trees, like a decrepit dog. Finally Mauritz arrives at his tryst. He and Belcula couple in Willy Molenaer's grainhouse, where their whooping and groaning harrow the field-mice. Oh, monstrous! Piers cannot bear to think of the indignities done to his Lady. How Belcula must suffer under Mauritz's weight, beneath his tyrannous nozzle, when she might be exalted by Piers, who alone in the world truly loves her.

Days pass in frantic strategy. Finally a plan is hatched. Piers, bolstered by desire, waits outside the grainhouse for the love-moans to subside. When Maur-itz emerges, bleary and drained, it is his rival who steals into the mealy den, bearing gifts of fruit and honey.

Within the hour, Belcula is ravished. Being twice her captor's size, she assists Piers in his efforts, dragging herself to his pigsty; where she scoffs his fruit and gladly submits to his veneration.

(For those who think it harlotry on Belcula's part so readily to swap lovers, I would invoke the zeal of the recent convert. For flesh has revealed its pleasures to her, as the soul may True Religion. Nor can Belcula's appetites be sated by one little man. Like Nature, her passions are changeable. She is various, bountiful, humid. The libations that men offer are as drops of rain on thirsty soil: accepted, absorbed and always insufficient. So rest assured, my friends, there is plenty of her to go around.)

Life in Piers' pigsty provokes some strange behaviour. Belcula reverts to a condition of hogdom (hogness? hogitude?) characterised by languor, flatulence and gluttony. What decorum she has acquired, over the years, in fecal matters is thrown (so to speak) out the window. Yet Piers is insensitive to his Lady's stinks. Through the sensual prism of his lust, she is gorgeousness itself.

« Varlet! Thief! Come out and fight! »

Thus the jilted Mauritz, having learned of his betrayal. With a great knotted stave he confronts the pigsty, taunting his brother into battle. Piers, unable to shag for the insults flying at him, buttons up his breeches and flings back the wicker gate.

For five hours their garboils rage. Mauritz the challenger (lithe, if you overlook his paunch) fights like a lion; Piers bites and gnashes, and only once conshits his breeches. At last, squeamish Morpheus draws her veil across the scene. Piers returns to his well-fed Amour, Mauritz to brood in his tent of hazel.

Daily from that time the brothers clash. Sometimes Mauritz has the upper hand, bashing spondyls, baffing optics, thumping omoplates. At other times Piers appears to be winning – that is, when he kicks his brother in the balls. Sometimes, to their groaning, Belcula adds a sleepy sigh or laid-back fart.

After ten nights of siege, grey-fingered Dawn rises yawning from the East. Piers, who has slept in a bruised heap outside Belcula's pen, peeps over his battlements to see the field of war deserted. A gladder sight still – since food has dwindled – is the roast pig left by Mauritz outside the gate. With merriment that even his herd – though presented with an image of its fate – seems to share, Piers drags the offering into the pen. Hungrily he snatches at the meat; when from the roast pig (which is a skin only) his foe emerges. A figure of armed insolence, redolent of pork, Mauritz brandishes a cleaver. No blackened eye or deadened arm will assuage his anger. The curse of Cain is in his blood, and Piers, seeing his death in his brother's eyes, shrinks back defenceless.

But hold your horses. Before a fatal blow is dealt, the Prize herself appears at the fence. The brothers must stare at some length to comprehend this simple fact: Belcula looking *in* from the *outside*. She smiles at her suitors casually, as one might greet cousins in the street, then snaps into an apple. Mauritz lowers his weapon, crestfallen. Piers drops his breeches, to empty them. Together, the lads fling back the partition to their Lady's chamber. Alack! At some point in the night, Belcula must have broken the wall with her buttocks (the breach is unmistakable) and wandered off in search of food. She has abandoned them both, indifferent to her allotted role.

Cheerfully, with a belch, Belcula departs. The brothers' limbs soften and chill; and their lusts shrink, sad, exhausted, to the size of strawberries.

Of pastoral pleasures & the Elevation of Learning

Within a month of her ravishment, our heroine is put to work as a milkmaid. The brindled cows of Cornelius Fuchs warm to Belcula's touch. Stolid, sopping nosed and slowly cudding, they gaze at her through long black lashes. Their udders are ponderous and big veined; Belcula squeezes and the jets trill into her pail. Across the meadow, the milking sounds like cicadas singing.

Is it any wonder, in such a setting, that appetites should swell? For whereas Nature has confined her baser creatures to a defined season for copulation, the lusty fires of womankind burn eternally. Even in her monthly bleedings (which are tides, I tell you, Pharaonic floods) Belcula cannot keep from frigging. The Fuchs boys vie for her attention, offering their inherited leers. The milkmaids, formerly so proud of their assets (a plump heel, a sexy overbite), seethe with resentment. Even the bull in the paddock is driven wild by the love-potion that seeps from Belcula's pores. Madly he bellows, rucking up great heaps of earths until, in an attempt to head-butt his gate, he knocks himself out cold.

One morning Belcula is charged with carrying milk to a customer. This is not normally a maid's task, but the boys of the farm are incapacitated by lust, and Mistress Fuchs is glad to rid the air of its infection.

And so, one hour after cockcrow, Belcula arrives at her destination. Pieter Hooch – friend to Oxford's Eruditus, author of the best-selling *Platonic Dialogues for Beginners* (twenty-eight copies sold) – is working in his study when he observes the milkmaid at his door. Dashing off his skullcap (which does nothing to endear him, baldness notwithstanding, to the Finer Sex), he rushes to her aid. Belcula gladly surrenders her pail and takes the coin that is folded, slowly, into her palm. Pieter Hooch talks quickly, bombarding the girl with incomprehensible words. Assuming herself fallen on a foreigner, Belcula turns to go. Whereupon the scholar – unable to contain his mental tumescence – invites the fascinating mute indoors.

« I am moved by the challenge of restoring her oration (he says later to the Molenaers as, flattered by a scholar's attention, they flim and flam over plates of ryebread). I putate most emphatically that, given my indefessible attention, she will be exprimerating – even cantabilating – within months. »

Nor (after offering a brief translation in the vulgate)

does Pieter Hooch expect remuneration for his work. It would be reward enough simply to help an innocent. Therefore, with pangs of reluctance, the Molenaers relinquish their daughter and Belcula is led, hand in clammy hand, to Learning's domicile.

For six months (when she isn't slipping out to see boys) Belcula undergoes rigorous treatment. With seemingly infinite patience, Pieter Hooch caresses her vocal cords; he puts his lips on hers to encourage enunciation, and strokes her downy midriff to stimulate good breathing. In all his experiments, he fails.

« *She is wholly untainted by sophistication,* Pieter Hooch writes to Eruditus in England. *Nor can she be corruptelated by poetical youth, lacking comprehension of amorous superverbosity.* »

Come Candlemas, he has engaged her to be his wife.

How Belcula gets translated

Flush with late-flowering love, Pieter Hooch devises a syntax of gestures for his bride-to-be. As soon as Belcula is asking her howdyedos and begging her pardons and troubling for the butter, he invites an audience to a demonstration of the 'Hooch Manulatory Method'. And who should offer a venue for this illustrious gathering? Why none other than Oswolt von Spewer. This merchant, eager to trade hospitality for prestige, inveigles lords and ladies into a hall where the family coat of arms (recently commissioned) is greatly in evidence.

There is a hush when a side door opens. Venerable in scholarly black silk, Pieter Hooch parades before the patrons his bride-to-be. It's like watching a sale at auction: all eyes admire the filly's tone and ossature, her sleek mane and strong teeth, and everyone forgets the pretext for the gathering. Belcula, glad of the attention, beams in virginal brocade.

« Honoribilous guests (Pieter Hooch says), I shall translate for you the gesticulatory colloquy of my patient. »

At first, the routine goes well. Belcula, when asked a question, kneads and pinches the air. Pieter Hooch enquires after her health and mental happiness. (Yes, yes, most excellent comprehension.) Pieter Hooch seeks Belcula's admiration of his methods. (Indeed, she is most fortunate.) And how did she come to be here, before these noble people?

To this question Belcula replies. In full. From the *very* beginning.

By the time Pieter Hooch realises what he's translating, it's too late to turn back; nor can he twist a tale that has been for so long repressed. Slack jawed, and craning as at a bearpit, his patrons learn of boar fur and hunting hounds, of millers' wives and holy water and dancing on the riverbank. Belcula has a formidable memory, and so do high born gossips. Pieter Hooch – weighing shame with duty, propriety with lust – has no alternative but to make an honest woman of the wretch.

Almost as planned, then.

The Drinking Woman's Tale

How Belcula, learning an important fact,
flashes her tits at Matrimony

It is the eve of the wedding, and Belcula is being clucked over in Fanny Molenaer's kitchen. Talk of a wife's duties has done nothing to dissuade her – after all, she sees no sign of obedience in her mother.

Now who, do you imagine, should shatter the ancient ritual of daughter-in-her-gown-on-the-kitchen-table? Why, Martin Bolerckx, of course: the bride's godfather. Beaded by sweat and boggle-eyed with beer, he refuses a chair and banishes cake. He shudders like a tumbler on a tightrope, who can neither advance nor retreat for apprehension. Belcula and Fanny watch the words rise, like unbidden bile, to his lips. Out they gush!

« Belcula you must know because you're getting hitched now it's out in part at least I was paid to shut me gob and when you just appeared like that no-one guessed it was you I thought you were dead that's what he told me stillborn well now you're not Christ forgive me I'm your Dadda— ! »

When he comes to, Martin Bolerckx is slumped in a corner with a vial of vinegar for sal volatile up his nostril. Fanny and Belcula, even as they fan and cosset him, wheedle the fellow for an explanation. Martin describes how, many years ago, Oswolt von Spewer had paid him handsomely for his silence. Silence on what? he'd wondered – only to be clipped round the ear and told that he knew very well what. So he'd taken the money, seeing no trouble in keeping mum on a subject he knew nothing about. Only for years it made his ears itch and his balls (begging pardon) shrink to the size of cherry-pips. What *was* this secret he was paid to keep? Then Martin did some serious thinking and, what with Hildegard's disappearance, confronted her father who told him about the stillborn bastard and Hildegard's confession and exile on the island of Whatsit off the Danish coast and where was he? The egghead! – sorry – Dr Hooch! When he made Belcula talk with her hands and the news got out it travelled to the tavern and, let's be frank, it doesn't take a genius to put two and two together, does it?

Belcula burns in her bridal gown; her blood simmers with strange new desire. All night long, beside troubled and unsleeping parents, she listens to the want in her veins. The following morning, in church, she looks through her garland at the red face of her grandfather and the blanched face of her father and the blotched face of her adoptive mother and the stiff face of her adoptive father and the chalky mask of her betrothed. She is no longer the woman she was the day before, except in one respect: that her flight from the altar is signalled by a flash of cleavage at the Host and a moony at the congregation.

By the time they find her gown splayed upon the grass, Belcula's journey to her birth mother is well under way.

END OF THE FIRST BOOK

BOOK TWO

Of the open road, & Flemish hospitality

Nowhere in Christendom (it is a certain fact) can the traveller expect a shorter or less uneventful journey than through the quagmires of our low country. Belcula is better set than most, wanting either a fast horse or an armed escort to save her. Add to this the fact that she's the most desirable woman ever to stray before inbreds and woodsmen and one might expect an unlovely end to our fable.

But you catch on quickly, I can tell, and know better than to despair at the start of a chapter. Belcula herself – urged northward by instinct, neither reading the stars nor caring a fig for the sun's itinerary – is blind to danger. Consequently there's something mysterious, magical, in her bearing, such that the most cut-throat of brigands can only stare (nursing his prick, aerating his pestiferous trap) at her passing. For all the lust that she inflames – and hundreds fidget in her wake, as though their wicks were dipped in stone alum – few men dare accost her. Lone loping wolves, snuffling up for a snack, are flicked like flies from her path. The rare undaunted hedge-thief is rammed by her breasts and trounced underfoot. For these – and trees, bogs, hamlets besides – are as so many hummocks between Belcula and her mum, to be trampled and passed over.

Fuelled by her heart's desire, our heroine ignores all

other wants. Excrement and urine she evacuates walking; to drink, when she must, a standing pool does the trick. Only food makes its absence felt, blackberries and crab-apples being meagre substitutes for sheep's brains and steaming tripe. So it happens, after three days' fasting, that Belcula's belly makes its stand. It is dusk, and in a forest clearing a cauldron froths over an open fire. The cauldron's torturers having left it unwatched, Belcula reaches down its neck with a stick. She stirs around inside for a time, then juggles a hunk of venison before tearing it on the tips of her teeth.

Now a first bite of meat puts one in mind of one's hunger and Belcula, finding herself ravenous, makes short shrift of the entire pot. Within an hour she is stretched out in belly-cheered sleep. She knows nothing of the robbers who gather around her like magpies about an upturned sheep. Blood-grimed fingernails flick at daggers; pig's-liver tongues lob and slobber. There is always, in the thief's profession, a precise pecking order. So the leader of the band – a wall-eyed churl with conger-eel teeth – approaches his victim with his breeches down. Belcula, sleepily turning at the nip of his blade, crushes the villain under her right tit. Wading in after him, his deputy expires, wedged like a furrier betwixt seals, in Belcula's cleavage. Whereupon the lesser bandits waddle, stark buttocked, to their deaths. One suffocates between Belcula's thighs. Two more, approaching stiff rigged from behind, are blown off their feet by a thunderous fart and have their brains dashed out on a tree trunk. When, yawning, Belcula bites off the privates of the sixth, the seventh bolts in terror. (This last bandit does not fly far. Cunning without brawn, he has an enterprising frame of mind, with which we shall be acquainted shortly.)

Darkness' hours creep to a timorous dawn, and nightingales, with their liquid song, bring Belcula to her senses. Noticing the bandits – stiffening in all the wrong places in the fire's dust – she assumes herself amongst the sleeping rather than the dead, and sets out unhurt (though stalked at a distance) for the city of Gent.

How Belcula, reaching Gent, strays from her own story

Once inside the city, my boys, you will notice a lean carrot-topped fellow – neither young nor old but weather garbled, sinewy and carbuncular – unpeel himself from shadows. He accosts, as might an ambassador, the travelling beauty: bows low and flourishes his pigeon panache.

« O queen of marvels, fairest flower, vouchsafe an ear to a humble servant. My name is, er, Scatologus, redistributor of wealth. I was leaving just now the Grainweighers' Hall, sunk in matters of financial weight, when of a sudden my eyes received the radiance of your beauty . . . »

This tack leaves Belcula cold and, tagging along after her, Scatologus switches: « Listen, love, you're in a strange city without so much as a liard to your name or a friend to turn to. It so happens I'm well connected: got a swanky townhouse. I charge no rent, only a contribution now and then – you could do it lying down. »

But Belcula's eyes are set on the house fronts, their handsome gables and blinking windows. Only when she passes a *kramieken* stall and inhales the breaths of currant buns does Scatologus see his angle: « Food you want? Me got food. Soup and cheese and fricadelles. »

This Belcula hears (as with the old, her deafness is selective). She drags the scrawny fellow to the food stall and, at his expense, nosily devours its wares. Scatologus is glad to part with ill-gotten moneys, knowing well that, after eating, a woman's more southerly appetites stir.

When Belcula has scoffed her fill (that's half a crate of pistolets and several hundred *strikken*) she abandons herself to her benefactor; who tries for himself the services he expects to sell. Their narrow bed in the fleapit inn creaks and travels till cockcrow. It takes Scatologus two days to wipe the silly grin off his face. Then he sells brooches, necklaces, silver-plate prosthetics. The revenue from these stolen goods he sinks into a house in the Patershol quarter, where he installs, at great expense, a sturdy four-poster bed. Next, with a trail of buns and sweetmeats, he lures his investment into the dwelling. Belcula snuffles into downy pillows. The clamour of heredity is dimmed. She forgets, like the lotus-eater, her journey's purpose.

The Drinking Woman's Tale

Of the world's oldest profession, with divers customers

It is the dead of night. All along the Geldmunt little rivulets of piss creep towards the gutter; there are puddles of yeasty puke congealing in doorways. Stepping over drunkards' legs, a dandy leads a weaver to his dwelling. The moonfaced weaver clutches a palm-greased florin; his long shanks seem to tremble under the weight of it. His feather-capped companion glances at the stocks in St Veerleplein Square: beneath the jaunty headpiece, could one look that closely, one would notice beads of sweat and a bobbing Adam's apple.

« You'll have the screw of your life (the dandy whispers). When she gets going, you'll be stiff like a horse, you'll wonder: is this really *happening*? »

The weaver, as he's ushered up a staircase, seems less than enthused by this prospect. When a door opens at the summit (assailing him with feminine odours) he visibly quakes. Yet, five minutes later, it is a dishevelled, new-made man who emerges and parts with a week's wages.

« Tell your colleagues » Scatologus winks. It is a sound strategy. Within a week, to Belcula's joy, five hundred weavers flock to her bed. These early comers, to coin a phrase, find a wet dream incarnate: an uninhibited buxom who gags at nothing and goes where housewives rarely venture. The vigour of coition is such that, in one day, Belcula works her way through the following:

Item, Armourers. 17

Item, Bakers 19

Item, Brewers, guild of . . . 3 (36 dropouts)

Item, Cripples 6

Item, Eel-trappers 29

Item, Friars (mendicant) . . 2

Item, Pickpockets 8

Item, Tradesmen. 63

Item, Weavers 98

With a fortune flooding in, the maître d' hires an army of discreet washerwomen. He commissions an architect to design a pulley system by which Belcula might be hoisted, unflustered, from her honeyed swamp and hosed down with rosewater.

To further satisfy his golden goose – he has seen what she can do, even in sleep, when slighted – Scatologus goes to the Vleeshuis and Groetenmarkt. With a clattering of nimble cooks he concocts delectable dishes. An hors d'oeuvre of potted veal, for instance, vegetable bouillon and piping *flamiche* tart. A main course of rabbit with prunes, steaming *karbonaden* and fat-boiled goose. For dessert, sugar-coated *krakelingen*, explosive choux pastries and toffee *barbelutten*. Finally (because he's done his homework and bribed a scholar to read Galen) Scatologus stuffs Belcula with aphrodisiac pine nuts.

He needn't take the trouble. She is to whores what Bayard is to horses: a sexual giantess. No kermesse

freak could satisfy her, not Polydor or Argayon, nor
hugely hung Gouyasse. Wallowing in steaming sheets,
Belcula utters her first words:

« More! More! I want more! »

The tricks of Belcula

The enterprising Scatologus, finding an insatiable sup-
plier to meet an insatiable demand, disseminates at the
Vrijdagmarkt a bill of fare. (He does not consult Belcula
about it. Whatever she does, she does freely, by her own
invention. For a lover that is unacquainted with precedent remains, *de facto*, the first lover that ever was.)
The services listed include:

the missionary	the tundish
the parson	the pearl tiara
the prostrate bishop	the pearl necklace
the passionate shepherd	the facecushion
the hoarding hamster	the footstool
the ostrich	the bullseye
the busy-bee	the joust-and-target
the languid slug	the mace
the dog-chasing-its-tail	the bastinado
the cat's ablution	the thrum-my-naker
the nodding donkey	the hornpipe
the drayhorse	the bladder pipe
the hobbyhorse	the rommelpot
the horse-and-trap	the *jeu d'harpe*
the handcart	the gay galliard
the wheelbarrow	the squatting gavotte
the crab race	the horizontal jig

the conch	the piggyback
the clambake	the leapfrog
the eeltrap	the stick-in-the-mud
the *moule au vin blanc*	the headstand
the prickly pear	the bellyflop
the split fig	the blind man's buff
the buttered parsnip	the Cyprian wrestle
the creamcake	the goat and cheesegrater
the gobstopper	the angry nurse
the blackpudding	the pillaging Hun
the clean-my-pantry	the thrifty Jew
the chamberpot	the lonely Turk

With publicity comes a better class of customer. Instead of journeymen, merchants come in points of silk, smelling of the grainhouse. Instead of weavers, clothmakers from the Lakenhalle seek relief – a little spasm of forgetting – from the day's low prices. The bedchamber becomes a catacomb of *petites morts*. Old men die, deliriously happy, of cardiac explosions; apprentices cream themselves at a glimpse of thigh, a flash of kirtle; frustrated husbands wallow in quim's bitter jelly. Soon the city's printers are proving their worth, circulating woodcuts of the divine anatomy; for the learned, poetasters print octavos in obscene Latin, panegyrics to Belcula's talents. Even Belfort tower's gilded dragon turns to watch, from his belfry top, the frantic copulations of her guildsmen.

Belcula, for her part, enjoys her men's enjoyment, getting her own pleasure when she can, from the few who come close to measure. But tempers *fugit*, as the saying goes. Lust's young dream will not last long.

*In which Pieter Hooch and Oswolt von Spewer
ally themselves against adversity, & we learn
something of their employee's pedigree*

It is the peculiar talent of civilised men to make alliances
with brutes, when they think it suits them. So Pieter
Hooch and Oswold von Spewer meet one afternoon in
the green-shaded courtyard of the merchant's home.
Pieter Hooch is gaunt, sober and clean shaven; he casts
a swift eye at his seat before folding himself upon it, and
lifts to his scholar's nose a discreet, ring-shaped po-
mander. Oswolt von Spewer, on the other hand, is
short, pot bellied and ruddy: he farts the ghost of
expensive meats and enjoys the stink. Pieter Hooch's
speech is orn- and Latin-ate, displaying like fruits the
harvest of new fangledness. Oswolt von Spewer (who is
fluent in English, French and German smut) speaks as
though Cicero had choked at birth and Demosthenes
been born a Scotsman. Yet despite these differences,
between Man of Letters and Man of Commerce there
flourishes the friendship of mutual need.

« It was my praestarility (begins Pieter Hooch) to
custodiate Belcula from her foedistical nature. For she is
unmatrimoniated and, *sine magistrum*, displays all the
libidities and infirmitations of her gender.

—Right (von Spewer nods), without a man to guide
her, she's not answerable for her actions.

—My meditarious operatics to inculcate a modicum
of moral comprehension deficerated, for her feral in-
canabulation cannot be erudited out of her.

—She's as wild today as the day you found her. It'll look bad with the wits, Hoochie, your failure to make a decent woman of her.

—Indeed (says Pieter Hooch), you loquate veraciously. Yet it must be timorated that, in the insectation of her sanguinious generatress, the neovestalite your daughter, she may also maculate the vendibilious nomen of Spewer.

—Come again?

—Now that your secret's out, Belcula may take her mother's name and so sully yours. »

Put like this, the situation demands strong measures. All day long these Pillars of Society hatch a plan for Belcula's capture. They settle (not without agonising) upon the infamous Griet von Antwerpen. Only such a creature – the pillager of Yves Gomezée, capturer of the eloped Duchess of Darmstadt and single-handed queller of the Oudenarde Heresy – can be relied upon to succeed. For Dulle Griet (as ungrateful citizens call her) is as avaricious as she is ruthless, and the gentlemen offer a handsome bounty for Belcula's return.

Within two days of their letter's dispatch, Pieter Hooch and Oswolt von Spewer are drawn to the casement by sounds of chaos outside. In the street stands Dulle Griet like a hunched, ill-omened bird. Aproned and armoured, she is followed by a mob of huswives; who, having looted Varenburg, labour under the weight of flour and cloth and silver plate. Dulle Griet herself stands eight feet tall: a dry, pinched, thin-lipped harridan. So terrible is her aspect that none could doubt her boast of having plundered Hell and returned unscathed. (Hell's-mouth being located, as everyone knows, in the far-off bogs of Ireland, it is useless doubting the story.) Nailing her employers with cruel eyebeams, Dulle Griet demands admittance to their home. Her voice is like a rack when sinews are stretched upon it.

With a creak of reluctance, von Spewer's door opens. Dulle Griet – leaving her mob to crow over its pilferings – skulks into the marbled hall. Her broadsword drags along the ground, spitting yellow sparks. She stands by the chair offered to her, and makes an inventory of the household's riches. Oswolt von Spewer and Pieter Hooch, plying their guest with unappreciated wine, explain the delicacy of the situation. Interrupting them, Dulle Griet leans in like a raven over carrion.

« I will find your fat girl (she says) and whittle her down to size. But I must have licence to use *necessary means*. »

At these words Pieter Hooch blanches; but Oswolt von Spewer, upon whose fortune the venture depends, has read no Histories, and consequently replies in the positive. Half satisfied, Dulle Griet turns on the equivocator:

« And you, the bookworm?

—Me? Omninotely. I laudate and comprobate my colleague's prudential dictum, without invidiation or exception.

—Is that a yes?

—Oh, you bet. »

Barely blinking, Dulle Griet requests an item of her quarry's clothing. Pieter Hooch hands over the bridal veil, and chills to his marrow at the touch of her coarse fingertips. Dulle Griet lifts the silk to her snout and inhales. *Pwoah!* Stink of cloying life juices. She memorises the quimsical stench: it lodges in her nostrils, that delight in nothing but the tang of coins. For Dulle Griet has a stronger flair than a truffle-pig, is pursued night-and-day by the perfumes of her greed and the musk of people's terror.

« In forty days (the huntress says) I will return. Have my money ready. »

Effusive and sweat-dripping nods follow her exit. Heaving deep sighs of relief, Messrs Hooch and von Spewer slide to the floor.

Outside, the mob follows its leader like a swarm its errant queen.

How Belcula meets her match, no match at all, & swears companionship to Dutchcap, from whom she will never part

Now Scatologus – pleased with his belly and his Toledo sword and the gold-frizzled plume in his bonnet – is invited one day, at dagger's point, to a house of pimps in Hoogpoort. Inside a low-beamed den he meets twelve copies of his former self: ragged, mashed-up scumbags with zits and warts and variations on the pigeon feather threaded through their caps. A spokesman emerges from their midst. Scatologus, who has been thinking quickly on the way, wisely ditches his offer of a cut-price gang-bang. He sits on the stool that nuzzles into his legs and listens.

These gentlemen (the spokesman explains) constitute the Board of the Guildhuis der Kopelaars. The guild is struggling financially: business is slow, see, unaffiliated competition is sapping demand. Of course Scatologus understands that prostitution has its rules, like any other trade. Perhaps he'd care to peruse these implements, the guild's own collection – careful, that's rather sharp – which his esteemed colleagues are itching to baptise?

Scatologus needs no demonstration. Sprinting accompanied into his house, he snatches money, pearls, widowers' rings; then, with a hefty bribe for passport, he vanishes.

Some hours later, Belcula awakes from wholly satisfying sleep to find no lover in her bed. Outside her chamber stoop no keyhole oglers, no priapic poseurs or clerical sniff-smocks. Checking every room of the house, she surprises neither red-cheeked virgin nor braggart shrimp-prick. In short, she is alone, buzzed about by silence. In this emptiness Belcula's blood beats again its former longing. Add to this the rude minstrelsy of tripes (her own, parping like a cornemuse) and inaction is no option. Draping a Moorish rug over her shoulders, Belcula strides out into the city. Northward she travels – making men, out with their wives, nod in admiration of their shoes – until she stops, flabbergasted, beside a beggar.

What can she find of interest, you wonder, in some scrotty bum: a gloomy-looking chewbeard with naked filthy feet? The beggar himself, floating vague eyes at his admirer, seems to ask the same question. He follows the direction of Belcula's gaze to the beached porpoise in his codpiece. It is a prize marrow! a monument! a mastodon of human cock! Belcula discandies to have found at last a pick for her lock. She falls to her knees in worship before it.

« Madam (says the stud), you admire my equipment to no purpose. »

Alas, the fellow, though possessed of a prick that falls to his knees, has no use for it beyond passing water. The ballock-sacks, which hung in their glory like purses for diamonds, now sag like nosebags, void of pride or purpose. In vain Belcula tries to stir the listless phallus. No amount of sexy dancing (though it cripples the censorious watchman) can rouse the giant from its slumber.

« Desist, dear lady. »

A gang of young rakes, former regulars at Belcula's table, jeer at the tramp and fleck his beard with beer. « Don't hope for guilders from him, darlin'. He's Dutchcap: the safest sex in Europe. »

Dutchcap looks sagely pained: he mimes the putting-on of a headpiece in explanation. « I prefer the name Nullifidius (he says). Because I believe in nothing, not God, not Man, nor even myself. »

A mob of scab-kneed schoolboys skips by, chanting: « Dutchcap, Dutchcap! Keeps a dead snake in his lap! » The butt of their taunting flicks a fly from his face.

« In my youth (he resumes) I was passionate, bellicose and potent. With my best pal Jan I served as a soldier – *lieutenant de garde* at Gravensteen castle.

« We were the city's greatest lovers, Jan and I, each as hugely hung as the other. Women of every class, from countess to country moll, fell Y-shaped at our feet. It was a rare day, I tell you, when we didn't have to wade through stockings to get to our watch. But here's the thing. Our pleasures we shared. And the double dose of pleasing oneself and one another brought us happiness, I mean real contentment – what the gods (who don't exist) hate most in mortals.

« Our downfall came, as Death does, in the guise of an angel – a very earthly angel. She was a chambermaid. Her name was Frida. » As he sounds the name, our narrator's eyes mist over. Still, believing in nothing, he sniffs up the phantasmic rheum and continues. « To describe her would be to belie her. No more enflaming beauty has ever crossed my path. (Until today, for what it's worth.) In Frida's presence men's eyes rebelled against their wills, their heads wandered, Gent was full of broken noses.

« Here at last, Jan and I agreed, was a wench made to measure. But Frida was not powerless to resist our charms: she was a strategist, a machiavella of the bed-chamber. Only one of her suitors, she declared, would enjoy her treasures.

« So, for the first time, Jan appeared in my sleep as a rival. I would wake up sweating, despairing, only to find the reality worse than my dream. Because Jan started making claims. He would lie outright to lewd comrades, saying Frida lay with him, had chosen him over me. So to protect my lady's honour (yes, from the slander of sleeping with a man other than myself) I challenged him to a duel.

« We fought like knights. That is to say, like brutes: swinging at one another with swords, kicking when the swords broke, biting when our legs gave. We hadn't found a noble venue. I was no Lancelot and Frida was no Guinevere. Nonetheless, I won. Taking my rival in a headlock, I whipped the rest of him sideways. He lay like a rag-doll in the cellar's grime – in that grey-blue loam – his head at an impossible angle.

« True to her invidious word, Frida offered herself to me. As I'd imagined a dozen times, she parted her gown. Her breasts spilled out of her bodice. Her incredible body was like thunder exploding in darkness. But with all her art and vigour she could not rouse me. I looked from those wet hungry lips to the blue snarl of my companion. And I knew that I had defeated myself. Neither of us would enjoy our mistress's favours. For I was impotent. Shamed. The bloodless effigy slumped before you. »

Belcula's eyes are brimming cups. She weeps to find manhood sunk so low. When Dutchcap concludes she wraps him in her embrace, calls him friend, soul mate, bosom companion. Dutchcap hangs meekly at her teat – believing in nothing makes resistance difficult. Proudly Belcula parades him, tucked like a rag-doll into her armpit. She brushes, with careful fingers, the mud from his seat. When his feet drag along the cobbles, she pulls them safely between her legs. When his baby-bald head emerges from her breasts, she waters it with tender kisses. And so an intimacy is born, which, by means of sighs and strokes, Belcula swears will never end.

« I don't care (says Dutchcap). As well follow you as another. » He tastes with his indifferent nose the perfume of her skin. « To the ends of the earth, if need be. »

How Dulle Griet picks up a scent,
& Belcula sets to sea six leagues from the coast

With her cohorts behind her, Dulle Griet sniffs a confluence of wealth and cesspools. Gent basks in a haze, unconscious of impending catastrophe. Dulle Griet stirs with her fingers the gold-capped teeth in her sack. It had been child's play to prize them out of that popinjay's head – that Sarcophagus – along with his confession. How he'd wreaked of *her*, stinking from every pore. The pamphlets in his pocket merely confirmed what Dulle Griet already smells: Belcula is in the city, disgracefully employed.

In actual fact, at this moment, both prey and prey's companion are boarding a Dutch merchant ship in Graslei harbour. (The vessel is bound for the North Sea, by way of river and estuary, transporting cloth to Bergen.) Yes, Dutchcap insists wearily as they walk the gangplank, it *will* be sailing north. Yes, the bo'sun whispers to his whistle, she *is* coming aboard. « Welcome aboard the *Profijt*, ma'am » enthuses the first mate. The ship's captain, normally so averse to passengers (resenting unsalable freight and the retching of landlubbers), proves remarkably friendly. He even offers the use of his own cabin, should the young lady want for comfort during the voyage. Dutchcap, plumping stoically for the hold, notes the stiff-breeched excitement of the sailors, their salt-coarsened faces insufflated by unholy grace.

Now it is said in Gent that its cathedral bell, invoking auspicious winds, speeds ships on their journey. Sure enough, just as Dulle Griet enters the city the bell Roland is set ringing. A storm heaps and grumbles on the horizon. Zephyrus cracks his black cheeks and sends the *Profijt* bucking towards the Westerschelde.

Ignorant as yet of her poor timing, Dulle Griet hastens through the streets. Her nostrils flap like blowholes as she approaches the cathouse. But when she reaches its gaping door and sees looters astride the window, Dulle Griet's stomach turns over. Thwarted! Her round eyes contract to blackness – with her mailed glove she tears a hole in the wall and, foaming, gobbles its paste.

But walls alone cannot slake Dulle Griet's rage. With a scream like the rush of air from a furnace, she summons her followers. Then she hits the city with her sword whooping: parts people from their jawbones, lops heads as though they were daisies. Fleeing for its life, the commonalty stumbles into the maw of Dulle Griet's women; whereupon it is trounced, pronged and cudgelled. Merchants and menials, lawyers and loafers, are trampled to death, flattened with rolling-pins, and their black-eyed, gap-toothed houses are set ablaze.

« To the river! » Dulle Griet shrieks, wading through gore and rubble. The horde turns in her wake, humping its plunder in rugs, putting the boot in where necessary, and generally behaving like your regular army.

On the east shore of the river some attempt is made at resistance. Regrettably, the city's defenders, after three weeks of Belcula, are too plain shagged out to fight. Barely managing to wheel out a single small cannon, they embark on a bad-tempered, sore-headed search for shot and powder. When at last the cannon is primed, a gravely post-coital captain lights the fuse. The shot flies over the heads of Dulle Griet and her rabble – over the burning rooftops of the Patershol – into a watchtower at Graven-steen castle; where it kills outright nine soldiers, three doxies and a dozen pimps who were attempting to rekindle business. To this day that ineffectual cannon can be seen guarding a bridge over the Leie and bearing the dread name of its intended target.

In spite of the stench, Dulle Griet sniffs at the harbour till she picks up the spoor. « A ship (she screams)! Find me a ship! » Her followers need none of Belcula's charms to secure transport. Butchering, with finest silverware, the crew of a Dunwich trader, these versatile women infest the ship's rigging and release her sails. Dulle Griet on the poop deck sifts the wind for the trail of an odour. « Raise the anchor » she commands, there being only one way to negotiate a river: downstream, to the sea.

END OF THE SECOND BOOK

A sudden thirst interrupts the Drinking Woman's tale. She smacks her lips and tries to moisten them with a dry, heavy tongue. Her audience – rapt, for the most part, by her performance – swiftly and without a word spoken refills her flagon.

'Good 'ealth!' the Drinking Woman gasps as she wipes her dripping chin. 'Now then. I need a quill and ink.'

All men on board pat their chests. Only the Monk is equipped. Warily, he hands over the tools of his vocation. And the Drinking Woman, pushing the Nun aside with her heavy hips, falls upon the ship's table. Pinching the Monk's quill, and coating it in wine, she sketches a map of Belcula's coming journey.

'There now. Any of you boys get lost on root,' she says when the map is finished, 'have a butcher's at this.'

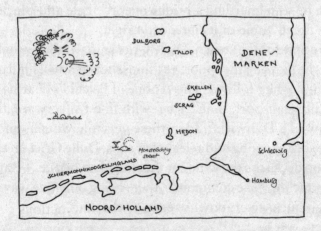

Whereupon, with a wink at our affronted Nun, the Drinking Woman resumes her tale . . .

BOOK THREE

Of sea monsters, & how Belcula
rids the ship of a pernicious specimen

Belcula sways on the deck of the *Profijt*, distracting the crew from its duties. Never before has she seen the sea, or felt its ancient heaving. Leaning at the prow, she fills her lungs until her bosom swells; the ship's figurehead, a busty siren, is dwarfed in comparison.

Dutchcap, too, is troubled by his companion's charms. Not that he disapproves of her liking for sailors. It's just that, as a nihilist, he's quite afraid of death; which sex, that postpones oblivion in its instant, can at sea quite likely hasten.

« Far be it from me (Dutchcap coughs into his fist) to take an interest in your amorous life – it's all right, sir, my back is turned – but might you not consider the perils of being distracted in these unforgiving waters? »

Bouncing upon the midshipman's face, Belcula concedes that, no, she might not. It is in no ways a malicious reply (*that* comes, muffled, from the sailor), merely a statement of fact. Belcula cannot conceive of any harm in pleasure. It is for Dutchcap to fret and tremble; and this he does, green gilled, below deck.

The *Profijt* sails up the Zeeland coast with a strong wind at her back. There reigns over the fractious crew of Dutch and Danes a sense of sensual kinship. Contrary to Dutchcap's bleak prognosis, ship's morale is excellent.

Until, that is, they tip Noord-Holland.

The cold grey waters of western Frisia – just off the coast of Schiermonnikoogellingland – teem, it is said, with great variety of sea monster. Credulus of Rotterdam writes of the rhinocerical Behemoth, dreaded for its halitosis; of the *groot zeekreft*, the flesh of which is highly prized by the French (who'll eat anything); of leopard-fish and *waterslang* and prophet-gulping Leviathan. As they enter that fog-accursed region known as the Monsterachtig Straat, the sailors aboard the *Profijt* begin to quake and gibber. Dutchcap, dreaming below deck of his flaccid schlong, is woken by Belcula in a state of high excitement.

« Can't you leave a man in peace (he groans)? You know I've lost my function! »

Accustomed to her companion's temper, Belcula points his ears to the sailors' cries. They hear a sinister scraping on the hull. Gravely concerned for her pillicocks, Belcula rushes to the hatch, forcing Dutchcap to follow.

On deck a fog has fallen, one so thick that not even his companion's girth can guide Dutchcap. He stubs his toes on ropes, brains himself on the yard-arm and, with a kind of grim satisfaction, snags his useless placket on a cannon's butt. « Help! Help! » the crew shrieks as the fog fills with scales. The ship's captain, stumbling by chance into Belcula's tit, begs on his knees for assistance:

« Help us, *juffrouw*, I implore you. How do we fight a fish we cannot see? »

Stirred to pity by the snap of sailors' bones, Belcula has herself tied to the mainstay. Then she swells up like a puffer fish and sucks in all the fog. Within three gulps the blue sky returns and Belcula – whose belly, like the alchemical pot, transmutes base elements – blasts from her fundament a fragrance of roses.

Deprived of fog cover, the *Profijt*'s assailant is exposed to view. Imagine, if you will, an octopus twice the size of an ox, with eyes like dishes and a snapping parrot's beak. Its flailing limbs, which tug at the rigging, reach as high as the crow's-nest, causing no end of grief to the crewmen.

The captain, fortified by a dram of hope, exhorts his men to combat. When no shots fly, however, Belcula lifts the cannon as one might a cucumber and presents herself to the gruesome beak.

« For pity's sake (Dutchcap wails), have a care for your safety! »

The octopus, stupid with hunger, tilts the ship on to her side, the better to get at Belcula. Expecting to receive a tasty morsel, it chomps instead on Belcula's cannon. A terrible indigestion of lead sinks the beast beneath the waves – whereupon it is devoured by its fellows.

In this manner Belcula rescues the *Profijt*. The waters seethe and simmer with fins, which Dutchcap ogles warily. The rest of the ship – including its sober dependable captain – can only gawp at its saviour and drool.

*On Dulle Griet at sea, with a
brief description of her maritime diet*

The same wind that speeds the Good propels the Bad. Dulle Griet, unlike her prey, takes no pleasure in the sea; for what wealth it conceals lies fathoms deep in wrecks, watched only by fish and bland, unclenching squid. Nor have the doggers boarded since Vissingen yielded any booty. No: what delights her (if vultures are capable of delight) is the chase. For two days now, the oblivious *Profijt* has sat on her horizon.

When a fog descends – a maddening odourless limbo – the pursuit is compromised. Dulle Griet in her rage beats her women's heads together. Even her favourites are lashed by her tongue, cursed to dryness, pox and penury. When the ship starts slobbering tentacles, then, it comes almost as light relief. Dulle Griet's women, released from her wrath, hook sharks and tusked eels; they flip them on deck, like pancakes, for butchering, and slip in their icy blood. Dulle Griet herself, snapping the spine of a kraken, sucks the eggy goo from its eyes.

Abruptly, the fog lifts. There is a sickening smell of roses. All about the ship glutted monsters roll. Whereas Belcula left the beasts to their digestion, however, Dulle Griet sees a fortune in the making. What won't taxidermists pay for specimens? At once she sets her women to work, scooping the dopey brutes from the sea as one may pluck tench from a ditch. The air fills with the slop and fizz of flaying. In one hour, I tell you, the Frisian sea is almost cleared of monsters. They become Behemoth pie and sea-slug stew, owl-shark paste and giant-squid soup.

As the hides are nailed out on deck to dry, Dulle Griet scours the sea for a speck of the *Profijt*.

How Belcula comes to the land of Hedon,
& what Rights they enjoy there

The republic of Hedon – a great joke among cartographers – is a lushly wooded island fringed by ivory sands. Emerging from its tree line, above phallic towers and mammarian domes, three mountains rise like the heads of submerged giants. It could be Eden, thinks Dutchcap, and he catches on his face the prickling of a smile.

As she nears the harbour, the *Profijt* passes a beach where natives bask like seals. These sunbathers are almost entirely naked. Buttocks are bisected by thin black filaments; men's parts and women's nipples are explicitly concealed in scallop shells. Dutchcap is astonished to see islanders smear ointment over one another's bodies. Belcula, meanwhile, stares transfixed, her lovely eyes glowing.

« Don't get any ideas (Dutchcap warns). We're only here for the morning, to stock up on essentials. »

Immediately, he regrets the phrasing. For Belcula is growing restless.

Now Hedon's harbour – which is overlooked on three sides by tall granite buildings – is crammed with statues: beautiful effigies, great sexed, with emptily symmetrical faces. Instead of Nature's sagging, pear-shaped vessels, here is Art's hyperbole. Boys and girls petrified *in flagrante delicto*, with a tradesman's name etched into their buttocks. The postures, too, refer to local trades. So you'll find oral pleasure on an anvil, say, heavy petting with a mackerel, or a barber's comb teasing alabaster pubes . . .

« My God (groans Dutchcap), there's no getting away from it. »

Beautiful live girls emerge from behind the statues. Surrounding the *Profijt* with baskets on their arms, they caress plums and fellate baguettes in a strange attempt, it seems, to sell them. Dutchcap, attempting to seem unflustered, offers to buy Belcula a loaf. But she is no longer at his side – nor anywhere else on board.

Dutchcap panics. He pushes through crates and hagglers. He elbows Hedonites on the gangplank. Amidst frenzies of plum-squirt and lewd salesmanship he searches. Without success. Defeated, he slumps on a bollard; where he is accosted, within a few minutes, by a bare-chested youth.

« Are you from the Gent ship (the fellow enquires in passable Dutch)? My name is Blandus Vlaag. Court warden. I've been sent to find you about a young la—

—dy, yes. What has she done?

—She's been taken into custody, I'm afraid. Non-Contractual Propositioning. Failure to Provide Certificate of Health and Hygiene. Refusal to Sign Consent prior to Mutually Beneficial Foreplay.

—What, she just pounced on somebody?

—Without the necessary documents. »

Dutchcap begs for clemency: Belcula isn't from these parts, he explains, she means well but lacks social graces. Nodding dully, Blandus Vlaag offers to escort him to the prison. « You can plead with my superiors » he says. So they hurry – one man muffled to his ears, the other barely clothed at all – through the island's capital.

In architecture and grace, Hedonopolis is little different from Gent. Only the frescoes of erotic couplings (triplings, quadruplings . . .) mark this town apart from its continental fellows. Also distinctive is the need, apparently felt by the citizens, to expose more flesh than the climate calls for. Dutchcap, though trying to attend to his guide, is distracted by skimpy skirts and projecting codpieces, and a thousand mirthless smiles.

« I guess your surprise (guesses Blandus Vlaag) at these proofs of our liberation.

—You were occupied?

—Preoccupied. By cranky hang-ups, outmoded codes of conduct. Sex on Hedon used to be fearful, snatched against strictures. But there was an uprising, the forces of repression were routed. And what had been a necessary evil became an Absolute Right. Inviolable and inalienable, predicated on Legitimate Needs. »

Dutchcap knots his perplexed brow. A schoolmarm, lining up her pupils in the street, barks for attention and checks for dirty palms. Now a rangy youth, tight stockinged and omnicured, approaches. The heavy matron indicates him with her finger, coos mechanically and joylessly pinches his bum. Whereupon the young man (not looking too put out) suffers on his hams the studious nipping of two dozen schoolgirls.

«. . . codified promiscuity (drones Blandus Vlaag) is taught in the classroom. In their first year, children learn posture and practice. By the age of seven they must be proficient in Mutuality (that's Ethics), Forms of Seduction (Rhetoric) and Finding the Clitoris (Anatomy). Needless to say, those that fail Basic Entitlement have to sit the year again. »

Dutchcap wonders what happens to those who fail consistently. There are many vagrants crouched, shunned and ragged, in the pissy side streets.

«. . . Hedon boasts a good body of literature on the subject: its necessity for health and the spirit. Sex is our principal source of employment. We have physicians for potency, spas to replenish stamina, workhouses to rehabilitate the Undersexed.

—Are there no taboos?

—Well, celibacy, of course. Look, it's either a perversion or an infringement of Basic Rights. Either way, transgression must be punished. We have prison for abstention, ostracism for the chaste. And *shame* (Blandus kicks dust in a vagrant's eye) . . . eternal shame for the impotent. »

«—But do you (asks Dutchcap) derive any *pleasure* from it all? »

Blandus Vlaag squints at the question, perplexed. He describes, slowly and at volume, the island's quotas on orgasm, the Bill of Spasmodic Equity . . .

« So we've arrived » interrupts Dutchcap, simply to stop the blather.

Here, indeed, loom Hedon's forbidding prison gates. Blandus Vlaag knocks thrice on the resounding wood, which groans open to admit them. Dutchcap quakes at the sight of gallows in the yard. In a dusty courthouse, he is admonished by magistrates with chest wigs and chasmic cleavages. Somehow the grovelling of a dumb foreigner appeases these justices. Released from her chains, Belcula rushes to embrace her saviour. Blandus Vlaag, caught up in the jubilation, shakes Dutchcap by the hand and makes a legalistically flawless pass at his companion.

Belcula, deeply confused, clings to her Dutchcap all the way back to the *Profijt* – which promptly raises anchor and escapes.

How Belcula visits the isles of Scrag and Skellen, & the speed with which she leaves them

As, having been mowed to the stalk, a patch of ground reshoots to rankness, so Belcula recovers from her ordeal. Within hours (you'll be glad to know) she is back at her old tricks, while Dutchcap swings alone in his hammock in the hold.

At dawn the next day the captain emerges from his cabin and, shutting his peeflap, charts a new course to Scrag and Skellen. Trade can wait: his ship's business is now m'lady's pleasure. « Though if her mother lives on these islands (he confides to Dutchcap), God help us.

—Why, what goes on there? »

The captain shudders. « You'll find out soon enough. »

For two tempestuous days, our friends pitch and stagger. Neptune toys with the ship on his belly: he dips her into his navel, where fish scales flash, then flips her on an outbreath into his foaming beard. Dragging himself to the hatch and ogling, pink eyed, a heaving molten sky, Dutchcap despairs. All of Creation lurches, nauseated, floundering to its end.

On the third day a rent appears in the blackness, a silver peep of light. It grows slowly as they sail towards it, letting down its golden braids. At last, blue sky yawns above them – sunbeams swim like jellyfish upon the hull – and a cry from the crow's-nest announces land.

As you can see on our map (hey, who's licked it?), the isles of Scrag and Skellen are linked by a causeway of granite knots. Though near neighbours, they could not be more dissimilar. Scrag is quilted with orchards and wheatfields – Skellen is desolate, barely tufted by grass and stunted rye. Neither island boasts a harbour, their jagged, wafered cliffs descending, at best, to low, sea-wracked shelves.

« We must explore them both » Dutchcap insists.

In view of the danger, the *Profijt*'s captain offers his services. Ruffling maps, he hands Belcula to the rowing-boat, then joins her in it. Resignedly, Dutchcap leans on the oars as the sailors wish Belcula good luck (each man secretly praying for her return). Then Dutchcap grits his teeth and pitches himself against the waves, catching – after three clean strokes – a jolting crab.

« Don't worry about me (he huffs), you keep at it.

Rocks? We won't hit any *rocks*. With my back turned to the shore? And you two lashing into one another? »

Dutifully, the captain surfaces. But his distracted navigation leaves much to be desired, and Dutchcap cricks his neck attempting to find a bearing. Finally he sees an alcove: scuttles into it with the seat of his breeches damp and the sweat dripping off him. Belcula, accepting the captain's gallantry, somehow ends up astride his ears, with her heels in his groin, before plumping down on the barnacled rock. Next the captain – greatly flustered both upstairs and down – hauls himself ashore, leaving Dutchcap to secure the boat.

Some minutes later our explorers are sunning themselves in a meadow (Dutchcap glumly on his belly) when they hear the sound of running feet. Looking up, they see a hedgerow shudder and disgorge a large, sweaty family. Mother, father, two sons and three daughters canter, floppy wristed, along a sandy track. On their foreheads they wear bands of calico; white cladding stuffed with straw encases their feet. Though clearly in pain, they push themselves to their physical limits.

« Something terrible must be happening » Dutchcap quails, imagining massacres. At the opposite end of the meadow a second family appears. These islanders, too, are on the run, making great show of their breathlessness, their Vs of sweat. I should say how *toned* they are, having purged themselves, through fanatical toil, of flab and looseness. When Dutchcap hails them they fix the ground (the fat skipper and his mate are *deformed*) and break into a sprint.

« Nothing for it (says Dutchcap), we'll have to follow. »

Yeah, right. Our threesome limps along the coast, falling ever farther behind, till it reaches a huddled village. Here the houses – which are wind hacked, decrepit, fringed by dead gardens – seem to puff and clatter from within. People never rest on Scrag. They run (on the spot if needs be), they leap and starburst. It's exhausting just *hearing* them: the hop scotching blacksmiths, the girls pumping iron.

The sound of so much industry makes Belcula hungry. Swiftly the captain cuts his purse. He selects a cottage and knocks at the door. For a time nothing happens; then it seems he has set off a clockwork mechanism – *clack*-tacka-tacka-*clack*-tacka-tacka – that opens the door. Nodding, the captain doffs his cap:

« Sorry to trouble you, sir. I can see you're busy. My friends and I are rather hungry. » He makes the global sign of grub and fondles his pregnant purse.

Curious Dutchcap sidles closer. He sees, in the doorway, a young man with a skipping-rope. The fellow is encased in gleaming muscle. The slightest pulse sets it rippling under rope-veined skin, as though his flesh crawls with restive molluscs; as far as his face the creatures have travelled, slithering expressively beneath the derma.

« Hongerig (the cottager pipes, surprisingly shrew-voiced in all that brawn)? Du bist, nee? Ich habbe multo tasty noš. »

Ah, a sailor's knack for the lingo! Pleased with himself, the captain folds his fat fingers across his belly. When the cottager returns, however, self-satisfaction spills from the sea dog's face. For he's confronted with a platter of celery, unsugared prunes and oatcakes so thin they crumble on sight. Please don't worry – the oatcakes are fat free and entirely unsalted! The captain, relying on a diversion, gestures his thirst; whereupon he is offered carrot juice, rainwater and concentrate of lettuce. Purely out of good manners, he buys a flask of rainwater and a brace of spry-leafed celery – which Belcula consumes like a cat attacking chicken bone, snapping with great hacks and sipping down the tatters.

« Might you know of a Flemish lady in these parts (Dutchcap enquires of Ajax)? She'd have come here many years ago. Name of Spewer? Hildegard von Spewer? »

Stretching solicitously the tendons of his knee, the cottager shakes his head:

« Ganz unlikelich. After eerstgekolonisten settle hier to beautify body – like Bog, great Gott, intending – since then niemand gekommen to Scrag auf dem ganzen Kontinent.

—I can't imagine why (side-mouths Dutchcap).

—Because them cannot HACK it! »

Now it is Belcula who interjects. Clapping Dutchcap's hand to her chest, she shares with him the eloquent tam-tam of her heart. Farther north, her instinct tells her. Her mother lives not here. So, having sought directions, our adventurers take leave of the skipping man and head for the rocks that link Scrag to Skellen.

Windmilling across the plashy causeway, Dutchcap mutters darkly. « Did you notice there were no elderly, no sick, no lame? » But soon they are on the other side, with fresh matters to attend to.

This second island, Skellen, is cold and dead thorned. The wind blowing across it makes twice the howl it made on Scrag – which simpers in sunshine across the sound. « Makes you wonder why *this* lot don't invade *that* lot » Dutchcap muses.

The reason's simple, actually. Unlike their Scraggite neighbours, who can't sit still for an instant, the people of Skellen can scarcely move. They lie beneath the beams of their decaying huts, sallow, gaunt and purple lidded. Belcula and Dutchcap try not to wince at the sight of brittle limbs and furry skulls and bulging, languid eyeballs. Remembering a celery leaf down her front, Belcula rushes with it to a starveling's side.

« What cruel famine stalks this land? » Dutchcap-the-indifferent asks tearfully.

The prone, vaguely feminine creature – too weak to take the celery – tautens her skull in suggestion of a sneer. « God (she croaks), how can you *live* with yourself?

—Well, I had no idea—

—Letting yourself go like that. Now I'm no oil painting, I'll grant you. But where, off this island, will you find better?

—B-better?

—If you lift up my head – thank you – you will observe how close I come to my Perfect Form. Did you wonder about my sex when you saw me? I'm more androgynous than ever.

—Oh well, I wouldn't—

—One day, quite soon I think, they will permit me on to the Walkway.

—Walkway?

—Weekly we congregate at the Walkway. Where Skellen's Perfect parade. No more than twenty yards: the plainest among us can rarely exceed fifty. In a straight direction I mean. Without collapsing.

—Collapsing?

—Have you come to join us? We get all sorts. Anchorites, hermits, fainting virgins. The competition is fierce. Its only comfort . . . that no one stays Perfect for very long. »

Confronted by a taut, yellow-gummed snarl, Dutchcap shrinks back, ceding his place to the captain. « Now look here (the bluff tar blorts). Does the name Spewer mean anything to you? Von Spewer? Does it? Mean anything? To you? Von? Spewer? Hildegard von Spew—? »

A tug on his coat tails suffices to stop him. Then with oomph and great speed the expedition retreats – across the causeway, through green fields and orchards – back to a leaky rowing-boat. Holes notwithstanding, it carries them as far as the *Profijt*'s ladder, to the boundless relief of the sailors.

What Belcula witnesses,
from a privileged vantage, of an island's pastimes

Hold tight, we're getting there, I promise. I'll skip minor incidents (the storm that sweeps them out to Siberia, the captain's fatal encounter with polar bears, Dulle Griet's sacking of Tartary) to concentrate on the Quest.

The skipperless *Profijt* bobs merrily at the base of mighty cliffs. Consulting what remains of the maps, Dutchcap declares this to be Talop: an island about which he knows nothing. Upon gaining the main-deck he is startled by deep, sonorous lowing. Whales, he wonders? Sea cows? Following the crew's example, he cranes his neck to see, on the crest above them, three robed figures blowing into conch shells.

« They must be hailing us (says the first mate). Let's wave back and show them we're frien– »

The rest is choked. A man has just fallen off the cliff.

To be precise, a man has just been thrown off the cliff, naked, to a gruesome end. The same trajectory is then traced by another, who forgets himself in his descent. A third man flaps his arms like a fledgling and is dashed on wolfish rocks.

« Right (says Dutchcap), I say we skip Talop. »

But Fate has decided otherwise. Three longboats have slipped from a secret cove and now bear down on the ship. Propelled by long black oars, these sleek boats carry ensigns – of a charioteer gazing at the heavens – and quite a few heavily armed soldiers.

« I am Leno (a patrician voice drawls), Chancellor to

King Commodus II of Talop. These crossbows are loaded. Who might you be?

—If you please (says Dutchcap, preserving with a length of canvas Belcula's modesty), we are traders on our way to Bergen. Won't you, um, step aboard? »

Within seconds, black-plumed soldiers have secured the *Profijt*'s deck. Browbeating the innocent sailors, they part to let the Chancellor through. It is all a bit theatrical.

« His Majesty requests an audience (Leno says baldly). You, sir, and this young lady. We shall return you, eventually, to your vessel. »

It is clearly unwise to refuse. The soldiers usher our friends into separate boats. Dutchcap searches for Belcula, and finds her at the Chancellor's side.

« I sense your curiosity (says Leno as the longboats advance) concerning the king's qualities. He is the island's guardian spirit, as was his father, our founder, before him. Measure, beauty, mind and science meet in Commodus like four streams converging. He is our Philosopher King. » Belcula – *uuah!* – yawns. « The ensign, of course, represents the Philosophic Life. The present king designed it. »

Having regained the hidden cove, the longboats mount a sandy bank. The passengers are disembarked; they climb steps cut into the bluff, at whose summit deferential peasants fall on their faces.

« You notice, madam (says Leno), the happy industry of our people. These were once fishermen, risking their lives at sea. Now they slave safely on dry land. »

It is dirty work: digging peat, cutting it and stacking it in mounds. The island is dotted with these black, empty hives. As for the peat-cutters' huts, they are barely larger than the mounds, their yards littered with filthy children. The party marches on. Eventually, the level bog falls away to parkland. Dutchcap admires, despite himself, the box-framed formal gardens, the mazes and a boating lake. « The seat of government » Chancellor Leno announces, indicating a palace of Doric pretensions, all peristyle and architrash.

Within, the palace is as gorgeous as its outside implies: a little too plush and candelabrous if you ask Dutchcap, but no one does.

Now we enter a banqueting hall, where king and counsel sit in meditation, their heads bowed over parchments. Chancellor Leno clears his throat; the king snorts on his knuckles. Leno scuttles over and whispers into Commodus's ear; the king leaps to his feet. « Welcome (he shouts, waking his counsellors)! Dine with me, dine with me! We so rarely have visitors! » But this is mere politeness. The king proceeds to talk, incessantly, through the oysters and the stuffed swan and the gold-leaf gateau:

« My father came to Talop after being exp—, after graduating from the Platonic Academy in Florence. Through pure epistemology he subdued the islanders. Now all have a function, and each man knows his place. Especially me. »

Letting his attention wander, Dutchcap observes his fellow diners. They are all variations on the theme of

Leno (himself a second cousin to the throne). Wise and otherworldly, perhaps, but also deadly bored.

« . . . the people are an extension, into lower weaker multiples, of their king. They love me as all natural things seek a unity, a higher unity, with their source . . . »

Now Belcula – having got over the feast – is showing grave signs of dullness.

« . . . mankind recalls only dimly the timeless Form of Justice. So justice, in most lands, is imperfect. But I, being virtuous, chaste and intemporal, have *perfect* recollection. I am sufficiently expert in everything to do without laws.

—So those men you threw into the sea (Dutchcap lets slip), they'd broken no laws? You just didn't *like* them? »

The gathered Lenos stiffen at their fingerbowls. « He means, your majesty, to understand the benevolence of your policy on literature.

—Thank you, Chancellor (says Commodus). Let me explain. Imitative art is at one remove from reality, yes? But *reality* is at one remove from *Truth*: the world of Forms to which I alone have access. The degrading arts corrupt the soul because they mislead, they exaggerate and denigrate, they make us *dissatisfied*. Those were poets we threw from the cliff. It was for their own good. »

Dutchcap's custard skins over.

« The first was a dreary sonneteer. The second, who fell I'm told in a shower of wet shit, wrote love poetry. Then Olympiodorus, the so-called satirist. Well, he just *sneered* at everything. In rhyming couplets. (The king shudders in recollection.) He made rather a fuss at the end. Typical of his sort. Never satisfied with their lot. »

Thus enlightened, Dutchcap sees the wisdom of biting his tongue. Yet, as the dishes dwindle, he dares raise the subject of Hildegard von Spewer. « Perhaps you extended your hospitality to her, long ago? You see, majesty, she is my lady's mother. »

Commodus splutters and kisses the tablecloth. A falsetto Leno speaks for him.

« We did once (he says) have the pleasure of the Abbess's company. She visited us from Dulborg, just a few miles to the north.

—Abbess, did you say?

—Abbess Hildegard, yes.

—JAYSUS GOB! »

Belcula shoves her hand down her front to slow her racing heart. But the king seems much recovered from his short fit. He didn't realise the Abbess had a *daughter*. And *such* a daughter. How *interesting*. He snaps his fingers for slaves to clear the feast. His counsellors rise and depart, like a clan at a wake, and Dutchcap is escorted, by a most insistent Chancellor, to a cosy prison – leaving Belcula alone with Commodus.

Whistling through his nostrils, and leaning oddly at the waist, the Philosopher King expounds his doctrine to the indifferent Beauty. « The cause of all evil, my dear, is matter. (And what a lot of it you have.) For a man such as I, the object of life is to escape earthly interests for those of meditation. (Why don't you slip into these undies? I designed them myself.) By purification . . . (He puffs and stares, groping in his ermine) . . . by purification one attains . . . intimation . . . of the Divine Mind and ECSTATIC . . . UNION . . . with the OOONE! »

Belcula looks at the little man frenziedly masturbating at her feet. She wonders, as he grunts and whimpers, where Dutchcap has got to, and sets off to find him. Her exit sends servile courtiers pouring into the banquet hall. These men know their duties to the king; unfortunately, they also know a wanker when they see one. Cries of scandal pursue Belcula down the passageways. At last she hears the yelps of her flaccid companion, locates his prison cell and frees him.

« This is a madhouse » Dutchcap declares as, hand in hand, they leave the palace and its formal gardens and the wretched bog and the secret cove with the bluff-carved steps. « To Dulborg? » pants Dutchcap as he works at stolen oars.

« To Dulborg and Mama! »
See? What did I tell you?

END OF THE THIRD BOOK

BOOK FOUR

Of Dulborg Abbey, & a mother's love

Wimpled, stern and dark browed, Abbess Hildegard scrutinises the new recruit. Several things trouble her about the girl. There is too much appetite in those dark eyes, the sensuousness – could it be? – of spoiled goods. Muteness is no flaw, of course, but it suggests hidden thought, the keeping of unsound private counsel.

« She's of good understanding (the guardian insists) and immensely dextrous.

—You realise you can never see your charge again, if we take her? We admit no men beyond the gatehouse, and only I have dealings with the outside.

—Naturally. It is my fervent hope to, er, preserve her innocence. »

Belcula, in stiff clothes, struggles to contain herself. All morning she has spent bound at the chest, coached by Dutchcap in the art of blandness. Now, in her mother's presence, her heart is full to bursting. She takes in, restlessly, the dark mill of the abbey, its blind granite ramparts and the dun, unbroken marshes beyond. The sea is grey, the sky grey, and grey the loam at her feet; yet Belcula inwardly beams. For this is her mother's landscape, familiar to the maternal eye. Honestly, she wonders, where's the sense in this dressing up? Why Dutchcap's ploy, when all that life needs is frankness?

Abbess Hildegard, continuing, offers a verbal tour of

abbey life. (This'll be old hat to one of us.) Nuns rise at three of the morning. Matins, Lectio Divina and Lauds precede a silent breakfast. Work begins at eight, ceasing for Sext and Noon Dinner, which is likewise silent. There follows silent prayer in cells, then silent work until Vespers; which precedes a silent supper until Night Prayer and silence. The Sisters of Perpetual Renunciation, she explains, are pledged to Obedience – the full surrender of the self to God, whose concrete expression is obedience to their Abbess, Hildegard. As a postulant, Belcula shall contract herself to lifelong enclosure. As a nun she will tend crops and manufacture Dulborg Liqueur – the most intoxicating liquid known to man – from which she shall abstain. Her only delight, in this life, shall be Prayer, Penance and Mortification.

Dutchcap, watching this formidable lady, marvels at how thoroughly, over twenty years, she has subdued her physical self. Clearly she has no inkling of her daughter's presence. Even when she inspects Belcula, turning and palpating her like a fruit, she does not hear what Blood proclaims: their womb-tied bond.

« What route did you take to find us? » asks the Abbess. (The Order, since she tightened it, receives few recruits; yet Hildegard masks her suspicions throughout Dutchcap's neutered account, listening gravely, until his praise for King Commodus makes her snort.) « Civilised? Philosopher! That homunculus, sir, is a pervert and a pederast. My visitation was piously occasioned, neighbourly – we sell our liqueur throughout the North Sea. Yet that . . . concupiscent . . . *beast* (I hesitate to speak it) dared of *me*, a votarist and virgin, request favours (may the Lord forgive me) of a *carnal* nature. »

Despite his face's evidence, Dutchcap is not in the least surprised; nor is he to learn of the Philosopher King's harem and his collection of androgynes. He notices, however, with interest, the wet-lipped zeal of Hildegard's denunciation. The Abbess catches herself in time – pulls Belcula to her breast and welcomes her to the community.

« Before you take the veil, young lady, I must know every recess of your soul. »

So we have reached the Moment of Truth. The world's histories are crammed with unmaskings, revelations, prodigal children – what can I add that might lift your spirits or prick your eyes? Dutchcap and Belcula drop their disguises. Abbess Hildegard, smothered in claims and kisses, skelters from amazement to denial. She stammers in defence of her chastity, smarts at irrefutable facts. Somewhere through that stiff habit, I don't doubt, the ghost of a ditch flits – she must hear the echo of a baby's cry. Yet despite a lump, a knot, in her heart that aches to embrace the fabulous, the Professional Nun prevails.

« I have dedicated myself to the Lord's service (she says). Before Dulborg there was nothing. It is quite impossible for me to recognise you. You are some devilish apparition, or a tasteless jest of Talopian devising. Therefore I implore you, GO AWAY! »

With that she retreats behind the gate, leaving our pals in dismay and drizzle.

The Drinking Woman's Tale

In which all seems lost, & most probably is

Belcula sits with Dutchcap in a swineherd's hut, banished to the dullest edge of Dulborg. Both are sick at heart and damp to the bone; nothing Dutchcap says can console his friend or stem the flow of her tears. Could he guess the worse that's to come, he'd spare himself the trouble and drag them off the island.

Because Dulle Griet – while we've been sobbing – has finally caught up with us. Out across the sea, a trail of devastation smoulders. Hedon fell first, then Scrag and Skellen. Talop, alone of the four islands, resisted; yet no number of Pythagorean engines could prevail against Dulle Griet's greed. As I speak, the deposed king Commodus laments his family jewels, which Griet lopped off and swallowed ungarnished. His former counsellors, that long line of ambitious Lenos, scrabble through the palace ruins, their minds on anything but philosophy.

So to the crunch you've been waiting for.

Dulle Griet's corsair, black sailed and batlike, couples brutally with the *Profijt*. Crampons, like long fingers, dig into her oaken flanks. Then, from the harridan ship, the huswives spill. Dutch vitals, Danish brains, paint the deck. The first mate, thinking in his peril of those on shore, tries to toll a warning: Dulle Griet catches him before the bell has sounded, breaking his back with the flat of her sword. Finally, when no Belcula has been plucked (like a grub) from the ship's splinters, the pirates flood the hold. Whatever glitters on twitching fingers, in gaping gobs, is prised out and stuffed into aprons. As swiftly as it had boarded, the mob abandons ship.

Now, from the corsair's belly, scullers are launched bristling with arms. Dulle Griet stands erect at the leader's prow. Behind her, the trusty *Profijt* sinks. The sails bloat and fart trapped air. The bow is last to disappear, rising above the spume like a bird's beak, until it too succumbs to the gluttonous deep.

Now follow me (if you can take it) into the gruesome throng of Dulle Griet's army. Any living thing – beetle, bird or lizard – that strays into her path gets pulverised and slung into the mire. See here (careful!), Dulle Griet's nostrils are quivering. The spoor is strong. She drops her basket and begins to run: running as some terrible lizard might run, every footcrash an affront to Creation.

In the swineherd's hut at the far end of the island, Belcula stops her tears. Like her boar-mother long ago, she smells danger and hears the baying mob.

« Don't go out there! » Dutchcap pleads, trying without success to restrain her. « Whatever's happening has got nothing to do with us. »

Unheeding, Belcula makes for the north cliff, from whose vantage she can see the besieging army. It is her first glimpse of the enemy: that shadow which has clung to our tale. And what a sickening vision it is, an infestation. Dulborg Abbey will not withstand an assault. The nuns on the ramparts, with mounting fervour, invoke the Almighty, their prayers almost drowning out Dulle Griet's ultimatum:

« You must surrender the wench Belcula. She is my

clients' property. Protect her and die – yield her up and live. »

It is no idle threat. Already huswives are scaling the walls, with darning-needles for crampons. Belcula, on the clifftop, cups her hands around her mouth. Before Dutchcap can stop her, she shouts—

On the Consequences of Propriety

Any tale is like a glass bell dropped into a rock pool. Encompassing within its eye a teeming world, it shows nothing of the Universe beyond. Planets spin, stories unfold, without our noticing; nor can turning our backs prevent them. So let's look away from Dulborg at this awful juncture. We've been neglecting the folks back home.

For Pieter Hooch and Oswolt von Spewer, time has run its course. Rumour has spread beyond Varenburg of their monstrous bargain; from flattened hamlets to the Patershol, Dulle Griet's victims march south, along the swath of her plunder.

Shaken from profound and scholarly sleep, Pieter Hooch rushes in his nightcap to the casement. His house booms and shakes; brick-dust puffs in light beams from the shutters. « Oh Lord, save me! » Panic stricken, he rummages inside a chest in his study, extracting neither bribe nor weapon but thick wads of erotica. He bids no fond farewell to his bride's pictures (bought off travelling pamphleteers) but stuffs them into the hearth. It is thus – prodding, bare buttocked, a reluctant fire – that the rabble finds him and drags him screaming to the merchant's courtyard.

Hundreds, meanwhile, besiege von Spewer's mansion. Recognising the gravity of his situation, the old merchant attends to essentials. He gathers together loose gold and jewellery, unfurling a rug to expose a trap in the floor. This secret vault is trigger-opened by a lewd latch: the prick of a marble cherub. But men break down the door just as his fingers touch the latch, branding an image for ever in their heads. There isn't even time for a merchant's curse. With impressive efficiency, the mob beats, rapes and dismembers the household, from kitchen boy to steward. Von Spewer's gold is taken, with deeds and Italian furnishings, as reparation, leaving not a beam behind.

From Pieter Hooch there is less to steal. He lived frugally, it must be said, with only an old crone to cook for him (and she died of fright before sport could be made of her). So violence turns instead on his books. Worthless illuminated manuscripts, first editions with authors' emendations, unfloggable crap from Constantinople, are winged and ruptured. A few titles are put to some use. Epicurus, for instance, is used as arse-wipes, Plato to pack apples, and Aristotle's *Ethics* serves as kindling.

I used the past tense just now because, in the time it's taken to describe these things (in that little heap of seconds), Pieter Hooch and Belcula's grandsire have been slung from a branch of the courtyard oak. Their heads knock together. Eyeball bulges at eyeball. A strong gust sends Oswolt's convex gut into Pieter's concave belly. The lynch-mob watches, numbly, the belated recrimination of their corpses.

In which we come to the climax – a misleading expression

« Over here! Come 'n' get me! »

Dutchcap's arms are flung about Belcula's legs, his face sinking earthward, where he would, if he could, hide in darkness, never to witness her crazy heroics. Belcula, undeterred, dances for Dulle Griet's attention, writhing like a worm on the angler's hook. Sexily she pouts, heaping her lustrous hair. And it works! Imagine a ruffle of crows picking over bones. Now drop fresh carrion in their midst and see what follows. Dulle Griet's guile is fled: moneylust devours her. Hissing, she ascends the escarpment with her women in tow.

« Holy God (Dutchcap prays), let's make a deal. My unbelief for a miracle. »

Above the nuns' shrill incantations, Dulle Griet gives out orders: « Open the net! We'll lime her like a lark, we'll cage her pretty plumage. » Dextrously the women unfold a weighted net. They arc out with it slung between them, forbidding escape. Confronted by the prospect of capture, Belcula lifts Dutchcap to her face and kisses his blinking eyes. Her breath is hot, animal, sugared. Then she replaces him in the grass and, bending at the waist, bares her peachy bum at the foe. This insolence – so unexpected, in the context – unnerves the advancing women. Only outrage from their leader starts them forward again.

Suddenly, at a speed too great to permit interference, Belcula has shed her virginal togs and thrown herself off the precipice. She makes no sound as she plummets, unseen, to the sea. The nuns wail on her behalf, three score voices pitched in despair.

Finding her prize once more eluding her, Dulle Griet bounds, with great disgusting strides, into the abyss. Cursing and bleating, her women follow, bundling over the edge until not one remains.

(*Regarding this phenomenon, Aristotle observes,* lib. 7 de Histo. animal., *how the Caucasian wolf-marmot – a most cruel and savage rodent – will, in pursuit of its prey, fling itself headlong from a peak – embedding itself most often in the mountainside. It takes no special learning to know that, like unicorns and basilisks, the Caucasian wolf-marmot is today extinct, lost to its blind appetite. The same is true of Dulle Griet, plunged to legendary infamy, and to whom the obvious moral applies*.)

So what, my pals, are we left with? Dutchcap on all fours, at Dulborg's edge, staring in grief and admiration at the far-below flood. That old-timer, the sea, looks unaffected by its remarkable meal. Apart from the odd rag and pewter plate, nothing of Belcula nor her hunters remains.

Dutchcap is still looking, almost lulled by shock, into the sea, when Abbess Hildegard sits beside him. She places (for her own sake) a steadying hand on his shoulder. And Dutchcap observes, with indifference, the black-and-white throng all about him, of nuns casting prayers at the water.

How Dutchcap gets his vigour back

Though masculine except in function, and so, by rights, *non grata*, poor Dutchcap is admitted to Dulborg Abbey. Four sturdy nuns carry him – he is limp with fatigue and sorrow – to bed in a white arid cell. Water is brought to him and the casement window (a rare luxury) opened for fresh air.

Implacable evening closes in. Dutchcap lies forlorn on the bed, his eyes drowned in the ceiling's whiteness, when into his cell comes the Abbess. Too broken to attend, he does not see the strain, in her physique, of irreconcilable feelings: the warp of metamorphosis.

« What was she like (Hildegard asks)? To sacrifice herself, she must have been a saint. »

Dutchcap cannot bring himself to respond. The Abbess looks long at his washed-out face; he seems not to feel her eyes on his skin. « Tomorrow we shall pray for her » she says, and quietly withdraws.

Later, at some station of his grief, Dutchcap's cell glows with unearthly light. It emanates not from the window, which continues to frame night's blackness, nor from any lamp or taper. Dutchcap props himself painlessly on to his elbows and sees, without surprise, Belcula naked at his feet. About her lavish curves radiance flares, like the eclipsed sun's corona. Dutchcap cannot look away from her face, its look of rapt beatitude. Her eyes like deep pools claim his own. Beneath that intent gaze he senses the weight of her breasts, her rosy nipples, the ample belly with its tides and labyrinths. Belcula lowers her eyes to license his. Dutchcap feasts on her fertile hips, the gathered bush and, divined beneath it, the pink inworked folds of her sex. Now Belcula mounts the bed and her friend's knees. Without astonishment (what *doesn't* make sense in dreams?) Dutchcap senses blood returning to his manhood. He takes life in Belcula's hands – she breathes upon him and he rises, mightily, to the occasion. Now they kiss, fusing wetly. Belcula shuffles gracelessly to straddle him. She spreads her tepid hands on his chest, her fingers in his greying curls. He presses and caresses and kneads her breasts. O! the look on her face, of alarm and welcome, as they couple. Each, after count-less Almosts, has found the Perfect Fit. For aeons, it seems, they mate. Seasons and landscapes alter, unre-garded, outside, until they come together with the force of mountains. Belcula licks the tears from Dutchcap's cheeks, and he awakes.

He lies, chilled, in the empty cell, across whose walls blear blue seams of dawn. Gathering up the threads of his mind, Dutchcap discovers, to his stupefaction, a hot stiff prick. (His own, I mean.) Poor lucky man, to be made entire again at just the wrong moment. Belcula – that gigantic fleshly force – is dead; all of Dulborg is in mourning; and Dutchcap, after twenty years' flaccidity, is confronted by a brash excited member. Joy and grief alternate within him. Think as he might of icy marble, it stands, like a bald and sunburned alderman, rigid with avidity. He plunges it into his water bowl to cool it; he rests it against the cold iron of the door latch, as in desperation one attempts to soothe a flea-bite. Above his cell the mourning bell tolls. The cloisters shiver with approaching nuns. Powerless to resist, Nullifidius (let's call him once more by his chosen name) leaps to the window and reveals, to a startled audience, the infallible proof of a miracle.

By the time the Abbess reaches the scene, a crowd has gathered to hear Nullifidius's story. How Belcula, coming to him in a vision, reawoke his dormant loins. Belcula the Prick Quickener, the Bringer-to-Life. Abbess Hildegard – fragile after a sleepless night and much soul-searching – does not clobber the nudist, or even reprimand him for scandalous behaviour. Quite the contrary. This further proof of her daughter's munificence transfigures her. (Sister Nun, you could learn a thing or two.) Bombing to the front of the crowd, Hildegard tears off her vestal uniform and plucks her tits to the wind.

So begins the reformation of Dulborg Abbey; which, if you'll be patient for a final chapter, I shall describe in brief.

Of Eudokia Abbey, its Charism & Practices,
& in which we bid farewell to our story

They call it Eudokia: a place of good will and contentment.

Immediately, Hildegard revokes the speaking laws. This results in an unstoppable flow of words, a great torrent of feeling and thought and song. Nullifidius marvels that Belcula, who barely spoke in her lifetime, should in death become the cause of such babble.

Armed with eloquence, Dulborgian missionaries set out for the mainland. In expectation of their return (laden with male converts) windows are knocked into every cell. The nuns demolish the enclosure walls. Clocks are banned, their ticking tyranny overthrown; for the body is its own timepiece. Diet, too, undergoes a transformation, on the principle that good food whets the appetite. As for furnishings, Eudokians don't much care for splendour. Function and comfort are their watchwords, luxury being confined to the beds, which are fragrant and sturdy and soft cushioned.

For centuries a blind place, unbroadened by mirrors, the Abbey's interior blinks with Venetian crystal, which some nuns fix to their bedroom ceilings.

As liberty takes root, the nuns banish the habit, dressing instead as pleasure dictates. Out go the wimple and the hairshirt; in come silk stockings, damask gowns and petticoats. Neither stay nor fainting bodice is to be found on the island, leaving the body to its own dancing, like a poppy in the field.

After a few weeks, the first men arrive, eager to embrace the new dispensation. Above the abbey gates they read this motto:

FAY QUI VOULDRAS,

that is, 'Do Who You Will'. Its author, Nullifidius, introduces the boys to the girls. Together with the Abbess, he neither punishes nor exhorts the Siblings of Perpetual Willing – encouraging instead by example. Only marriage is forbidden, which seeks to fetter wandering lust. You won't hear, on Eudokia, the language of Need or Duty. Desire, after all, requires no excusing.

Finally, in Belcula's memory, Nullifidius builds a pleasure garden in the Abbey's cloister. At its gate, on a marble plaque, this simple verse is inscribed:

> Eudokia Abbey
> Welcomes all;
> Be you great
> Or be you small,
> Visitor, be happy!

*

There is a version of this story that ends with Dulle Griet victorious. Another, saving Belcula in the belly of a whale, spits her out on Atlantis's shore. But *we* finish as we started – with Hildegard tipping her arse (now quite a bit larger and less pneumatic) to receive her ardent lover. Nullifidius, as he crampons on, still believes in nothing; he just keeps the fact a secret, for his happiness' sake.

Thus I conclude my scurrilous life of Belcula Bolerckx. May God grant her bliss.

Explicit liber Bos et Gallo.

The Nun's Prologue

For a time after the telling, the listeners sit cross-legged. Only the Nun, incapable of tumescence, speaks her mind.

Nun. What fanciful lies! It's a proven fact that fat girls given to licentiousness are vulnerable to disease. And if not sickness, then worse: death in childbed or the shame of bastardy.

Fool (having mastered his jester). But Sister, surely Brides of Christ commit polygamy on a daily basis?

Nun. Passionless people are Chosen by God to keep Him company in the small hours. It is desirable to live without physical love. Adam and Eve in Eden had no need of increase.

(*Choristers. Mankind had no cause to grieve/Until Adam fell on Eve!*)

Nun. Passion overheats the brain and is bad for the body; and that which is bad for the body is bad for the soul. Give in to lust and Death will catch you, coming at you in the night with glowing eyes.

Choristers. Barking like a hound.

Monk. Yelping like a fox.

Drinking Woman. If Death's ugly I'd kill myself. I should have him a pretty youth, with big hot hands.

Nun. Would you, now?

Drinking Woman. To take me in his arms till I swoon.

Nun. You would fall for a handsome Reaper?

Drinking Woman. So long as he has all his teeth.

Nun. Oh, think seriously on your soul, woman. Let my story answer yours.

The Nun's Tale

It is haymaking time in the Year of Grace thirteen hundred
and thirty-seven. A traveller, gazing down from a particular hillside, might see the houses of a village gleam, like
glazed loaves, in the sunlight. In fields hard by, the villagers
toil as at every harvest, with all but the lame at the task.
They scythe and sweep and fork up the hay; heaped carts
blunder; horses strain. For though kind Nature is heavy
with fruit, soon the leaves will fall, the sap will sink in every
root and Winter come, baring her widow's face.

This particular year, a pretty, plump-chested girl
walks apart from her companions. Her name is Agnes.
Shading her eyes with her hand, she turns to face the
declining West and scans the horizon. Every hour she
stops and looks; and whenever he can, Wilhelm the
miller's boy leans on his hayfork to watch her. What
does she look for in those distant blue hills? Does she
dream of Love and High Adventure? The older men
tease Wilhelm for his musings and he blushes, clearing
his head as a dray-horse shakes off flies.

'Why don't you speak to her?' says the miller, keen
for his boy to marry. 'Moping and moaning never won
a woman's heart, no matter how deep the feeling.'

Sure enough, Wilhelm, being young, has worked

himself into a passion for the girl. With every day the sickness that poets call Cupid's poison worsens, and still the boy dares nothing. The object of his devotion stands strange and sainted to him: he cannot hope for a cure.

Agnes seems equally preoccupied, to those who know her. For months she has lived in her imagination, meeting her family only at mealtimes and for prayers. She begrudges none of her daily duties, for her mind floats above the chores like a feather on the breeze. Agnes lives elsewhere. The village boys feel like clouds in the indifferent skies of her eyes.

As sleepwalkers, then, Wilhelm and Agnes move through days of early autumn. One evening, as smoke from the fields stands ghostlike in the trees, they take the same path through the woods and fall, having no alternative, to talking. Imagine Wilhelm's delight when Agnes speaks (about the harvest, about the weather) in clear, mortal's German. She even blushes, he thinks, when once he claims her eyes with his. What sweet delight, to meet a goddess and find her approachable! Wilhelm bids Agnes goodnight by the bridge, resolved at last to woo her.

By the first snowfall he has advanced to uneasy friendship but no farther. 'Don't love me,' Agnes begs. 'We're brother and sister in longing but I cannot love you back.'

Perhaps it is to prove her detachment from the working world that, one bright December morning, Agnes disappears. The village, where at times of tragedy the many join to help the few, rallies to the rescue. Men dredge the icy brook but find nothing. Search parties skirt the fringes of the forest to no avail. Wilhelm sickens with fear. Every danger, from wolves to bandits, gnaws at his sleep. He mourns her loss as though he were Agnes's husband: deeply, bitterly. The miller watches his son's agonies and suffers. Every heart burns in a sharp frost of grief; so that the thaw, when it comes, is sudden and scolding.

'Agnes! She's alive! It's Agnes!'

Wilhelm awakes running. Pulling on his coat he dashes out into the cold, creaking morning. Villagers have gathered outside Agnes's house. They bob and sway, like young corn, to catch a glimpse inside.

'What is it,' Wilhelm asks. 'What has happened?'

'The girl's returned,' says the blacksmith. 'They say she's raving – dressed for midsummer – with flowers in her hair.'

When Agnes within hears Wilhelm's voice, she calls for him. The villagers part, all eyes, and Wilhelm moves through them into the dark interior. He finds Agnes's parents clinging to their ragged daughter. Agnes's face, escaping a quilted blanket, is round and pleading like a child's. Her naked feet, frost-swollen, are garlanded with wilted daisies. Her unkempt hair is threaded with rosemary and columbine, with pansies and violets, withered all.

'Dear friend,' Agnes says. 'I have tumbled from Summer back to Winter. Where I have been – what happened to me – seems impossible when I speak it.

'I went walking by the brook, there were rowanberries I wanted to pick, you know the spot. Somehow I lost my way – my thoughts were elsewhere – and soon the trees had closed about me. Night began to fall, my coat was torn by brambles, the cold bit at my face.

'Just when all seemed hopeless, I heard the crunch of hooves on snow, and a knight appeared before me. His armour was of silver (in the snow it shone like the moon) and the charger was white, high and handsome. He came to save me.

'Well, I must have slept, for I don't recall our journey. When I awoke I was in a great stone hall. The hearth stood empty, as in high summer, yet the air was warm.

'For a week the knight attended to me. He clothed me and brought me these flowers and I drank nectar from a *glass* and never thought to leave. Why should I? Until this morning, when I fled, I awoke – no, I found myself – back here, by the rowan trees.'

Of course, the villagers, when they hear it, doubt Agnes's story. People who must struggle to live resent the claims of dreamers. *She's touched in the head*, folk mutter, *she's cracked, a fibber*. Wilhelm finds himself unwelcome in the afflicted house, while the loose talk of villagers outside wounds him. Like the maggot in an apple, curiosity gnaws at Wilhelm, until he decides, with the blindness of ardour, to clear his lady's name.

Far from his friends, forlornly he walks. On the trunks of trees he etches his initials, hoping to retrace his route thereby. But losing his way is the least of Wilhelm's cares. For the cold is a cruel law and he must bow before it. Sharp snow blinds him; freezing rain stings him; the trees are fanged with icicles. Out of the darkness he hears the huff and snuffle of unglimpsed wolves. Still Wilhelm carries on. In the corner of his eye he glimpses the hem of Agnes's skirt, her garlanded foot; in a reverie he starts at her breath on his frozen face.

On the third day, as cold, coppery sunlight pierces the wildwood, Wilhelm prises himself free of brambles, trips on a root and falls into a clearing. For an instant he thinks he has found the knight's dwelling-place. But his eyes behold no great stone hall, only a woodsman's hut, ramshackle and rudely built. Wilhelm knocks at the door.

'Who's there?' growls a voice within.

'A traveller,' says Wilhelm. 'I'm lost and seek to know my whereabouts.'

He hears a sighing, shuffling movement behind the door. It creaks open, a fraction only, and a spear-shaft is pointed at his throat.

'I'll tell you where you are,' says the woodsman. 'You're in the wrong place – clear off. I've seen what's happening in some villages, I know what's coming to others.'

Thinking himself met with a madman, Wilhelm retreats. As he edges back towards the tree line, he cannot contain his question. 'Do you know of a knight in these parts? A silver knight on a white charger? He has a home, a great stone hall, where flowers grow out of season.'

'That's all I need,' the woodman wheezes, 'a crackpot.'

*   *   *

That whole day it snows without let-up. Wilhelm clutches his wet clothes to his chin and shudders. Hope and heat drain from him. Towards dusk, as he wades through deep new snow, his head sinks on to his chest. His quest has been foolhardy: there is no knight to discover. He will perish out here needlessly, lost in the thorny maze. And what a release it seems to die, to sink like snow in deep blue drifts of sleep. Wilhelm sighs and falls, longing for death as for a lover.

He awakes to find a dog licking his ear. Wilhelm does not cry out. His trembling fingers touch cold matted fur, a wet snout. With a surge of energy, the boy pulls himself free of the snow. The dog arches its back in play, barks and makes off through the trees. Wilhelm follows, flailing at dead branches. His feet at last find strong ground. The dog stops once to make sure that it is being followed, then leaps on. The trees are parting now, melting before Wilhelm's hope. At the forest's edge he finds the clearing and is free.

The snow survives here only in patches. Plump drops plash from the trees; about their roots bright meltwaters dance. How is this possible, Wilhelm wonders, a thaw so suddenly? For his village is clean of snow, as though a giant had breathed upon it.

'A miracle!' Wilhelm rejoices. And runs – so fast his legs can barely keep up with him – into a village choked by Pestilence.

* * *

The worst of nightmares has broken from sleep and taken terrible form on earth. Wilhelm trudges through disaster's wrack. Stray dogs and cattle roam the streets. Door after door is daubed with a cross. In the mud of the churchyard a long pit gapes.

'My son,' whispers the priest from his sanctum, 'leave the village!'

'But I just did.'

'We are being punished for ungodly ways. You must save yourself.'

Wilhelm staggers, dreading the worst, to Agnes's house. The door is bolted shut: a rough red cross condemns it. Wilhelm pounds on the wood, until at last a neighbour ventures from a window.

'They're walled in with it,' the old woman says. 'Only the girl's gone.'

'*Gone?*'

'Fled to the woods.'

Wilhelm, as he stumbles home, fastens to this hope. He feels Agnes living still. She is his True Love: Love is stronger than Death.

The miller his father is dead and buried. Wilhelm's uncle sobs in the doorway. Drunk, with a sweat upon him, he clutches at his nephew. Wilhelm, from too much grief, retreats. He wants to crush that gibbering head, to stamp it out like a weevil. Instead he helps his uncle to bed and forces water upon him.

'The Plague Maiden,' the old man rasps, 'the *Pest Jungfrau* came. The sun was shining, it was midwinter spring, we meant to enjoy it. Then *she* appeared at the window, waving a scarlet kerchief. We spoke to her, not knowing her. But she gazed right through us – as though she's no business with the folk she kills but rather with someone she can't find.'

Wilhelm hears these piteous ravings but he does not credit them. Indeed, he can manage one thought only. That his father is dead. He has no one. Save Agnes. When his uncle's eyes have shut in sleep, Wilhelm runs from the house. If she lives, he knows where to find her. Abandoning the stricken village, he retraces his route into the forest.

Agnes sits, breast deep in wild flowers, under the shade of the rowan trees.

'Keep back!'

Those are tears that pearl her cheeks. 'Keep away,' she pleads. 'I am cursed.'

'Thank God you live,' says Wilhelm, wading through flowers towards her. He imagines their bodies embracing, mingling and turning to steam, their blent drops settling on the petals as dew. But Agnes panics at his approach; she staggers backward like a crab. A scarlet shawl falls from her shoulders; she snatches it and pulls it over her eyes.

'Don't touch me!' she shrieks.

Wilhelm stops, startled. Slowly and with great patience he crouches, as one might to coax a bird to one's palm.

'Wilhelm, I am cursed,' says Agnes, lowering the

shawl. 'My parents, our neighbours: all that know me perish.'

'How can you hurt me, when the very ground you touch springs to life? If you wish it, I will go. But only to the glade's edge, where I will watch over you.'

Night falls, as warm as Midsummer. Agnes settles beneath the rowan trees. Wilhelm, having taken himself off a short distance, sits until sunrise, maintaining his vigil.

Birdsong wakens her. Agnes sits up from her flowering bed and meets her servant's longing eyes.

'Are you well?' she asks. 'No sneezing, no head-aches?'

'None.'

'No fever, no thirst?'

'None.' Wilhelm hesitates before speaking again. 'What happened to you in the forest? I went in search of the knight and his hall. I went to defend your honour. But I found nothing.'

Agnes contemplates a poppy; her face is like the fields after rain.

'Like you,' she begins, 'I know what it is to love. And so fiercely that death loses its sting, if one could die for Love's sake.

'Last spring, I met a soldier by the brook. He was resting there on his way to war. He was tall and fair, with eyes like the dawn. Behind his smiling eyes I saw the sadness of a life without roots.

'I brought him bread and milk. He told me of the valleys and the plains in the world beyond ours. And as he spoke he set down roots into my heart.

'When the time came for him to set out, we kissed and pledged to meet again. How could we not? I was his kingdom and he was mine – and where else do journeys end but home?

'When he was gone it was high summer and the sunshine mocked my misery. You think you love me: I *know* I loved him. In night's darkness I kissed his mouth and felt his arms about me. I looked for signs of him on the horizon. I walked with him in the evenings as Winter closed in. And one day I came here, as I said, to pick rowanberries.

'The air was clear, so sharp, and the forest I saw was beautiful. Not as in Summer, when all is lush and green, but a still, stark beauty. It lured me like a song into the trees. Deeper and deeper I walked, until I was quite lost. When night began to fall I was afraid: I could do nothing to save myself. So I knelt and prayed to my lover, chanting his name over and over. To keep myself from feeling the cold, I imagined every detail of his face and body. I put him on a white horse, and decked him in bright armour.

'You must believe me, Wilhelm: when I saw the knight through the trees, even though it was dark, I knew his armour was silver and his mount as white as snow. He put his gloved hand out to catch me. I could hear the horse panting as it approached. I put out my hand and shut my eyes. His hand caught mine – I was swept up on to the saddle and saved.

'All night we rode, and when I awoke I was in a great stone hall. Wilhelm, no one from our world has ever known such comfort. My bed was wide and soft; I awoke to music and drank nectar from goblets of singing crystal. And I renounced my old life, as one forgets a dream.

'My host visited me every day. He never removed his armour, nor even his helmet. He seemed shy of me, keeping his distance. Although his face was hidden I felt his eyes upon me. And I knew him for my Beloved.

'One night I kept myself awake for him. At last, the door to my chamber opened. I shut my eyes fast and pretended to sleep. I did not hear him enter; I heard no footfalls, nor his breathing as he knelt at my side. I thought once I felt his hand in my hair, though it could as easily have been a breeze. How I longed to open my eyes and see his face, and touch his cheek with the back of my hand! But my courage failed me and when I scolded myself for falling asleep it was already morning.

'Swiftly I stole from the hall of delights. I found him at the forest's edge, looking from our garden to the winter wastes beyond. *Take off your helmet*, I said. He did – and I saw the face of my remembered love, unblemished by welt or weal. *The ghost of you*, I said, *has taken form in the present. I find you exactly as I lived you in my heart.* Hardly breathing for joy, I unbuckled his armour. At last there was only his shirt above his nakedness. My fingers ached to feel him beneath the wool.

'Just then – oh God – just then a cloud passed across the moon. And in the darkness I saw his eyes glow white, infinitely cold. I was afraid and, startled, I touched his hand for comfort. It was cold as clay.'

Crushing the poppy in her fist, Agnes begins to weep.

'When the moon floated out from behind the cloud, I saw the flowers shrivelled at my feet. And he, my True Love, was gone. Leaving no trace but the armour scattered about the wilting glade – pus flecked and *stinking of plague*!'

Agnes's fingers fly to her eyes, and she screams as her nails fill with blood.

It was impossible to calm her from a distance. Wilhelm fought with emotions for which he had no name. He thought of his dead father, of his uncle's grief, and he felt the chill of despair grow its crystals about his heart. He needed *life* – and Agnes was warm, she suffered and loved like him, though martyred to illusions.

Seeing her subside, exhausted, into the bloom and spray, he jumped to his feet and broke the charmed circle. The flowers sighed and fell before him. He reached his fainting love and held her in his arms. Her hair sifted like sand through his fingers; he dabbed the scarlet shawl in her wounds. And Agnes, too weary with hunger and horror and grief, suffered the boy to kiss her gaping mouth.

Explicit liber Pest Jungfrau.

The Prologue of the Penitent Drunkard

A silence of great discomfort descends upon the censured boat. The Monk chews the creases from his nose; the Fool grins wrinkles from his brow. The Choristers, however, and the Drinking Woman, take less trouble to disguise their displeasure, plugging their noses at the Nun's story as though at some drifting miasma.

It is (perhaps surprisingly) the Penitent Drunkard who clears the air.

Penitent Drunkard. Your story, Sister, is about credulity, and how we heed our illusions at our peril. Have you much experience, I wonder, in love?

Nun. Certainly not, sir.

Penitent Drunkard. But you speak with such authority.

Nun. It is a legend I heard in my youth.

Penitent Drunkard. But embroidered by a rich imagination.

Nun. That is, ah, a legend based on well-known, verifiable facts.

Penitent Drunkard. Oh, we need not trouble ourselves with *facts*. I'm alluding to Truth, looming above us on its huge hill. To scale it you must shun the obvious routes.

(*Drinking Woman*. I liked him better when he was throwing up.)

The cryptical gentleman turns, vomits overboard, and quite casually resumes.

Penitent Drunkard. To understand the world, we flit between History and Myth. Myth, of course, is more trustworthy. Literal untruth, it cannot claim to be anything other than what it is . . .

Choristers. Codswallop!

Penitent Drunkard. Yes, I have a story. And it's a true story. But is it a True Story? I've spent so many years intoxicated that I no longer know for certain. But I'm being obscure, am I not, before I've even begun.

The Penitent Drunkard's Tale

Like many young men of humble birth but lofty aspiration, I longed as a boy to enter the Tower. No other band of men – not the Templars of old, nor our Saviour's disciples – belonged to so rare and secret a code as the Brethren. Little was known of them, beyond that their number was limited at any one time to seven; that their calling, once entered upon, could be abandoned only in death; and that they were sequestered from the world beyond their supposed labyrinths. Even the priests – whom by nature will brook no competition in respect – spoke of the Brethren in hushed, nervous tones. For the cleric's duty is to shepherd his flock along the paths prescribed by Scripture: he is a perpetuator of God's Law only. The seven Brethren had a greater calling. They were inventors, adding to the very storehouse of Creation.

Being young, and feeling myself inclined to greatness, I spoke of nothing at home but gaining admission to the Tower. My father (whom I honour now, too late, as the wisest of men) warned that the life of the Chosen was, for all its honour, a lonely and a loveless one. He explained how God endows us all with energies: how for most men these are spent in toil and their line's continuance. My father could not determine whether the Brethren were breakers of God's Law or blessedly exempt from it; what was certain, however, was the sacrifice required of them. At the time, these words meant nothing to me. My remembered self – barely a self at all – is now an empty chamber echoing with dead voices. Sometimes I think it is myself speaking, not my father, and that I am, in the vapours of drink, confusing my father then with myself now. For when I conjure his voice it is mine I hear, imploring me too late to renounce ambition, to choose sublunary life in all its safe banality.

Nobody knew the Tower's history. Constructed of brick and bitumen, windowless, it seemed a thing of the ancient past and of an opaque future. At a good pace one could walk around it in under an hour. A traveller, craning his neck to discern its summit, was liable to strain himself, for the Tower stretched high into the heavens. All sunshine long we shivered in its shadow. Uncomplaining. For none but lunatics rail at mountains: the sane toil, as they must, in the cold valleys.

Though forbidding as a keep, the Tower was not impregnable. Yearly, at Pentecost, young hopefuls would present themselves at its Eastern Gate, carrying or dragging their inventions. As a child I used to watch, with friends, the fortunes of those acne-pitted contenders. To all the Gate, with a groan of pulleys, opened. On all the Gate, with a groan of pulleys, closed –

ousting them, blinking, on to the sand. The discourage-ment, for the rejected, was total, and I spent many hours studying the anatomies of their discarded inventions. Painstakingly I articulated the skeletons of clocks and music boxes. These contrivances, without exception, owed too great a debt to existent instruments. Their timorous makers had, for the most part, done little more than tinker, adding a new cog here, a superfluous runnel there.

My own contribution – when, aged eighteen, I joined at last the queue for admission – had in its favour great originality. It was a footpedal-activated egg-whisk. I didn't doubt for a moment that it would triumph for me. Its domestic usefulness was indisputable; the problem of bulk could be solved with just a little investment. Standing in line, my imagination seethed with such dangers – of theft, sabotage, or expeditious plagiarism – that I hid the egg-whisk beneath my cloak. Even when the Eastern Gate opened to admit me, my fear was focused on the outside world and it was with relief that I stepped inside, leaving behind my nameless competitors.

Once inside the Tower, I forgot myself entirely. I have visited great cathedrals since: those echoing spaces are as log cabins in comparison. How do I describe the scale of it? It was like walking upon a plain at night, a space so vast it could exist only in the open air. Yet this landscape was walled on all sides, with the sky bricked out above me.

I turned at the sound of the Gate closing. The daylight

thinned to a sliver and was gone. My eyes rolled blindly; I heard footsteps and had to repress my panic. Suddenly a shard of light punctured the blackness. The ignis fatuus flickered, paranoiac, then asserted itself. I beheld, in that Chaotic darkness, a grey monkish figure bathed in cobalt light. Livid sparks tumbled from his torch like water. The man spoke, urging me closer. I extended a foot and found solid ground. To master my nerves I focused on the torchbearer. It must have taken me two minutes to reach him. I saw as I did so that he was standing by a stone well. Following my gaze, he swept his torch above his head to reveal a metal chain straining high into the obscurity.

'There's a five-hour climb to reach the winch,' he said. 'I am Brother Nester. You will accompany me and show me your invention. You will then, most likely, leave.'

Before I could reply, Brother Nester had plunged into the oceanic darkness. Keenly I followed his torch; water vapour as thick as dust evaporated within its blue halo. The air in the chamber was dense and ancient. It shifted and swam, transected by currents of cold and warmth. I was afraid of that protean, unearthly element: my mind populated it with phantoms. After several silent minutes, the darkness ahead of us began to resolve itself, solidifying to brick and mortar. I felt the inner wall of the Tower looming above me. It lured us in; we were in its pull, like insects enticed into the gluey skin of a pond.

We came finally to a heavy, anthracitic door. Brother Nester stroked the side of his torch and its blue flame perished. As darkness closed back over us he knocked thrice upon the fossilised wood. A latch was lifted within and the door opened. The light inside, though artificial and subdued, was at that moment as welcoming as sunlight in winter.

'Enter,' said Brother Nester, 'we have much to get through.'

As I stepped inside, I thought I heard something breathing behind the door. A hollow sense of dread prevented me from enquiring further. I followed Brother Nester doggedly through the bewildering passageways. They were lit by wall-hung lanterns, whose phosphorescence made the stone floor glisten underfoot. In this penumbra my mind worked furiously. If I was in the Tower *now*, where had I been previously? Some kind of courtyard? Perhaps the Tower was hollow, like an ancient oak whose core has rotted, the living husk enveloping nothing?

We stopped at a door indistinguishable from those we had passed already, a door seemingly wrought of petrified wood. My guide opened it himself, admitting me into a narrow library. I had never seen so many books in one place. Brother Nester sat down at his desk and opened a bookmarked ledger. 'Proceed,' he said.

Nodding, I uncovered my machine, squeezed the trial egg from its cotton-padded pouch, and set to work. Brother Nester watched the demonstration with impassive grey eyes. Every so often he would bow his head and scrawl scratchily in the ledger. My egg-white was worked quickly into a froth. I offered the foam for inspection but Brother Nester declined to test its consistency.

'Where did you get this?' he asked gravely.

'The bowl?'

'Not the bowl. The whisk. Where did you find it?'

'I made it.'

'On whose specifications?'

'On my specifications.'

'The shoulder brace? The waist straps?'

'Yes.'

'The two-bolt stabiliser? The non-friction spinning helix?'

'Yes, it's all my work.'

Brother Nester scrutinised me, as though I had interesting runes on my forehead. Then he excused himself and slipped through a panel in the bookshelves.

Alone in the musty chamber, I sank miserably, fearing failure. Wallowing in self-pity, I noticed Brother Nester's ledger closed on the desk. Reasoning that I had nothing to lose, I yielded to curiosity and opened it at the bookmark. Not daring to turn the book in my favour, I scanned the writing upside down. This hardly mattered, for Brother Nester's notes were obscure at any angle. The lettering was cramped and illegible, as though thousands of mites had been crushed in careful rows between the pages; at irregular intervals I saw smudges that might have been technical diagrams.

Suddenly I heard male voices approaching. With no time to shut the ledger, I stumbled back to my stool. Six men, all clothed in grey like Brother Nester, squeezed through the panel into the library. I realised I was surrounded by the Brethren, and their features blurred in my apprehension.

'What's your name?' asked Brother Nester.

I told them. A silent conversation ensued, each man turning to the other with much nodding and stroking of chins.

'This is Brother Ludwig,' said Brother Nester at last. 'This, Brother Heridus. These gentlemen are Brothers Greda and Œp – who collaborate in everything. This is Brother Kay, who will show you to your dormitory.'

I gasped like a fish, half comprehending.

Brother Nester shut the ledger and continued. 'Tomorrow we shall meet at Theory in the chapterhouse, where you shall take the Oath of Vocation. Let me keep your device. Welcome to your noviciate.'

With a welter of emotions I confronted my triumph, torn between bewilderments of joy and trepidation. Yes, I had succeeded where so many hundreds had failed. I had fulfilled a lifelong ambition. But the brisk inscrutability of the Brethren unsettled me, and as I was escorted by Brother Kay to my dormitory I swallowed back my questions. Bitter and brackish, they stuck like crusts in my gullet.

After many convolutions we ascended a cold, echoing staircase.

'The Tower has many miles of stairway. As the years go by, you will become familiar with many of them.' A gaunt, angular fellow, Brother Kay bore himself with meticulous equanimity. His voice was soft and shorn of modulation; I found little comfort in it. 'Every novice,' he continued, 'is an explorer. He must find his way gradually in the Tower, bringing to light its obscure corridors. It isn't easy, but the rewards – creatively speaking – of our life far outweigh the rigours.'

We arrived, short of breath, at the place. Brother Kay ushered me into a long, high-ceilinged room the height and volume of an upturned galleon. Row after row of narrow iron beds led to a washbasin, altarlike, at the far end of the room. The beds were made, and clean. They were unoccupied.

'Tomorrow,' said Brother Kay as he left me, 'you will begin to understand.'

I shivered, haggard with anticipation, alone in the deafening silence. The word 'homesick' cannot begin to describe my desolation. Imagine yourself admitted to a hospice for the sick; imagine lying in the deathbed of strangers, gazing at an unfamiliar ceiling. Concentrate on those cracks, the warps in the wood, those inexplicable stains: you have looked your last on life, on love, and every corpuscle of your blood knows it. That is how I spent my first night in the Tower. I feared I was dying, or already dead, and in the inscrutable darkness I wept bitter tears. I imagined my parents – proud, grieving – continuing the business of life without me. Of my house I pictured every nook and corner, as though by sheer mental effort my spirit might return there. Finally, in that night without bearings, I entered the maze of sleep. My dreams – the last for many months – were of entrapment and suffocation. I found myself stuck fast in some sort of burrow, unable to turn either left or right, hauling myself forward with clumsy, clodden hands.

I was still scrabbling in the dust when I awoke to the ringing of bells.

Although there was no daylight in the Tower, artificial light shone in squibs from the rafters, and I was glad of it. I arose and dressed. Peering into the washbasin, I found that the water had been replenished overnight.

I was still puzzling over this mystery when Brother Kay entered, carrying a white gown and sandals.

'This is the Gown of Inception,' he said. 'Follow me, it's time.'

We set off wordlessly for the chapterhouse. Occasionally we would pass a hall or chamber, my heart twitching each time in expectation. But those rooms were empty and our destination still lay far off. The interior of the Tower, I tell you, was like a patchwork of interlocking buildings, as though an entire city had been compressed into interconnecting cells, so that windows opened not on to exteriors but other interiors, and one flight of stairs ended with the beginning of another. I lacked the effrontery to ask questions about the ceremony and its particulars; no doubt my being kept in ignorance was part of the tradition.

'Here we are,' said Brother Kay, summoning me from my musings. He struck a heavy black door three times with his cane. From within, a sonorous gong sounded thrice in reply, and the door heaved open.

The Brethren were already seated as we entered the chapterhouse. They were dressed in solemn grey, their faces grave with self-importance. I bowed humbly to each in turn: it seemed a sensible gesture.

The dark bearded one, Brother Heridus, stood up and spoke first. 'Welcome to the Tower. You've been chosen by our Master—' He paused and glanced significantly at the others. '—Gerboš von Okba – for the position of novice. You will learn from each of us, copying our endeavours until you find your own path. Innovation, originality and specialisation: these are our watchwords. *Per ardua ad astra*. Over the centuries this Tower has produced many great minds . . .'

'Ourselves,' butted in Brothers Œp and Greda, 'very much included.'

'Central to the Ceremony of Inception will be your anointment. Your place in the world, your status in the eyes of God, set you apart from human dross. You are *pueris rationalis capax*. That is to say, you are Chosen.'

Brother Heridus spoke with deliberation, licking his lips and savouring his words: it was a most authoritative performance.

'You must now relinquish your civilian clothes. They will be incinerated and the ashes returned to you. This is called the Purgation. Brother Kay will then officiate the putting on of the Gown of Inception, so called—'

'—because you are as yet but a notion,' interrupted Brother Nester.

'—in the mind of our Master.'

Now Brother Nester struck a pose in front of Brother Heridus. The two men jostled briefly for prominence. Brother Nester triumphed in the end through sheer bulk. 'The putting on of the Gown,' he declared, 'is called the Edification. For as the years pass, you will amount to—'

'—a tit-tit-Tower of Thought.' This from Brother Ludwig. 'Let us be your fif-fif-flint—'

'—that your works may illuminate the world—'

'—that dwells in te-te-terrible darkness.'

There followed a scuffle, as the three Brethren attempted simultaneously to descend the dais. Brothers Greda and Œp, who were musicians, struck up at first a fanfare on whistle pipes, before slapping their brows at the mistake and switching to a stately anthem. Brother Kay tugged and flustered at my shirt. 'Hurry,' he said. And I undressed, surrendering my garments to the floor.

I won't trouble you with the particulars of that flushed, bad-tempered ceremony. I was mauled and hauled into the white Gown of Inception, with Brothers Heridus, Nester and Ludwig vying to officiate. They spoke in several languages, only two of which (Latin and Greek) I recognised. The lion's share of the speechifying was in a guttural gibberish that made the Brethren hawk up great spumes of spit. Finally, with great solemnity, I was spattered with rancid oil and presented with an urn containing the ashes of my layman's clothes.

The six Brethren then hassled myself, and each other, into an antechamber for the Inception Banquet. I was too dazed to fret about the brown matter that occupied our dishes. In the table's surface (polished to a sheen, a lake's surface in moonlight) I noted my reflection. Already my face had changed. Robed in white, it belonged to some precocious seer, had shifted into adult gravity. I sat at the table surrounded by sounds of mastication. The Chosen ate with little delicacy, jabbing open their mouths, rolling food from cheek to cheek and probing the toothy interstices with noisy gastropodic tongues. Over dessert of what resembled steamed prunes and sour cream, my superiors broke into heated intellectual debate, little of which I comprehended. Absorbed as I was by the occasion, it did not occur to me until later that the Master himself was absent.

I soon grew accustomed to Matutinal Summons. Since we had neither sun nor moon to go by, Time in the Tower was an intellectual construct, observed with tintinnabulation by Brothers Œp and Greda, who granted each hour its unique melody.

Allow me to describe the daily routine.

Matutinal Summons brought the Chosen to the Refectory for breakfast. Always our bowls awaited us, and I grew eager to understand the serving system. Who prepares our food? I asked, tugging at sleeves. Who changes my bed, who keeps the Tower *working*? Alas, conversation, though permitted, was rare. Every mind chewed over its own concerns, and I could not elicit the briefest explanation for anything.

(A word, if you please, about the food. It was never clearly identifiable. It had a dark, dank, crushed quality. Mushrooms were transmuted into soup and purées; meat was snail-rubbery and anonymous; for want of vegetables deserving of the name, we swallowed thin green filaments redolent of bog-moss. Whatever the dish, the Brethren scoffed it hungrily, blowing to cool their forkfuls with stale fungal breaths.)

After breakfast there followed the Call to Industry, when the sated Brethren traipsed off to their respective workshops. The first work hour was devoted to Theory; the second to Composition and Refinement. The third and fourth hours were taken up with Crafting and Implementation.

Luncheon was announced with an engaging *organum*: one bell maintaining a steady note in a low register, the other singing out high above it. Visibly it lifted the spirits of the conundrum-gripped inventors. They would gather with a spring in their step, smiling almost at their meeting. Conversation then was fast and furious; but when the Resumption Bell tolled, it ceased in mid-flow. The Brethren, who only seconds earlier had been leaning across the table in fervent disputation, bowed their tonsured heads and trudged back to their studies.

The afternoon was divided evenly between Creative Progress, Total Perplexity and the Tearing of Papers. At last, when all extraneous notes and stillborn enquiries had been consigned to the dustbin, the Brethren would sit at their desks and Nap for twenty minutes until Evenbreak.

Supper was a very different affair from the midday meal. On weekdays the Brethren assembled in the Red Room; on Saturday it was the Scarlet Chambers; on Sunday, the Solemn Apartments. Regardless of setting, it was the custom for one of the six to recite from the Book of Instruction.

The Book, also known as The Guide, also revered as The Blueprint, was not for my novice's eyes. My only experience of its hundred chapters (it was thick enough to brain a horse, if such was your bent) was hearing the Chosen recite selected verses. None of which I understood. For the language of the Book of Instruction consisted of a throaty garble, mere vocalisations unchained to 'things'. And yet, if I let my attention wander, my ear tingled sometimes with recognition. The lilting verses, their clucks and clicks, the slushy consonants and sliding vowels, registered profoundly somehow, like smells from childhood. Intrigued, I asked the Brethren to teach me the language. They declined, avoiding my enthusiasm with vague, abortable hints of help to come. Brother Heridus, the Tower's polyglot, when begged for a translation, retreated to his workshop muttering of colic. The motto on his door – *Salus extra arduam non est* – exhorted me to work, yet my curiosity went a-begging.

On the training front, too, I found myself frustrated. Although I devoted many hours to each discipline, visiting by rota one workshop after another, the Brethren proved reluctant to involve me in their projects. I floated sadly in a limbo, excluded from all but the simplest aspects of my superiors' studies. Perhaps – I came to reason – the Brethren's indifference was *proof* of their engagement? Less an abnegation of responsibility than a policy dutifully enacted? Surely my exclusion was part of my training, requiring me to match inquisitiveness with investigative flare? Since most Great Discoveries are made in spite of hindrance, I was to show initiative and acquire an education through stealth, to snatch textbooks when the owner's back was turned, to sneak looks at blanketed prototypes. It was with some measure of satisfaction that I formulated this theory. The Tower had thrown up its first enigma, and I had cracked it.

What, then, of the different disciplines? What did the Makers make in their dusty, disordered workshops?

Let me begin with the eldest of the six. A small, neat man with eyes hard and bright like a blackbird's, Brother Ludwig specialised in Mathematics, Logic and Geometry. On his door were inscribed words from Plato: ἀγεωμέτρητος μηδεὶς εἰσίτω. 'Let no one enter who does not know geometry.' Had I been able to read Greek at the time, I would have been prohibited. But as I didn't, I wasn't.

The workshop itself was hillocked with papers. Parchments of blotched, spidering sums lay on every surface. I found, in the disorder, many geometrical implements, but soon grew tired of mishandling them. I realised (with some relief, I confess) that I could expect no induction into the occult world of figures from Brother Ludwig: he had better things to do than explain himself to a nin-nin-innumerate tyke like me. His stammer, as you will have surmised, was no symptom of bumbling amiability. Brother Ludwig was fired by fat reserves of scorching odium. He scowled and seethed through his work. He threw up bustling, multistoreyed equations with dazzling speed, clacking his chalk on the foggy blackboard with electric loathing for the physical world and its frictions. For his mind moved faster than his fingers could follow, sending him stumbling over the symbols like a sprinter in a sack race.

'Damn this board to hell!' he would scream as yet another chalk exploded in his grip. Everything – especially clueless boys – distracted him from the purity of numbers. I was simply one more material intrusion on his abstractions, and he huffed and murmured darkly when I watched him working. Still, it pleased me to follow his frantic calculations. When they came to naught, he spat and swore without a trace of verbal impediment; when they came good, he treated himself to fingerfuls of damp, fudgy ooze, which he cultivated in a frosted jar.

Above Brother Ludwig's scrawlings I preferred my visits to Brother Heridus. Preoccupied as he was with his life's work – *A Lexical Compendium of Everything, as*

Spoken in Every Tongue of the World, with Footnotes & Appendices – it took him some time to recognise me, his lazy-lidded eyes drifting nebulously above my head.

Although he would not be drawn on the Book of Instruction, Brother Heridus granted me, in time, the occasional lecture on lexical quirks. He spoke, for instance, of the Laplanders' many words for snow, or the purity of Icelandic, which reaches into its box of old words to assemble new ones. I strained to catch him speak of Mari and Mordvin as heard on the Volga; of Udmurt and Zyrian, which roam the wastes of Arctic Muskovy; of Ostyak and Vogul, which never venture from the Ob Valley of northern Siberia. He told me of the Shang dynasty texts incised on tortoise-shells and cow horns; how the Chinese rebus, which took pictograms of concrete words to indicate abstract ones, borrowed the pictogram for *dustpan* (*ji*) to signify personal pronouns (*qi*), until over time *dustpan* ceased to mean *dustpan*, and the selfless word got its character stolen. In a voice cracked with mental strain, Brother Heridus explained how words are forever making and unmaking themselves, fragmenting and reassembling like quicksilver spilt on a slope. He told me of patois that live, unwritten, only in the mouth; of dialects so rare that one family cannot comprehend its neighbours; of words that live like parasites and change their meaning when they climb upon another word's back.

'So many,' he exclaimed. 'How can I cope with so many?'

I must confess I was somewhat in awe of Brother Heridus for the breadth of his learning. How I longed to ransack his overburdened bookshelves for the Babel they contained! Without doubt I would have done (the Nap offered a theoretical opportunity), had it not been for the philologist's extreme vigilance. I was forbidden, strictly forbidden, you understand, to touch the very *bindings* of his books without prior permission.

I asked for permission. It was refused every time.

More forthcoming, if only from the tenacity with which I feigned enthusiasm for their work, were that inseparable pair, Brothers Œp and Greda. When they caught me plucking the strings of a stray mandora, I became their entire audience. Certainly I was glad of the attention; though I was unable to take pleasure in their latest composition.

'This is an entirely new direction in music,' shrilled Brother Œp one morning as he sprinted to the positive-organ. 'The world won't be ready for it for decades.'

'For centuries,' corrected Brother Greda, who manned the bellows.

'We call it dodecatone music!' After punching or pulling the stops and inspecting the flues, Brother Œp landed hands first on the keys, announcing as he did so their 'Organ Piece in Dodecatone Form'.

'It'll blow your brain!' said Brother Greda discouragingly.

It was ghastly: a depressing, pluvious, bladder-pinching noise that left the ear hankering in vain for shelter.

There was no crevice, not one familiar outcrop on that sheer, unaccommodating wall of sound.

'Isn't it beautiful?' cried Brother Greda, stark haired in the organ's wind.

When the hourglass indicated Luncheon, the Brothers stopped to toll the bells. I was relieved to escape. But over mulchy food I began to hunger for a second performance. It worried me that the Chosen could produce material of such poor quality – it brought into question the mystical value of our calling – and I needed to be sure of the music's deformity. Brothers Greda and Œp whooped at my interest, and over the next few days I endured several times the 'Organ Piece', until my mind learned to intuit its new language, and I no longer winced at the music but frowned with sombre perplexity at its flayed, arid beauty.

Beauty of another kind was to be found in the workshop of Brother Kay. More specifically, in the weapons of Conquest and Persuasion, to the refinement of which his life was humbly devoted. He was unique among the Chosen for decorating his workshop with the proof of his labours. Instead of antlers for trophies, his walls were keen with halberds and harquebus, with armour joints and arrows and many-sighted crossbows. Only a draughtsman of inhuman patience could have put on paper the complexity of Brother Kay's armoury: cannonballs clustered like grapes; webs of steel inspidered by Grecian shields; blades of steel arranged as great Fortuna's-Wheels on the walls.

Touching the pink tip of his tongue to a sharp incisor,

the happy incumbent welcomed me with a familiarity quite at odds with his earlier behaviour as my guide. There is, it seems, no endeavour more conducive to perpetual invention as weaponry. It made the otherwise monotonous Brother Kay quite giddy with eloquence:

'Poets will tell you that love is the Big Theme. But the momentary spasm, the misery of Love denied, are as nothing in the life of Man. War – now war is the great subject. When you've devoted years, as I have, to the technical challenges of conflict, you will understand that all life aspires to it, that mankind hankers most for the silence of a battlefield when the carrion crows move in.'

One lesson absorbed by every novice everywhere is the privilege of seniority. Brother Nester, who was it transpired the youngest of the six Brethren, was assigned to the manufacture of Domestic Utensils. His work ranged from the culinary to the horticultural, with special attention given to matters of personal hygiene.

'The disposal of human waste,' he told me in a rare address, 'is the greatest challenge facing humanity.' Despite such declarations, his interest seemed less than enkindled by his work. His eyes were given to glazing over, leaving him hunched up and gaping like a carp, a tendril of drool hanging from his chin. On the one occasion when I tried to nudge him from this catalepsy, there emerged from his throat a thin whimper, as of some animal agonising in a trap.

I took advantage of Brother Nester's mental absences to explore his workshop. I discovered scythe-tongued machines for trimming grass, glass belljars for saplings, spiked trowels and hoes with gyrating mandibles. I unearthed vegetable choppers and carrot dicers, toothy vices for crushing garlic, ginger-root slicers, automated mandrake harvesters for the superstitious, water-powered pestles in granite mortars. Amid shelves of tiny carcasses I found glutinous limes, bug-shaped baits laced with poison, slug-melting salts and viscous flybane. Finally, in a dank recess, I encountered basins equipped with angled water jets, hot-air-venting cupboards, eternally looped handtowels and mushy soaps that smelt of tar and ambergris.

One afternoon, I think it was during Total Perplexity, I dared to reach under Brother Nester's drawing-desk, where I had earlier noticed several objects hidden in sackcloth. Casting a nervous eye at Brother Nester's drooling, empty features, I curled my fingers around a most familiar shape. Incredulous, I flicked back the cover and discovered . . . *my egg-whisk*. At first I assured myself that this was quite legitimate, that none of the Chosen would choose – would need – to pass off another's invention as his own. To put my mind at rest, I scrutinised carefully the footpedal-activated device. And found that it was a clumsy, scratched copy of my original – a forgery of the prototype. I could scarcely believe the evidence; only its metal solidity persuaded me to acknowledge its significance.

Brother Nester was a plagiarist.

* * *

Curious, is it not, how perceptions alter according to our expectations. Whereas before it had suited my ambitions to overlook oddities, after the discovery of Brother Nester's duplicity I could think of little else. The stolen egg-whisk was my Pandora's box: out of its gaping lid slithered a thousand suspicions. What was the Tower? Who kept it functioning? *Where* was Gerboš von Okba?

Days passed in issueless speculation. All things on which my eyes alighted seemed altered within, as in autumn, when the sap sinks, every leaf is the intimation of its fall. During work hours I continued to wheedle an education out of the Brethren. At night, intending to catch the person who replenished my washbasin, I fought to stay awake. It was impossible: after Supper I was bone tired. My mind, as soon as ear touched straw, sank like a stone into swimming waters. Unreplenished at my waking, I recognised on the Brethren's faces the same pallid masks of men who cannot dream.

Brother Ludwig was my first port of call. Knowing the fury that my presence inspired in him, I took to sitting within his line of vision, still and stupid throughout Theory and Composition. The strategy, for all its tedium, paid off soon enough. As he chipped away, Brother Ludwig contracted astigmatism from his attempts to wipe me from the corner of his eye. When finally the spasm in his left cheek became unendurable, he bit into his chalk and spat the dust in my face.

'What is it you want?'

'Want, Brother Ludwig?'

'You've been sitting there wa-wa-watching me like an owl. Don't you see, I can't *work* in these con-condi-tions—!'

'When did you start work on your theorem, Brother Ludwig?'

Taken aback, the old man squinted suspiciously. 'Why?'

'I've been meaning to ask you.'

'And for this you've been du-du-driving me up the wall?'

'Have I, Brother Ludwig?'

The mathematician squeezed the flesh from his cheek-bone and tutted into his palm. 'If I tell you,' he said eventually, 'will you promise to sus-sus-sod off?'

I sucked air through my teeth, as though pained by the question. 'All right.'

Brother Ludwig massaged his skin and nodded. 'I first formulated my theorem – that is, I took it on – forty-two years ago.'

'*Forty-two years?*'

'And three months.'

'Do you think you'll ever finish it?'

'Don't be a cu-cu-cu impertinent.'

Such was his mission. The lifetime pursuit of a proposition that was, for all anyone knew, infinite and insuperable. True to my word, I leapt from my stool and made for the door. As I lifted the latch, an afterthought, as it were, struck me.

'Brother Ludwig?'

'What is it now!'

'Can you tell me the theorem?'

'Don't be stupid, boy. After all this time, and so close to the solution, what do I remember of the problem?'

Ink stained, Brother Heridus was red about the eyes, as though I had interrupted him in the process of chopping onions. I tampered vapidly with his collection of oriental paper-knives, judged his mood, then asked after the progress of the *Lexical Compendium of Everything*.

'It's like draining a lake with a ladle,' he said, his eyelids drooping.

The time was Total Perplexity. With the Nap still a distant prospect, Brother Heridus's vigilance would not withstand a lengthy siege. I adopted a ruthless strategy, though it started gently enough with flattery. I could not, it seemed, praise sufficiently the unresting scholar. Servant to his Olympian task, scorning sleep for study, was he not, I asked, another Atlas, shouldering a globe of Thought? What could he want with the mortal's balm, sleep? Sleep, placid harbour to the storm-tossed bark. Sweet Morpheus's embrace, Nature's restorative – nourishing Sleep?

In five minutes he was snoring, his head buried in his arms on the workdesk. I nudged him to be sure and he mumbled incoherently. Then, crouching into long, slow strides, I approached the prohibited bookshelves. Leathery, lead clasped or veined with silver filigree, the books suggested from a distance the scaly carapace of a lizard. My fingers trembled as I reached for a

handsome edition of Dun Scotus's *De modis signifi-
candi*. As I edged the book from the shelf, however, it
began to smoke. Or so it seemed until, alarmed, I flung
back the marbled bindings and sneezed into a Sahara
of paper dust. I turned in panic but Brother Heridus
still slept. I waited for the blizzard of decomposed
words to settle, then replaced the book's empty casing.
Its fellows, chosen at random, fared little better. *Doc-
trinale puerorum*, its wisdom avidly absorbed by mites,
exhaled black powder like a puffball; Janotus de
Bragmardo's *Decrotatorium neologium* stank of fun-
gus; *Palabras muertas de la Mancha* dripped orange
spiders.

My head spun as I gathered the dust with the edge of
my sandal. Brother Heridus had no books! Was he
working, then, from memory? It occurred to me that I'd
never so much as glanced at his work-in-progress.
Grown careless of discovery, I sifted through his papers
and scrutinised the seemingly endless notes towards his
Lexical Compendium. Although no linguist, I had to
credit the evidence of my own eyes. Here were thousands of nouns, of verbs, all invented. Ingeniously,
Brother Heridus had fabricated tables of tenses, phan-
tasmagorical grammars, etymologies and textual attri-
butions. All elaborate, meticulously constructed and
quite, quite useless.

Brother Heridus stirred beside me; his eyelashes
fluttered. By the time he sat up, I had shut the door
behind me.

*   *   *

Like proud new parents, Brothers Greda and Œp displayed their shining L of brass. I was called upon to admire it from every angle as they held it to the light. Yes, I agreed, magnificent – what was it? Cooing like doves, they fixed the piece to a wheel in the butt of a hurdy-gurdy. The handle (for such it was) snapped at the first crank.

'Of course,' the Brothers chimed, viewing the brass I, 'it's only a prototype.'

Recovering swiftly, they assaulted the organ and polished its gleaming pipes. When Brother Greda began to hum an old favourite, Brother Œp snapped his fingers and sat himself before the stops. Brother Greda grabbed hold of the bellows.

'How thrilling,' he shrilled, 'an impromptu recital!'

It was a stale routine: their pretence at spontaneity, my fake gratitude. When the 'Organ Piece' was quite finished, Brother Œp turned to acknowledge the acclaim which I dutifully offered.

'Isn't it moving?' said Œp. 'I saw you in my mirror, fighting back the tears.'

'It gets better every time,' I replied. 'Do you have a copy I might study?'

'A what?'

'A copy.'

Brother Œp paled. Brother Greda blanched.

'You know – sheet music?'

'Sheet music,' Brother Œp echoed.

'Yes, for notation. You do write your compositions down, don't you?'

'Well, in our heads . . . that's why we train . . . muscle memory . . . it was the Master who *ow*! . . . We'd make a start right n*ouch* . . . !'

They were not creating a new jig: Brother Greda was kicking Brother Œp in the shins.

'Do you mean to say you can't read music?'

'Since when,' said Brother Greda, 'has *that* been a prerequisite of genius?'

'But how can you remember,' I said, 'without notation, the work that's gone before?'

'Music,' Brother Œp retorted, 'is a propulsive, ongoing process.'

'Oh,' I nodded, and left them to their circular devices.

Unique among the Six to escape my suspicions was the armourer, Brother Kay. Sensing my mood, perhaps, he devoted an entire morning to my edification. He explained the mechanics of the siege-turtle, demonstrated the wind-measuring anemometer and sang the praises of Greek Fire, a gelatinous incendiary used by the Ancients before gunpowder took the poetry out of battle. Brother Kay's self-containment was, I realised, symptomatic of his technical skill. For to fashion blades or assemble the rainbow viscera of a bomb requires, in his words, inhuman precision. When, within a sealed mouse cage, he demonstrated to me the potentials of chlorine gas and phosgene, I made myself as attentive as possible. Brother Kay waited until the squealing had stopped inside the cage before drawing his conclusions.

'Of course,' he said, 'wind direction might prove a

problem. So you see the usefulness of the anemometer. Also, I'm experimenting with napthenic and palmitic acids. Like the Greek Fire, they have real *staying* power.'

It was an undeniable truth: Brother Kay was a man enamoured of his work.

As day was succeeded by featureless day, the Brethren became incapable of hiding their antagonisms. Feuds raged, couched in languages of civility and learning. Like the shifting air at its centre, the Tower's political atmosphere was protean and unstable. From one day to the next new alliances were forged, new rivalries born. In the Red Room, in the Scarlet Chambers – but most starkly in the Refectory – the Brethren scrabbled for pre-eminence.

One morning I descended at breakfast to find the Refectory empty. Bowls were laid out, their contents coagulating, untouched. I had just sat down, having no alternative, to a grim meal when I heard voices from behind the crimson arras. Summoning courage, I crept up to and folded back the faded material. The arras was a screen to a secret chamber. Its panel door was ajar. Through the sliver I beheld an oak-panelled room almost bare of furnishings. Assembled about a lone, ornate chair stood the six Chosen.

Brother Heridus was holding forth, in several languages, on the subject of leadership. As he spoke he shuffled, almost imperceptibly, towards the throne-like chair. Meanwhile, though with less subtlety, Brother

Nester eked out a similar trajectory, interrupting occasionally, with scornful yaps, his rival's oration. To the left old Ludwig fizzed with outrage, yanking his hair until it stood like floss on end. To the right Brothers Greda and Œp fidgeted, grimacing as though caught in a sandstorm. Only Brother Kay seemed unexcited; he stood, set back from the fray, as still and impassive as an empty coat of armour.

'. . . and that,' concluded Brother Heridus as he deftly covered the throne, 'is why I can safely say, *in sacer verbo dotis*, that the right of succession demands my speedy and undisputed election.'

Brother Nester spluttered. 'On what basis?'

'*Non est discipulus super magistrum.*'

'Don't you patronise me, Heridus.'

'*Ego sum quis sum: dominum in divino veritas.*'

Brother Nester, enraged, sought an alliance of convenience against the lexicologist. 'He has no claim: he's trying to bamboozle us with his fancy doggerel!'

To which Brother Heridus replied:

'Antipericatametanaparbeugedamphicribrationes-merdicantium!'

This impressive ejaculation pushed the dispute into freefall. Brother Heridus, puce with effort, stood upon the chair and swayed from its crest. '*Chaultcouillons! Pantofla merdorum! Scheisskopf!*' In reply Brother Nester flicked imaginary fleas from his crotch. '*Furfuris!*' Brother Heridus shrieked. '*Simium! Improbe mendax!*' Brothers Œp and Greda, grinningly attentive, transformed into scrap-rousing voyeurs. Brother Ludwig, unable to produce a Latinism of his own, provided a ground base to the obscenities: '*Ca-ca-ca-ca-ca-ca* . . . !'

In the midst of all this, my ears bristled at the softest of sounds: a slithering breath, a breathed cough very nearby. The Brethren also heard it and froze in mid-expletive. Inside the room, on the other side of my panel, something caught their attention: some being, some skulking obsequious servant. Steadily, bidden by a hidden gesture, six pairs of eyes travelled to my face.

With infantile logic, I shut the panel.

When, after a suitable interlude, the Chosen returned to the Refectory, they found me seated in stiff affectation at my bowl. Guilt wafted between us like an intestinal odour. The Brethren assumed their seats and feigned, as I did, an appetite. Only Brother Nester was incapable of belated subterfuge. He dabbed angrily at his food, sighed, amassed a heaped spoon of sludge and flung it, with ballistic skill, at Brother Heridus's scalp. The missile landed with a low, dishonest *mlup!* Somewhat astonished, I braced myself either for a food fight or murder. But nothing happened. Brother Heridus dripped and munched on regardless. His neighbours, white knuckled as they gripped their spoons, hunched over their bowls in pretended torpor.

Finally, provoked beyond endurance, Brother Nester shrieked: 'You're all *arses*!' The arses stared intently at the table. 'What this place needs is young blood. Some vigour. A bit of bloody *fun*!'

'*Nihil . . . ante . . . discipulis.*' Brother Heridus grinned.

The rioter huffed – all spent – and sat down. How we all ached for the Call to Industry! When at last Œp and Greda got up to sound it, we shuffled quickly apart.

Judging the moment propitious, I loped off wolfishly in Brother Nester's pursuit. Humiliated by his petulant outburst, he would surely be unable to refute my allegations. I followed, with jaw set, his tensed back. Once among his things, however, I searched in vain for my evidence. The two egg-whisks were hidden, no doubt, among dozens of objects that squatted, shrouded under sheeting, on the workshop floor. Horned and humped in their brown skins, they looked like ruminants grazing dust.

Blandly, oh so casually, I asked Brother Nester about the clutter.

'It's mine,' he snapped. 'All bloody mine, you understand?'

'You should move it. Look at the space it's taking up.'

Brother Nester paced the floor like a caged bear. 'Can't do that,' he muttered.

'Why not?'

'Upper Storeys.'

'What are the Upper Storeys?'

'Where he's meant to take the bloody things for storage.'

'Who is?'

'The Master.'

'Why doesn't he, then?'

'What?'

'Why doesn't the Master take the bloody things for storage?'

For a moment I feared Brother Nester had slipped back into vacancy. His jaw slackened, his head lolled and his eyeballs flickered white. But there was no escape for him this time, no convenient unconsciousness.

'Uh – has nobody told you?'

'Told me what?'

'I thought you knew.'

'Knew *what*?'

'Gerboš von Okba is dead.'

As I lay in bed that night (waiting for sleep like a shark to drag me under) I wandered through the coiling maze of the Tower. Up convoluted stairways into silent corridors, from workshop to chamber I floated; thence, midge-like, through the soapy canals of the snoring Brothers' ears, into their brains; where I swam through quaggy tunnels of cerebrum before plunging finally into the crimson slurry of their veins.

There was a faint knock at my door. I opened to a perspiring Brother Nester. 'What I told you,' he whispered, 'about you-know-who. Nobody needs to know that you know. More especially, nobody needs to know that you know because I told you. That he's *psst*. You know: *fft*. You know?'

Brother Nester's breath stank of drink. I looked at the spittled lips, at the beard-mottled chin. I gave him every assurance of my discretion.

'Thank you,' he gasped. 'Oh, thank you, thank you.'
He shuffled backwards into the corridor, his clammy
hand still trapped in mine.

'Just tell me one thing,' I said. 'The Master, how did
he, as you say, *fsst*?'

Brother Nester's face narrowed. 'He was a genius,
you know. One of the greats. But a *thief*. Yes – he stole
my ideas. No sooner had I finished some prototype than
he claimed to have a working model.'

'He stole from you?'

'Jealous. Couldn't abide competition. Least of all
from me – the 'boy'.'

'How did he die?'

'Heart attack. Found him blue in his bath. His bath
water was black.'

'And when was this?'

Brother Nester glanced furtively into the gloom.
'Eight days before you joined us. We buried him quickly
– it's the custom. The dead get twenty-four hours in
state. Then it's into the Vaults for ever.'

'The Vaults?'

'Clever dicks' graveyard.'

'Where is that?'

'They.'

'Where are they?'

'He's in the Ninth Vault. Look, I must go. Someone
will notice.' I gladly relinquished the fellow's hand and
he slunk back to his chamber.

True to my word, I never alluded to the matter of
Brother Nester's indiscretion. Nor (although it was

common knowledge almost immediately) did any of his colleagues. Over Luncheon, however, I endured glances of curious reappraisal, such as a dog might train on a caterpillar that has rolled over to expose an array of poisoned quills. By evening my dormitory was an open confessional, as my previously intractable superiors came calling, anxious to tell me the actual manner of the Master's demise.

Brother Heridus brought an offering: an apple, a real one, that I devoured to the stem. 'Whatever he's told you,' he said without preamble, 'you must discount as malicious slander. Brother Nester is embittered by insatiable ambition.'

Instead of speaking, I sprayed white apple foam.

'The Master's death was a great loss to us all. But it was an accident, nothing sinister about it.'

'Fimiftur?'

'We found him lying on the floor of the Velvet Chambers. Clasped to his chest was a copy of Hythlodæus's *Pseudepigrapha*. No doubt he'd mounted the stepladder to reach the book and slipped. Neck broken. Terrible business.'

Relieved to have unburdened himself, Brother Heridus burbled recondidly ('. . . a splendid text, lucid, in a most limpid style . . .') until – prompted by my explicit yawning – he scarpered.

Minutes later I was cocooned in blankets, listening to Brother Ludwig. He offered me a slab of his finest fudge, which I bravely accepted. It was a clever tactic on his part.

'When I first saw you I knew: this is a fu-fu-fine young man. Intelligent, attentive, not easily swayed by pop-propaganda. Let me assure you, Gerboš von Okba did nothing drastic. Optimism shone like . . . in every . . .' He pinched the gimlet folds of his neck. 'Besides, he disapproved of such things, on a philosophical level.'

I wanted to interject but my mouth was a viscid morass.

'Poor Gerboš. Dead-dead-dear friend and colleague. We found him in his bed. As though in sleep, his face was serene. I placed my hands on his feet. They were cold as any . . . as . . . well they were cold.'

I chewed and winced and sucked with all my might. 'Ow bib ee by?'

'Stopping of the stomach.'

Hunched at my bedside, Brother Ludwig fixed me with round, pellucid eyes. 'As I am the oldest surviving member, you understand, the Master's post is mine. Mine by Law. Gerboš and I were like *this*,' (he crossed two fingers) 'but those upstarts, Heridus and Nester, are blocking my path.' His tone softened, as a fly softens in acid. 'Boy. Good, honest boy. I need your legs.' A grey claw scuttled to my knee. 'You must go to the Upper Storeys. I can't. Gug-gug-gout. Fie-fie-fibrous degeneration. Once there, head for the Master's Library. There's a ca-ca-case, a casket containing the cuk-cuk-cuk. The cuk-cuk. The cuk-ack-Constitution!' Brother Ludwig panted, collecting himself. 'The cuk-cuk-document confirms my entitlement.'

Painfully, I swallowed the insoluble gunk. 'The Upper Storeys, Brother Ludwig? How do I . . . ? Where would I . . . ?'

'Sleep on it, lad.' The old man tilted himself to the vertical and, adopting the ancient's privilege, pretended not to hear my questions which pursued him to the door.

The following morning, in the Refectory, I greeted Brothers Œp and Greda with a complaisant smile. The faces that met me seemed unusually cheerful. They served me water from the jug (a rare courtesy) and took an avid interest in my drinking. Later on, in their workshop, they tampered with valves. I gazed without interest at their finicky efforts. When I suffered a fit of coughing (my throat had flared up quickly since breakfast) the couple tutted with concern.

'Bad, this,' said Brother Greda. Through eyes brimming with tears, I saw them lean their heads together. 'It might be the start of a fever.'

'Tower Fever.'

'He'll want to treat it.'

'Or it might run away with him.'

Alarmed, I tried to speak, but the pain was a splinter lodged in my gullet.

'There's only one remedy.'

'Memling's Catholick Ailment Cordial.'

'But Œp: do we have any Memling's Catholick Ailment Cordial?'

'No, Greda: we don't have any Memling's Catholick

Ailment Cordial. But I know where we could find some.'

'Quick, man, tell me!'

'There's a ready supply in the Upper Storeys.'

'Of course! In the Upper Storeys.'

'Our friend might, while he's there, since it's on his way—'

'—bring us the Master's books on composition—'

'—on notation—'

'—on melody—'

'—since it's on his way.'

A plump, folded map was pushed into my pocket. My throat raw, my hands trembling at the end of mile-long arms, I was escorted from their workshop. The couple, as they steered me, spoke nostalgically of the deceased: he'd been their friend, they said, their critic, I was not to forget his books. But what, I managed to ask as they fussed me through the door, had he died of?

Greda. 'Apoplexy.'

Œp. 'Griping in the guts.' (*Beat.*)

Greda. 'Griping in the guts.'

Œp. 'Apoplexy.' (*Beat.*)

Greda & Œp. 'Wind.'

After Luncheon I retire sick to bed. The Brethren in the Refectory seem barely to note my departure. But as soon as I've peeled back starched new sheets, breaking their seal with my toes, my commiserators trickle through bearing gifts of fruit and fudge. 'Of all the disciplines,' says Brother Heridus, 'mine was closest to the Master's heart. Gadgetry was infantile, music imprecise, mathematics inhuman. Whereas Adam's first task in Eden was to name the beasts in his service. (Bless you.) For years we worked together, the Master and I, binding roots, excising galipots, galls, all the bloatings of parasitisation. (Would you like a handkerchief?) I'm not mistaken, am I, in thinking you a linguaphile? (Wring it tight, see, dry as new.) Might you, when you're better, visit the Upper Storeys on my behalf? I'm struggling on the Baltic languages, you see. It's difficult to work in conditions that are less than perfect. I have a list of titles. Excellent chap! I won't forget this kindness, when I am placed to reward it.' I sink under a dark membrane. 'A toe-toe-token of my appreciation; don't eat it all at once.' Brother Ludwig's face is close to my face. 'I know what they've told you – Heridus, the organ-monkeys, Nester's cack-cack-crapulous lies.' Palpation of my forehead by a moist, suctorial palm. 'The Tower listens. At night she looks in upon herself, searching me out. A great womb of brick.' Dry chalky fingers nudge at my lips and deposit on my tongue a tasteless bolus. When it is swallowed, Brother Ludwig's liquorice breath comes hot upon me. 'Gold and jewels beyond your dreams, when you find the document.' A rictus, like a moon waning. Someone looms over me. His bright blue eye winks. Brother Nester stands behind a torch, which blinds me from seeing his face. 'My inventions,' he hisses. 'Stolen. Everything stolen. Then you come. Who are you working for? Ludwig? The corpse? *Who?*'

*   *   *

My fever lifted like a mist. The pain in my throat was gone, my nose unblocked. I lay wide eyed in the stare and hush of the dark, my mind washed clean as a stone.

Something moved in the darkness. My heart clenched. Nothing for the time of a held breath. Then again: the sound of water slopping in a pail. The same, trickling into a stone basin. Gingerly, icy limbed, I reached for the flint and taper beneath my bed. I stroked the floor until at last I felt the taper's wick, its oily neck and the casing of the flintlock. A whisper – faint as a shrew's paw on paper – of someone stirring. I felt cold eyes upon me. Quick, convulsive breathing like a rat's. With the agility of terror, I struck the flint above the wick, dazzling my own dark-adapted eyes. An earthenware vessel crashed to the floor. In the blurred fringe of my sight, beyond the spark's blue ghost, the carcass of a butchered fowl scampered from the light.

'Stop!' I cried, and the fear in my voice shocked me.

Blinking to ease my scalded retinas, I distinguished the ghastly creature more clearly. Not the monster I had imagined, it resembled rather a naked, malnourished child. The head, which was bald like that of a fledgling, was hooked into the chest and hinged, by a misshapen neck, to sinewy shoulders. The vertebrae were a brute's knuckles warping the skin.

'Please,' I croaked, 'I'm not going to hurt you.'

But the child, as it gripped the door latch seemed not to hear. This, and the limited reach of my light, forced me into pursuit. I flung back my sheets, and in doing so snuffed out the flame. By the time I had relit my taper, the creature had disappeared down the benighted arteries of the Tower.

My skull throbbed with the beating of my heart; my heart was a hunted animal. All about me I sensed enmity. To conquer which, I tasked myself with taking stock of my situation. What did I know? That opponents within a fractious community had marked me as their pawn. That I was to be their errand-boy and, perhaps, their battlefield: as vying powers, wary of one another, fight their wars in the fields of vassal states. In the masque of my mind, I paraded the Brethren across the dormitory floor. Heridus the forger. Ambitious Ludwig and his rootless equation. Greda and Œp, unable to save their music for posterity. Nester, overwhelmed by the clutter of his inventiveness. To what measures might not such men sink to attain their goals? Obsessively, I replayed their struggles and tried to imagine the various deaths of Gerboš von Okba.

I walked to the clothes-peg and shook my gown from its hunchbacked languor. A document fell into my palm. I unfolded Œp and Greda's map and laid it across the floor, pinning its timid curling edges under dormitory beds. Then, taper in hand, I scaled the Tower's image.

The exterior was, as I knew, blind. Perhaps, many centuries ago, great windows had been sealed, bricked up to turn the Tower in on itself. Within its fastness I found whole districts of unsuspected space – the lot decorated with fabulous illustrations. *Cryptozoology Rooms (extinct)*, which once housed the horns of unicorns, vials of mermaid milk, pickled homunculi, the furballs of a sphinx, golem dust, gryphon dung and an egg-laying vole with the beak of a duck, which the cartographer dismissed as the work of inventive taxidermists . . . A *Sand Cabinet*, complete with cool oases and the occasional mirage . . . *Hot Spring Baths*, long since cooled by Time . . . cavernous assembly rooms whose floors and ceilings had collapsed . . . temples and kitchens and vomitaria abandoned to slugs and whatever spiders can prosper without light. The fraction of the Tower which the Brethren actually used was small in comparison to these regions: the scale, perhaps, of the liver in the body of a man. With my finger I traced the route (drawn in charcoal by Œp and Greda) that would lead me to the Upper Storeys.

At my bedside I trimmed the wick of my lantern. I filled the glass crucible with oil and set it alight with my shrinking taper. From my amateurish study notes I tore a shred of parchment and copied, from the map, the details of my route.

I opened the door of my dormitory and stuck my head out into the corridor. For a wild instant I imagined I was standing on the edge of a promontory, that inches beyond me the ground fell away to steep and certain peril. 'Nonsense,' I said aloud. My voice echoed down the corridor: how I longed to catch it and fling it back into my mouth. But the sound travelled unheeded, I hoped, and it drowned in silence, a loaded, forever-about-to-shatter silence that set the teeth on edge. I crossed myself twice and launched off into the labyrinth.

What was it like, that secret, bidden-and-forbidden journey? I can only compare it to ingestion. As food is pushed through the oesophagus, so the darkness, like a muscle, constricted behind and dilated before me. The first minutes I spent in familiar territory. My breathing sounded to me louder than my footsteps; my legs, I knew, were carrying me, but I barely felt them. By the Baths I was pursued by the slow dripping of the water pumps. I passed the chambers of Heridus and Nester without daring to listen for sounds of their slumber. Then the latrines, imagining the stone seats, the cold suction of the air on one's hams and the mute drop into the pit below. I ascended a narrow staircase. Past the Scarlet Chambers and Brother Ludwig's cell, with its door latch fringed with razor blades. Up a second spiral staircase I crept, fastidiously quiet. The third and fourth floors contained the workshops, as well as the cells of the musicians and Brother Kay. I scrutinised my improvised map but the turnings took themselves, as though body were clever where spirit was dim. Puny Theseus unaided by Ariadne, I left at every juncture a chalk cross to aid my return.

The fifth floor was unknown territory. The walls of the tunnel gleamed in my lantern-light; their surfaces were irregular, ridged in places like the roof of the mouth, and the paving crackled wetly underfoot. At last I came to the ultimate flight of stairs. High above me I thought I distinguished a blue smudge of light. I gripped the stair-rail with my free hand and looked into the hollow sockets of a skull. Not an actual skull, I quickly assured myself; rather, a sculpture in oxidised copper, neatly framed by fibia and tibia, with the lettering **IX. Requiescat in Pace** uncurling, like an eel, from an empty eye socket. The sculpture embossed a heavy door. I had found the resting-place of Gerboš von Okba. But without any sense of triumph. In truth, that grinning head sent me scurrying up the damp, resounding staircase towards the Portico of the Upper Storeys.

The climb was greater than I had anticipated. The glistening floor blacked out beneath me; I was fixed betwixt air and ether. I slowed – aching in limb and weary in spirit – some distance from the summit, and distinguished clearly the mist of light above me. I meant to consult the map but my fingers pinched nothing. Far below, sucking damp where I had dropped it, sat the parchment.

'Don't worry about that – you've arrived.'

We shall take as spoken my reaction to this disembodied voice. My lantern fell from my hands and clattered down the stairs. Gluttonous darkness swallowed me from head to foot.

'Have you fallen?' asked the voice. 'I'll send a torch down to you.'

Frozen by sweat, I watched in dismay a blue flame sink towards me on the end of a rope. My thoughts spilled in all directions. Taking the torch when it reached me, I contemplated retreat back down the steps.

'You needn't escape,' said the voice. 'Climb up, since you're here, and join me.'

Will-sapped, I obeyed. The last yards of that climb

were a Sisyphean torment. At the summit I met my defeat in the form of Brother Kay. A second torch hung, perilously I thought, at his side; beneath it glinted what looked like the sheath of a blade.

'I must have startled you,' Brother Kay said softly.

My gaze drifted towards the Portico of the Upper Storeys behind him. Twenty feet high and wider still, it was hewn of wood as black as charcoal and patterned with quincuncial beams. The lintel, of solid marble, was inscribed with ancient and inscrutable lettering.

Solicitously, like a parent shielding his child from cruel visions, Brother Kay interposed himself between me and my goal.

'Do you have the key?' I asked.

'There is no key.' He placed a hand upon my shoulder. 'You're tired after your exertions. I will accompany you to your dormitory – you will sleep. And we will never speak of our meeting thus, in one another's dreams.'

Familiar, jocund even, Brother Kay escorted me from the scene. Like the owl, he said, he was liveliest in the small hours: upright against the prone millions. As we walked, he began to whisper about his preoccupations. Was I familiar, he asked, with phosgene? With holy toxins that kill blackamoors but spare Christians? With poisons that lie latent in water and twist enemy foetuses into pretzel-knots?

'Of course,' he said, 'poison is all around us. Everything that lives, in decay, provides it. All you need to harness its power is a swab, a vial and a strong stomach.'

We descended our third flight of stairs and I could not lighten his monologue with interjections of my own, no matter how pertinent. Something in Brother Kay's tone, his very amicability, warned me to pay attention.

'In the last years of the Tung dynasty,' he said, 'there lived a master poisoner. His name was Lu Jung. He was chief eunuch to Chiang-hsi, the Emperor's beautiful and ambitious sister.

'Now the Emperor, K'uang-yin, having neither wife nor child, had no heir but his nephew, Chiang-hsi's son.

'On the Heir Apparent's ninth birthday the crimson-lacquered labyrinth of the Palace filled with screams. Servants stopped and bit their cheeks, fearing the worst. But Emperor K'uang-yin was not being strangled – no conspirators' blades hacked themselves between his ribs. He was howling at an image of his death, at the word-shadow of it, as predicted by a soothsayer. His enemies, he was told, were plotting against him; do what he might, he would not outlive the year.

'So the Emperor gathered about him his most trusted retainers, and Prince Chu with his mother was banished to a distant tower. Sealed within the Citadel, guarded by two hundred men, K'uang-yin neglected his Empire. The Huai and Yellow rivers silted up with pirates; nomads seized the salt wells of Szechuan; the rice-fields went untended. The greater his isolation, the more the

Emperor feared for his life. Cooks were forced to taste their own dishes, ministers became kitchen inspectors, and K'uang-yin grew thin on air and suspicion.

'It is impossible, however, to provide against Fate. One night the Emperor retired, troubled, to his chamber. They found him at dawn, stiff as a terracotta statue. Sublimate – that's mercuric chloride – inflames the heart, traps urine, blocks every orifice. He had suffered, effectively, a slow implosion. All witnesses wondered at the manner of K'uang-yin's death. His favourite catamite – with whom he had retired for the night –was never found, either living or dead.

'Official mourning is a most convenient moderator of emotion. Government cannot take the veil. So young Prince Chu became Emperor within the week, his mother the Empress Dowager – and Lu Jung the wealthiest commoner in Kaifeng. The Empress Dowager Chiang-hsi, in whose hands effective power lay, avenged her brother's murder by ordering the executions of his Inner Circle. Her sòn, the new Emperor, watched the corpses swing, like crows, from silken ropes.

'And so began a happy commonwealth, you might think. Ah, but Chiang-hsi's ambition could not be sated and she began to covet her son's divinity. Rumours spread in the city of a demon stalking the Palace, intent on the Boy Emperor's life. The Empress Dowager, acting as any mother would, confined her son to a pagoda for his security. She surrounded him with guards, and even the boy's favourite tutor, loyal Lu Jung, was obliged to withdraw from his presence. Bereft of companionship, the Emperor endured the hours playing with his pet dog. He nuzzled its wrinkled face, he groomed its bristly coat. The dog was at liberty to wander the Palace grounds. Upon its return the boy would sniff from its fur the forbidden fragrances of his home.

'Withdrawn to his sumptuous apartments, Lu Jung concocted his most remarkable poison. What he needed was something odourless, slow to rouse but quick to work. There were a dozen strange deaths in the city slums before he was able to fulfil his mistress's desire.

'One morning in the Jade Garden, Lu Jung found the Emperor's dog uprooting an orchid. From his deep pockets the poisoner withdrew a saucer and a vial of specially treated milk. (Lactose, you see, leaves a residue in saliva.) The dog, having finished its treat, scampered home and Lu Jung rinsed the saucer in a fountain.

'Now please don't think for a moment that the child was intended to suffer. The juice of the plant *Potamentis* provokes delightful visions – whatever one desires most is granted. The Emperor Chu, believing himself winged like a dragon, plunged from the pagoda's roof into an early grave. Leaving the throne free for his sorely grieving mother.'

Brother Kay searched my profile until I had to meet his black, glinting eyes. 'I myself am working along similar lines,' he said. 'From the *Achaemenis* herb, I can squeeze melancholy; from belladonna, unspeakable hallucinations. My favourite, antimony, has neither taste nor odour. No more than a pea's weight will kill a man; a pod's worth will bag you six. The antidote, by the way, is locked in the roots of *Enula campana* – and that doesn't grow in these parts.'

The threat was allowed to settle and take root. I could feel it uncurling like a seed in my stomach. I had to speak at once, for the silence itself was poisonous and a pretence of blitheness my only salvation.

'What happened,' I croaked, 'in the end, to the Empress Dowager?'

'The greater her power, the more suspicious she became of her subjects. So she ordered her guards to kill every servant in the Palace – and when it was done, she poisoned the butchers' salt rations. She herself died three months later, unattended, of bedsores and starvation.' Brother Kay's expression was so mild that he might have been describing the weather. 'But don't worry: Lu Jung survived. The talents of great men are required wherever power shifts.'

We had arrived outside my dormitory. Brother Kay stopped in the doorway, as though we had just returned from a night on the town and were keen no longer to put off sleep. I walked, feigning grogginess, to my bed. Brother Kay, at the threshold, bade a brisk farewell, and I was left alone with my fear.

Breakfast. The Chosen were seated at steaming bowls. I watched the slow labour of their jaws. Brother Kay had anchored himself in a book; Greda and Œp shared a daydream; old Ludwig inspected a chipped fingernail. Brother Heridus with his spoon was nudging a drowned weevil to the rim of his bowl. Brother Nester seemed transfixed by the grain of the wood of the table. To test their resolve, I hogged the saltcellar. But nobody, not even the salt-mad Ludwig, troubled me for it. I pretended to concentrate on my porridge, patting its skin. When I looked up, eyes scattered like fishes. I was being scrutinised. After the Call to Industry, there would be fawning and pleading, and hands on my knees.

Sick to the guts with anticipation, I pushed my bowl into the centre of the table. The Brethren's brows flickered. I tipped my spoon sideways and sticky globules of porridge flattened on the place mat. 'This food stinks,' I announced, trembling. 'It's trash, it's swill, I wouldn't feed it to swine.' I threw the spoon at the wall: it glanced and clattered. But the Brethren were deaf as stones. I tasted the years of intrigue and fear, the unspeakable fetor of their crimes.

I had to get out. The walls were screaming.

I rose and excused myself. Outside the Refectory, I began to run. They wouldn't follow me: mired in habit, they would settle, disgruntled, at their labours, each thinking I was with a rival.

From Nester's workshop I stole a chisel and a wooden hammer.

Then on – second thoughts snapping at my back – following my chalk tracings. Pain stabbed at my feet as my sandals slammed and slapped on the pavings. Fired by danger, I travelled down the damp obscurity of the fifth floor and stopped, panting, at the skull-embossed door.

The keyhole gaped like a mouth, suggesting a complex bolting mechanism within. The bolt itself, a metal tongue one inch thick, looked invincible. I fitted the chisel against it and struck a blow with my hammer. The bolt itself stood firm but the lock shot out of its frame. The door, thus loosened, swung open. Under the strain, its hinges buckled. It hung there, hesitating. Then the hinges snapped and – *crash!* – it fell, a giant's domino. The dust floated like smoke, scorching my throat. I unhooked a torch from its rusty bracket on the wall and entered the Ninth Vault.

The Vault was cavernous. I have stood since in the antechamber to a subterranean labyrinth, the mouth of an Alpine giant where stalactites as thin as straws, in numbers greater than the bristles in the right-whale's gullet, hang from the domed ceiling. In that natural cave my flame would touch the sloping far wall, granting me a sense of finite space. But in the Ninth Vault my torch could barely reach into the throat of the darkness. I found myself surrounded by stone sarcophagi. Many had buckled with age. Some were plain, like sealed baths, others were lidded with sculpted effigies. A foot of one sage, who clasped in his sleep a compass and sceptre, crumbled to dust when I placed my hand upon it. I stared at that magus of worm-eaten wood. How skilfully the sculptor had captured the lines on the brow, the downturned mouth, and the smooth almonds of his eyes; with what symmetry his flowing locks descended, like rivulets, into the purling confluence of the beard. I shone my torch at the side of the sarcophagus in hope of a plaque. My pleasure at finding one turned to shock – the cold blow of a fatidic discovery.

Hic depositum est Corpus
GERBOŠ VON OKBA
Hujus Turris Magistri.
Obiit 23 Die Mensis Maius
AD 14—. Anno Ætatis 66.

I brought my face up against the Master's epitaph. Escaping from under the edges of the plaque, like the limbs of something crushed beneath it, were the tendrils of an earlier inscription: loops and arches of an obscure alphabet. In the stone beneath the lid I felt with my fingers the rough, recent sores made by the Brethren's chisels. The effigy of the ancient occupant had been reattached only in the most peremptory fashion, with thin dabs of mortar. Placing my torch on the floor, I dared myself like a schoolboy to push against the sarcophagus lid. It moved, a fraction only. I got to my feet and, pushing with my hands and thighs, was able to dislodge the lid further, frittering the sandy paste. With my chisel I chipped away the stubborn crumbs of the mortar. Then, using the tool as a lever, I prised a gap between wood and stone. Since my torch was on the ground I could not see inside the sarcophagus but, by God, I could smell it. I improvised a mask from the torn sleeve of my gown and wrapped it about my nose and mouth. I was trembling and my skin prickled from the dust. I gave the lid a final shove of such violence that I lost my balance. Only by gripping the far rim of the sarcophagus did I avert plunging my hand into the distended belly of the dead Master.

You cannot imagine the triumph of my vindication. Despite my retching, in spite of the dread, I had brought the Truth to light. Quite literally. The corpse's hands were withered claws, the fingernails grown long and black. The feet, which poked through a dusty white shroud, were curled at the toes like a sultan's slippers. In contrast to his sculpted predecessor, Gerboš von Okba was – had been – clean shaven. Dry wisps of cadaverous hair were a downy halo about the mottled scalp. His face was muffled as though from mumps.

A livid gash travelled the neck from ear to severed ear.

I sat in the dust beneath the blown-out lintel and listened to the flap of the Brethren's sandals. Past sullen torches on the walls, I focused on the staircase summit. Violently it coughed them up. At that distance it was impossible to distinguish tonsure from tonsure, to personify any individual. As they approached, however, the mass unravelled, with Brother Kay nodding into the lead. Heridus and Nester, entangled, were attempting, even in their common goal, to overtake one another, while Ludwig (miraculously cured of gout) kicked his legs out as though to be rid of his feet. Bringing up the rear, Greda and Œp nipped at everyone's heels.

I was unafraid. I stood to meet them and they stumbled to a halt, their momentum lost to my stillness.

'What have you done?' panted Heridus, gripping his sides.

'Sss-sacrilege!'

'Punish him!' Nester coughed. 'Flay him in the arm-pits!'

The Vault's entrance gaped open behind me. Pale and thin lipped, the Brethren peered into it. I held my tools in cruciform at my belly.

'What,' asked Brother Kay (undaunted by my accusing eyes), 'have you to say for yourself? Desecrating a tomb is an infraction of Basic Law.'

'I see,' I said, 'and cutting your Master's throat is only a misdemeanour?'

Brother Kay's lips parted silently.

'That's slander,' said Heridus. 'Shut him up!'

'I don't understand,' Œp implored of his neighbour. 'What does he mean?'

'He means rot!' said Ludwig.

Zealously, I pointed my chisel. 'Brother Ludwig, remind me: how did Gerboš von Okba die?'

'I told you: stopping of the stutter-stutter—!'

'Stomach, of course. Brother Heridus, you told me the Master died of a broken neck, did you not? When he fell, reaching for a book?'

Heridus blinked. 'Er, yes. *Pseudepigrapha.*'

'Brother Nester, is it wise, do you think, to read manuscripts in the bath? After all, it takes less than a heart attack for an accident to happen.'

Nester never flinched; oily droplets gathered on his brow.

'And who' (I asked of Œp and Greda) 'ever heard of *farting* to death?'

The Brethren huffed in defensive, foul-breathed indignation. Only Brother Kay stood collected. 'If you are to indict us on any charge graver than embellishment,' he said, 'you will not find a more propitious moment.'

I looked from face to sour face – and felt the strength of their hatred. 'By all means,' I said. 'I want you to ask yourselves why I have done this. What were my motives for opening the Master's tomb and putting myself in danger? I might have ignored my suspicions. That would have suited me better. After all, I have realised my boyhood dream – here I am, in the Tower, one of the Chosen.'

'Not yet,' said Heridus. 'You're not *yet* Chosen.'

'Curiosity,' I said. 'The curiosity essential to learning spurred me on. From Brother Nester I learned that the Master was dead. From the rest of you, I found out enough contradictions to guess at something sinister. For weeks you've kept me in ignorance. You won't translate the Book of Instruction and yet you accuse me of breaking its laws. It was only a matter of time before I opened that tomb in search of the Truth . . .

'At first I didn't understand how the Master's killer could have escaped detection. You were all present at the entombment. That bloody gash – still visible after weeks of decay – was unconcealed. Therefore every one of you must have seen what I have seen.'

'So which of us did it?' said Heridus. 'Who's the murderer?'

'Brother Heridus, you were often alone with Gerboš von Okba, were you not?'

'Yes. I told you, we worked together.'

'Of course, on your masterpiece.' I aimed the blow with precision. 'I've seen the crumbling condition of your library. Paralysed without books, you despised your dependence on the Master. So you sought his death.'

Heridus was ashen faced. 'You've touched my library?'

'Yes, Brother Heridus, you had motive and occasion to slit his throat. Those oriental paper-knives in your study are much too sharp, wouldn't you say, for the simple task for which they were intended?'

Greda stared bug-eyed at the accused. 'So Brother Heridus killed the Master?'

'Nonsense!' Heridus shouted.

'Nonsense,' I concurred. 'Brother *Ludwig* had the more obvious motive. As the eldest after von Okba, he was first in line for the succession. And yet he was getting on, wasn't he? His life's work, that rootless theorem, will never be finished. He had nothing to lose by the Master's death and everything to gain by it.'

'*Me?* I'm skin and bones! Incapable of murmur-murder!'

'If you can manage five flights of stairs without collapsing,' I said, 'you can cut an old man's throat. As for instincts, you've demonstrated your violent temper often enough.'

'This is all very entertaining,' said Brother Kay. 'But what is your evidence?'

'Plenty, of motive. Brother Ludwig wanted me in the Upper Storeys to find the Constitution that would officialise his Right of Succession. He tried to bribe me with gold and jewels – glinting baubles which he knew to be worthless in the Tower.'

Nester suddenly sprang to life. To everyone's astonishment, he seized Brother Ludwig by the throat and attempted to throttle him. Ludwig hovered gurgling an inch above the ground, his colleagues apparently unwilling to intervene.

'Grip any tighter,' said Brother Kay finally, 'and you *will* be the murderer, Nester.' In an instant both strangler and stranglee subsided. Ludwig gasped, like a flounder, on the floor.

'Yes,' I taunted. 'That *would* have been useful, Brother Nester. Kill a suspect in a moral rage and you have a corpse on which you can pin anything.'

'Don't go on,' Nester cautioned.

'Of course, when it comes to brute strength – the sort required to split cartilage – Brother Nester has the lion's share. We're all familiar with his work on pest control. That glassy stare when he disembowels some helpless rodent, was it the last thing von Okba beheld, as he bubbled and gaped for air?'

'Motive?' demanded Brother Kay.

'Brother Nester had talked himself into the role of victim. The Master, he reckoned, was stealing his inventions. Why? Because Brother Nester is the Tower's unrecognised genius. Perpetually aggrieved, he seethed with murderous intent.'

'I killed no one!' shouted Nester. 'But the Master *was* a thief.'

'No,' I replied. 'You may have talked yourself into believing that, but it's a fiction. You see, Brother Nester . . . I know about the egg-whisk.'

'The what?'

'The egg-whisk.'

'What egg-whisk?'

'*My* egg-whisk. The invention that won me my noviciate. At our very first meeting you coveted it. Unable to tolerate *my* talent, you were working already on ways to appropriate it and pass it off as your own.'

Brother Nester shook his head. 'That's not right—'

'I found the model in your workshop! Your copy of *my* original!'

'So the conspiracy grows,' Brother Kay intruded. In his eyes I thought I saw an oblique kinship, an understanding that cuts through enmity. 'Which of us is the murderer, according to your Grand Theory?'

'I've not come yet to our musical friends, Brothers Œp and Greda.'

'It's not true!' Œp shrieked. 'There is no gash, he died of belly gripe!' Brother Greda carefully, as though placating a child, folded his arms about Œp's chest.

'Brother Greda,' I continued, 'do you deny that you were ready and able to poison me, if it could advance your cause?'

Greda was deaf; with the thumb of his left hand he stroked Œp's neck.

'One morning you confessed to me that you can neither read nor write music. That task fell to Gerboš von Okba. Both of you, I say, were as dependent on the Master as Brother Heridus. And dependency breeds resentment. I myself have suffered from your malignancy. You slipped me a drug, and called its effects Tower Fever, simply to blackmail me into your service.'

'Yes,' said Greda. 'But it wasn't *our* idea . . .'

Again, Brother Kay interrupted: 'I have a question. Whichever of my colleagues perpetrated this (shall we call it dastardly?) crime, why hasn't he entered the Upper Storeys and taken that which he killed for? If your man has no qualms about committing murder, surely he won't hesitate before a little theft?' Brother Kay's eyes were bright with pleasure. This was a gauntlet that I had to pick up.

'Mutual distrust,' I replied. 'I've witnessed your disputes over the succession. Up there, above those stairs, lies the fulfilment of all your ambitions. You gather about it like jackdaws round a well, in mutual deterrence.'

'And the solution,' said Brother Kay, 'was to make *you* the thief?'

'Exactly. I was the common factor in their plans.'

'*Our* plans?' protested Heridus. 'What are you saying?'

'Isn't it obvious? The knife wound to Gerboš von Okba's neck is too deep and too wide to have been made with just one cut. And why slice from ear to ear when a mere nick to the jugular would have sufficed?'

I watched them tremble. I was marble to their flesh: the Tower's Justice.

'The Master, I say, died not from one blade but from many. You conspired together, united in loathing – and in a frenzy you butchered the old man.'

For an instant all things stood in suspension. I was a sculpted David captured in his triumph. But Time – intolerant of our lives, which distort it – bit the sneer off my face. I was in mortal danger.

'Beastly!' the Brethren hissed. 'Monstrous!' I have witnessed, in my travels, the savage broils of Barbary apes. In like manner did the Brethren heave and shiver and bare the pink of their gums. I stumbled back until my calves struck the first rung of the staircase. Suddenly the Brethren surged towards me. I swung my chisel. There was a noise like a seam splitting and Brother Œp fell, clutching his face. Screaming, shrill and childlike, assaulted my senses. I swung my hammer at the flurry of faces. Bones broke – I felt the retort in my teeth. With my calves crushed against cold metal, I turned and lunged up several steps in a single stride.

I cannot recall my climb. The fury that pursued me must, I think, be the product of later imaginings, filling lacunae where Memory dares not venture. With clarity, however, I feel myself tearing from the summit step and cutting my knuckles on its serrated lip. I had nowhere to head for in that dark, uncharted territory but the

Portico. I ran to it, praying in my blood that it would receive me.

I crashed heavily into the wooden beams. My fingers found the iron ring – tightened – and the door heaved open.

There was barely time as I jumped inside to glimpse the Brethren, like screaming harridans, devouring the distance between us. Shuddering, I shut the door and dragged the bolt across it. I listened for a time to the impotent rage of my enemies. At last their clamour subsided; fists and feet and fingernails beat themselves out on the ancient wood; the Brethren turned away.

I did not move for some time, childishly absorbed in picking torn skin from my knuckles. When my breath returned I counted slowly to ten.

Then I turned around.

At my back stood the huge Portico – greater than any cathedral's, a fitting seal for the Upper Storeys. And yet I was trapped in a space no bigger than a storeroom. Ahead of me was sheer brick. To my left, in the penumbra, I sensed unevenness. Tentatively I reached out and felt broken masonry, torn and splintered wood. Up above it there was a richer seam of darkness, a void. I turned my back on the rubble and kicked, by accident, a pile of papers; they fluttered away from me like pigeons. Some few steps later, I struck a low dune and fell. Paper, in sufficient quantity, is protean: part Air (the lightness of its components), part Water (its treatment of foreign bodies), it is also suffocating Earth. Ahead of me, as far as I could tell, were steep cliffs and quarries of the stuff. On hands and knees I negotiated it. The surface papers slipped beneath my pressure; I slowed for fear of disappearing into a drift. Soon I lost all capacity to progress, as with every inch gained I was slipping three. Either foolhardy or courageous (I make no great distinction), I began to burrow. With claws and elbows I dug, as a rabbit shovels leaf-meal between its hindquarters. Suddenly a giant's hand dragged me down. I plunged through the great mound's core – emerging, in a flurry of papers, like a salmon tossed clear of a waterfall.

I looked back and discovered that I had slipped through a hole in a sheer, otherwise unbroken wall. The hole itself, still foaming papers, was not the work of a mason. Its roughness, and the brick powder gritting my fingertips, indicated haste, not method, in its making.

Before me ran a long, dark passage that dwindled to a distant aperture. It was an image, a false perspective – for after a few metres I stubbed my nose on a painted wall. The pain made me curse; my voice was aberrant in that unpeopled place. What was I to do? All the illogic of my impeded dreams was taking material form in the Upper Storeys. I kicked the trompe l'oeil with vindictive zeal.

It moved.

I pushed again and must have tripped a mechanism, invoking the thrum and whirring of cogs.

Slowly, with great mechanical languor, a low wooden door emerged in the wall. Still bearing traces of its former, red-lacquered glory, the door could not have been above twenty inches high. It seemed so childish that I giggled, and fell to my knees to turn its tiny brass handle.

I opened the door and found that it led into a small passageway: dank and dismal, with ribbed uneven walls. Crouching low, I looked along the passage into the grandest library you ever saw. How I longed to wander about among those massive shelves and thick volumes! But it was a terrible strain to squeeze myself through. Shards of brick embedded themselves in my knees and forehead. Blood and sweat oozed into my eyes; copper and salt on to my tongue. Just before its orifice, the passageway contracted, until there seemed to be no possibility of further movement. Ever since Plato described his Charioteer, Man has lamented the Animal in him. But I would have died that day had I been all Mind. It was physical rage that saved me – there was no resisting it; the pressure built until I became my scream, a birth-cry. I burst, like a bung from a bottle, into the inner Tower.

The library's floor was a circle, a spacious O. Books everywhere, in sufficient profusion to daunt a Methuselah. From a fixed point in the centre, seven staircases gyred upwards into the highest shelves. I gawped at the high domed ceiling and its tarnished mosaics. Did I discern there the Pleiades? Were those the Planets, connected to God's crankshaft? I might have climbed a staircase to be sure. But few would take my weight: they rattled uninvitingly when I shook them. Instead I browsed the lowest shelves. Beginning at 'Hades', I plucked at *Haematologia*, the *Haggadah* and *Hagiographœ Sanctori*; at 'Haiku' (thirty yards farther on) I gave up. I should add that the floor of the chamber was turfed with great heaps of books, all piled together in no discernible order, without observance of the alphabet. Looking at those learned hillocks, I wondered had they been salvaged from elsewhere in the Upper Storeys? Rescued – but how? Carried down rickety staircases – by whom?

Determined not to moulder in this room, I selected and climbed the sturdiest staircase. Soon, as I approached the ceiling, books closed ranks on me. Another dead end. I was learning quickly, however, and I scrutinised the spines. Sure enough, I found the switch, a book that protruded visibly. I pushed *Hortus Paradisus Terrestris* and a panel opened above me, sliding back with a sigh.

After another tight squeeze I clambered into a second, identical library. It too was a refuge to homeless books. There were the same seven staircases; or rather, there were three still standing and four mangled stumps feebly bolstered by planks. The bookshelves, heavily lumbered, ran from *Parloir aux Pîtres* to 'Perpendicular Tracery', a prospect which would have depressed me utterly had it not been for the distraction of Brother Nester's inventions. For in this second library I discovered the fate of that inventor's work. It sat, dusty and neglected, wherever floor-space permitted. I lifted sheets and glimpsed handles, axles, greasy fuel rods. More interesting, my restless eye decided, were the skid marks on the floor. These were grazes in the marble, scars that indicated the movement of heavy instruments. It was child's play to follow these marks to their destination. They disappeared under a wall. No problem; a simple push of every book and eventually the panel opened. I stared down a garbage chute, a straight drop into the unknown. What lay at the bottom I could only guess, picturing the articulated bones of rejected prototypes, an inventions' graveyard.

High above me something creaked, a wooden groan. I looked up until my throat skin strained. One of the ceiling panels, which had before been shut, gaped open. It was impossible to look away, though I wanted to with all my frightened mind.

There was a head. It emerged for an instant only, though that was long enough. It was small, allowing for the distance, and dwarfish. A turquoise headscarf framed large, albino-red eyes (yes, the irises were unmistakable) and the creature wore thick leather gloves that resembled the paws of a bear. I cried out, 'Stop!', and immediately the apparition disappeared, shutting the panel after it.

What alternative had I to pursuit? The staircase shook and trembled under me. But it held firm. At its summit I searched for the latch mechanism. I did not read the title of the trigger-book, seeing only the motion of the panel when it opened for me. I squeezed through the aperture, scraping my neck painfully in the process.

There was no sign of the dwarf in the third library. But my dread of repetition, at least, was allayed. Here one could dream, if one dared, of finitude. For there were no more staircases. The books on the shelves were inscribed with lettering from an unfamiliar alphabet: all knots and ribbons. The most striking change, however, from its predecessors was the denuded floor. My eye delighted in the absence of clutter; delighted, that is, until the light source faltered and I was plunged into darkness.

This was no gentle twilight, to which the eye in time adapts. It was as though deep, primordial waters had filled a breach in Space. Insulated from Nature, the Tower was darkness itself. Darkness, the darkness out there, cannot be banished; it waits, is waiting, for the Universe that aspires to it. Creation's expiration, the last of light. When the stars and moons, the endless fires of constellations, when all that is now and will be is sucked into a particle smaller than dust, and Chaos reclaims its dominion.

I floated for an indefinable time in the void. Oddly unflustered, indifferent. Yes, I might have stayed there for ever – suspended, oblivious – had the Tower taken pity on me. But I was not to be spared. A lone beam of light dissected the darkness. Shrill and white, it shot out from the floor. Then another. And another: each as concentrated as the first, I mean undiffracting, shedding nothing from its blade-path to the air around it. Thick and fast the beams appeared, as though I were in a box that someone was piercing with a pin. The white rays sliced and crossed the air, like the web of the Viking wyrds who measure and cut the cords of our lives.

The nearest beam to me seemed to hum – no, to sing, as a crystal glass sings when you stroke it with a wetted finger. Charily, I broke its path with my left hand: there was no burning. Keeping my hand skewered on the shaft, I crouched low to scrutinise my illumined palm. And there, somewhat crumpled by the lines of luck and life, was the face of Brother Heridus. He stared out of the palm of my hand, as small as the head on a shilling, and snarled. His blood stained teeth he washed with his tongue. Then, very tenderly, he probed his face with his fingers. Odd as it may seem, I could not hold back my laughter. Like some ludic deity, I held a human soul (most human, since most private) in my hand.

Every beam, I realised, was the inner sight of a reflective surface somewhere in the Tower. I watched strange and familiar places through the eyes of pots and pans, through mirrors and pendula, through the candelabrum that spidered over the Refectory table. Using my hand as a canvas screen, I observed the hidden life of the Tower, quite unknown to the watched, when watched there were. Most of the rooms, it must be said, were unoccupied, while many apertures, though lit, contained only fog, which might have been the glass or the contents of the chamber, I don't know.

Much too clear, however, was the beam that showed my dormitory's fumigation. The fumigators

were children, similar in shape to the servant I had
startled previously. With difficulty (for they were
maggot small in my palm) I observed these wretches
as they dismantled my bed. I shouted at them to stop
but they turned their backs to me, unhearing. Finally,
with what resembled incense-burners, they banished,
as one might an infection, all trace of my residence. It
didn't really matter. They merely confirmed what I
knew already. That my life, as I had come to understand it, was over.

Still, my useless power fascinated me; the voyeur in
me triumphed, with his Greek god's eye. Here was
Brother Ludwig, rubbing ointment into his ankle. Here
was Brother Nester, stripped to the waist and scourging
himself with a flail. And here, look, lay old Œp, with
Greda fussing over him. Greda unpeeled a gauze; Œp's
eyes drooled a fluid like egg-white.

Horrified, I turned my head. Exposing, in the process,
my right ear to the light shaft. Into that waxy canal –
pelting the tympanic membrane that thrums the malleus
that beats the incus that taps the stapes that tickles the
cochlea that prickles the labyrinth that jangles the nerve
that feeds the brain, whence it will never ever fade –
came revelatory sound. 'How can I play again,' Œp
gibbered, 'how can I play?' Greda brought him no
comfort. From his throat escaped a long, low moan
of grief.

I cowered in the blackness, jabbing at my ear. 'I've
seen enough!' I shouted. 'I want to get out now, if you
don't mind!'

To whom was I speaking? Certainly not God. Between a cruel inscrutable Absence and a cruel inscrutable Presence, I hope for the former.

Up ahead of me – if it's possible to speak of directions – a narrow crack of colour, a rent in the void, appeared. It yawned from a rectangle, slowly, into a square. A square of orange light that, as my retinas reminded themselves of their function, evolved into a hatch. I saw books. More books. A wall smothered with the fucking things. It was enough to keep me rooted to my spot. Only the reappearance (first the headscarf, then the ghastly red eyes) of the dwarf stirred me from suicidal stasis. Without him – the dwarf – I would, I swear, never have moved again, nor stirred, until another came to remove my bones.

'Who are you?' I demanded of the apparition. 'What do you want from me?'

The dwarf did not scamper off. He moved to the edge of the hatch, so that his face was obscured in silhouette. But he could see me. I did not appreciate my disadvantage and said as much, in colourful terms. The dwarf replied, I thought he replied, with inscrutable jargon. I blew a raspberry. The dwarf blew a raspberry. I made an obscene hand gesture.

The light returned.

The hatch to the new library was more spacious than others I might have mentioned and it was easy to lower myself through. My sandals touched carpet. Softness! I stared, incredulous, at the cause of that forgotten sensation. Then the dwarf spoke, in a language that, for all its obscurity, sounded itchingly familiar. I looked obliquely at him, scorning his ugliness, noting the garish headscarf. He pointed to the walls, which were book-lined, yes, but also stacked with implements of every Science. A polyhedron representing geometry; mechanical appliances for domestic usage; woodworking tools; a pair of scales; a bell; an hourglass; a magic square of sixteen numerals, whose every line combined to thirty-four. There was also a casket, glass fronted and empty. When I had slaked the thirst of my curiosity, the dwarf gestured me towards a large, black, hardwood table. I did as I was bid and sank – what comfort! – on to a cushioned stool.

'This is the Master's library!' I exclaimed, and the dwarf concurred with his eyes. 'And there's a door. Right ahead of me, an ordinary, spacious, easy-to-use *door*.' (I'm not a man of complex needs.) As a proprietorial gesture, I clasped my hands in front of me and brought them down on a wax-sealed scroll. I looked at the scroll. The dwarf looked at me. I picked up the scroll from the desk. The formal script upon it read, quite simply, *Novicius*.

'This can't be for me,' I said stupidly. But the albino had slipped already through the door, and no amount of protestation would bring him back. The scroll, in my puzzlement, weighed heavy in my hand. I shrugged and with my thumb broke the wax seal. For years afterwards, in reference to this moment, I was to dream of sarcophagi: of opening them and breathing on dead Masters. Some of the corpses had deep grooves in their wrist-bones, where long ago a ritual knife had ploughed its fatal furrow; others sported between their eyes a third, uneven socket.

The document was the work of Gerboš von Okba. It was his suicide note.

As you read this I am dead at last. These will be my latest Words – latest of too many Millions. For what Posterity do Manuscripts enjoy, stored Fathoms deep in Vaults? Unadmired, what is the Beauty of a Waterfall? Only in your Mind can I exist, for a Moment, for a short Moment longer.

The Brethren, if I know them, will have concealed from you the Manner of my Death. This is to be expected. Outside, my Corpse would be inhumed at a Crossroads; for Mankind, no Matter how brutish his Life, heeds like an Animal the instinct to continue; Suicide terrifies him by the Depth of its Subversion; so he buries it out of mind, in unhallowed Soil.

You have met Meshech. His People are the Servants, who speak the Language of the Book. Their Skin, over the Millennia, has lost, from lack of Sunlight, all Pigmentation; their Skeleton has dwindled; their Eyes, adapted to the Penumbra, could not endure the Light of Day. They are the Tower's Corpuscles; as we the Chosen, absorbed from Without, are the Tower's Food. Meshech has outlived me, as a Manservant must his Master, until a Successor is found; whereupon a new Manservant, promoted from Darkness upon ancient Criteria, shall take his Place. It was Meshech's instruction to wait for you; to show you something of the Anatomy of the Upper Storeys, including the Seeing Room; & finally to lead you to my Confession. Dead as I am, your

The Penitent Drunkard's Tale

Presence in this dark Mill is my doing. I have set you on your Journey; left Clues for you. You are the Proof, unacknowledged by your Brethren, of the Tower's accursedness.

At the Death of one of the Chosen, a Novice is found who will return our Number to Seven. It is customary for the Novice to be selected on the novelty of his Application Piece. I, however, inverted this Rule. My strict Instructions for your Admission were: That your Application Piece should _exist already_; that, quite independent of the Tower, you should have made a Discovery identical to that of one of your Superiors. No doubt Brother Nester will resent your imagined Plagiarism. And yet everything over which he toils I possess already, catalogued & tarnishing somewhere in the Upper Storeys. For the Tower contains all Knowledge: it is the great Sea from which, unwitting Fisherman, Mankind recovers his Learning, his Art & his Musick. Only the Divine Will has distanced us from Compleat Science. Many Storeys and their Libraries have suffered Collapse; entire Regions & Districts are sealed off. Hundreds of Servants live and die in the Upper Storeys, whose only Function is to salvage displaced & buried Material.

Yet the scale of this Degradation cannot undo the Truth. What Scholars and Thinkers term Human progress is mere Recapitulation. Just as your Invention — thought up in Isolation from the Tower — was simultaneously original & unoriginal, so with Everything that the Chosen build: we are permitted, at best, to make Rediscoveries - to stumble across that which was formerly ours. The Imagination is not free, since Invention _outside Creation_ is Impossible; & Nothing is made that does not exist already in the Mind of God.

For Years I was able to put this Knowledge from me: I

gave myself Work, & Work's Rituals, to sustain an Illusion of Purpose. What is the Purpose of Ritual? Continuance. What is its meaning? Continuance. The Tower is Nothing *but* Continuance - to no Ultimate Goal - at the Cost of immeasurable Sacrifice.

At last a Time came when I could endure no longer. You will have discovered, no Doubt, the awkward Truth concerning Brother Heridus's *Lexical Compendium of Everything*; namely, that our scholarly Friend is endeavouring to *manufacture* Language. Do not judge him too harshly. The Upper Storeys contain Hundreds of invented & stillborn Tongues; while of those Languages currently in usage, or which have been recently discarded, or which were current in Antiquity but are spoken no longer, the Lexicographies have long ago been written. Brother Heridus knows Nothing of this. His forgery is merely his Response to the Predicament in which I - by omitting to provide him with Philological Material – have placed him. For I have thwarted him in his Work.

To Brother Nester – who thinks me a Thief – I have done likewise.

To the Musicians, Œp and Greda, I have done likewise.

To Brother Ludwig – whose rogue Theorem I first proposed – I have done likewise.

To Brother Kay - when his Ingenuity has faltered - I will have done likewise.

You may see the Irony; it has taken *me* Years to glimpse it. The Tower has outwitted me. Like some cunning Leviathan, it regulates itself by turning its Enemies into its Servants. For I had decided – in my Disillusionment – to poison the Tower from within, to slow *its Functions, to Block its Arteries with inefficient and obfuscating Government. Yet in so doing – by giving the Brethren a petty Enemy against which to struggle – I have distracted them from the Reality of their Redundancy. Intending – as did, no Doubt, my Predecessors – to destroy the Tower, I have unwittingly shored it up.*

The decision, then, to end my Life is taken in Weakness. Conditioned as I am by Fifty Years within its Confines, I am not the Man to end the Tower. Perhaps you have the Strength? Perhaps you will do the necessary & terrible Thing? I die in such Hope. That one Day a Man might come to the Tower – when, for no purpose but its own Continuance, it has eaten ten million Souls – & that, seeing through its Walls to its empty Core, he will finish what God started.

I remain, Sir, in Dissolution,
Your most humble Servant,
Gerboš von Okba

When I had finished the Master's confession, I read it again; then I read it, from beginning to end, a third time. As after a heavy meal, I sat digesting its rough nutrients. How, I marvelled, had the Brethren managed to deceive themselves over so many years? Were there not clues everywhere, for those willing to find them? Take, for instance, the manuscript which von Okba took to his fatal bath. The *Pseudepigrapha* is a theological study of the 'Apocalypse of Shinar', an apocryphal text recounting the fall of the Tower of Babel. The 'Apocalypse' contradicts Genesis in one important area. Yes, Babel falls; but its lower storeys, like a tree-stump, survive. Now Hythlodæus (the *Pseudepigrapha*'s author) ascribes the 'Apocalypse' to the Old Testament prophets. But Hythlodæus, as the linguist Heridus must surely have known, means in Greek 'dispenser of nonsense'; while *pseudepigraphos* translates as 'falsely ascribed'. Nowhere outside the Tower (believe me, I've trawled every library in Christendom) is there so much as an allusion to the 'Apocalypse of Shinar'. The book, then, is an *invented* invention: the work of Hythlodæus himself. But who was this Hythlodæus? None other than Gerboš von Okba! He had invented the 'Apocalypse of Shinar' for no reason other than to study it – to give himself work. His bath water, when they found him dead, was stained not red but black. Not just blood, then, but ink also. It was the ink from the drowned book: the *Pseudepigrapha* washed blank. Did he take the book with him, I wonder still, to hide his forger's tracks? Or as a pointer to the perspicacious mourner, a clue to the whole subterfuge?

Such was my intellectual excitement that I failed to notice the closing of the door behind me. Only when the eye-beams of Brother Kay bristled my nape did I turn.

He stood in the doorway, his gown changed from grey to clerical black. Keeping his distance, he made a soothing gesture with his hand. He cast his eyes about the room, noting as I had done the abandoned tools and devices, the orphaned books, the expectant bell and hourglass. As Brother Kay browsed, I sat, knees beneath the desk, my head at ninety degrees to it, unable to move either one way or the other, like a stressed spring. Brother Kay blew the dust from a black-leather-bound book and parted it at the frontispiece. The tissue paper was stuck to the engraving; he tugged at it gently but it would not loosen.

'It's the albumin,' he said obliquely. From beneath his soutane he produced a thin knife, which he applied carefully to the glue. I stared at the blade that sliced the tissue paper so keenly. My eyes – which often betray me with their butterfly whims – flickered up to Brother Kay's face. He was looking at me. 'A protein,' he said, 'Used, very often, in the manufacture of parchment. Egg-white contains it, naturally. Blood plasma also.'

He stroked with his thumb the edge of the blade, as though the operation might have blunted it. My tongue cleaved to my palate. I worked up saliva to loosen it but the muscle felt sluggish and swollen, alien almost, in my mouth.

'It goes without saying that the others want you punished.' Brother Kay slammed shut the book and replaced it on the shelf. 'You got away very easily.'

'The Portico was unlocked.'

'Naturally: when you have fear and custom, who needs locks? My colleagues observe the Law. That's why we are here and they are in their cells, licking their wounds.'

Brother Kay ambled to the opposite wall. I was obliged to turn bodily in order to keep him in my sight. He ran an idle finger along a ledge, testing for dust, and leaned proprietorially upon the shelves. He had not put away the knife.

'This was the Master's library,' I ventured.

'Yes. It is.'

'How did you get in?'

'There are many entrances. I chose an easier one than yours.' As though in afterthought, Brother Kay's face lit up. 'Do you know what today is?'

I did not.

'Today is the day I take up the reins of power. I am the new Master. Everything you see here is mine.'

With slow relish, I unfurled my trump card, the refutation of Brother Kay's vanity: Gerboš von Okba's testament. When the scroll was taut between my fingers, Brother Kay approached to peer at the print.

'An attractive script,' he said.

'Perhaps you should read it.'

'I already have.' Brother Kay tapped his fingers along the blade of his knife, like a flautist miming a scale. 'The Master, in his late illness, lost all reason. He suffered from hallucinations visual, aural and olfactory. I diagnosed acute psychosis. Those delusions, I tell you,' (pointing at the scroll) 'are worth less than the parchment they are written on.'

'Why should I believe you?'

Brother Kay looked at me witheringly. 'The Theory of Archetypes? Exhaustion of Learning? On *this* infantile planet?' He slammed his hand on to the table; he would have taken the scroll but I snatched it away in time. 'Gerboš von Okba was no flawed martyr. He withheld his books out of political expedience. To be certain of our allegiance. You see, the power structure in the Tower is centrifugal. Everything revolves around the Master. It's a process so ingrained in the Chosen that few ever become conscious of it. Only I did – and in so doing, proved myself fit to rule. That is the only truth of the matter.'

'In that case,' I retorted, 'what was the cause of von Okba's madness?'

'Old age. Heredity. Protracted solitude.'

I brandished the scroll; it angered me to see it tremble. 'You're claiming he made all this up? Despite the evidence?'

Brother Kay about-turned. In his hands he held the Master's hourglass. Calmly he turned it over and gazed at the fine jet of sand. 'Reality is a heavy burden. Whoever wins must stare it out.'

'To gain control over your colleagues?'

'It's in the order of things. The blind beggar gets his earnings stolen.'

There was no escaping where this was heading. I spoke slowly, guarding his eyes with mine so that he might not see me fold the scroll into my gown. 'I understand. But what, exactly; is the *purpose* of your power?'

'Power.'

'But for what?'

'Power.' Brother Kay could not keep from smiling; he placed an indulgent hand on my thigh. 'It's a question no king needs to ask himself. He knows – like the wolf knows. Power is not the means to an end, it is the end in itself.'

Not daring to squirm under his touch, I poured my refusal into my silence.

'Morality,' said Brother Kay, 'is the consolation of the defeated.'

Thus concluded our conversation. At knife-point, Brother Kay urged me to relinquish the stool. I did so, and ascertained from the pressure of the blade at my throat that I was to move to the door. We staggered, my captor and I, across the room, like characters in a dumb-show. I saw Brother Kay's arm at my waist fumble for the latch. Right a bit, I said. His fingers fastened like a spider to its prey and the door opened.

We entered a dim corridor. I could not see its end. There was air, a strong draught, coming from somewhere. We waded – Brother Kay's knees in the back of my knees, the bony rest of him pressed too close to the rest of me – for ten, perhaps fifteen yards, until we discovered, in an alcove to our left, the draught's origin. It was a gaping hole in the floor, a chute of some kind. Yes, a disposal chute, like the one I had discovered in the second library. A squat figure armed with a scimitar uncurled from its shadows. It was the dwarf, Meshech; or so I thought, until he lit a phosphorus flare to reveal a face even uglier than the one I expected, framed in the same turquoise headscarf.

I should state that I absorbed these details at the exact instant of illumination. My eyes adapted faster than

those of my executioners to the light. The dwarf made
the mistake of looking directly at the flare: his red eyes
shrank from its efflorescence like polyps into their
shells. Emboldened by necessity, I seized Brother's Kay's
wrist and – pushing the blade from my neck – dispatched, with my right elbow, a savage clout to his ribs.
He fell back somewhere behind me. The grimacing
dwarf took a swipe blindly. I did not think. My hand
of its own accord seized the flare, my legs worked and
the floor disappeared beneath me.

For a gaping second I was in freefall. I am not
physically courageous, nor an enthusiast for pain; so
it was with closed eyes that I plummeted, for a few feet
at least, and with a scream of agony that I struck, with
my coccyx, the wall of the duct. I endeavoured, to
manage the pain, to adopt a foetal position; but this
had only the effect, by my falling forward, of replacing
my rump with my nose, which (my nose) bore the brunt
of my descent. I had just managed to roll to a dignified,
feet-first position when abruptly the chute – which had
been at an incline of some sixty degrees – steepened to a
vertical drop, thus ensuring that parts of me that had
escaped bruising heretofore were given a painful look-
in. I screamed, a bright star falling, and was cast on to a
jagged heap of refuse.

I lay groaning and bleeding on the gently spilling
mound. The flare lay three feet from me, glowering in a
trench. It, and the meagre area that it illuminated, were
all that I could distinguish. For I was in cavernous
blackness. I crawled forward until I reached the flare,

around which my fingers tightened. Slowly, from this abject posture, I raised myself, like a penitent, to my knees. There were beneath me paper and wood shavings, machine parts, torn cloth, glass shards; and sweetly cloying matter, cold and heavy like peat, that packed hard under my nails. Curiosity, even then, got the better of me, and I used my flare to investigate. I buried my finger in the mulch and then inspected it in the light; it was rust coloured. I looked more closely at the ground. There was a stain spreading out from a small rock some two yards to my left. I reached out to turn the rock in my favour, and pressed my thumb into the flexile softness of an eyeball. It was Meshech. His torso, stripped of its clothes like a hare of its skin, lay some way off, contorted by its fall. Quietly I pressed the face back into the mound.

Through dull horror I became aware of noises, a susurration of scurrying bodies. As when, standing in observation beside an ant-hill, one hears of a sudden, from imagined silence, the unignorable rustle. I remembered to be afraid. I had to move, since nothing but a duct separated me from my would-be assassins. I stood up, that my sandals might protect me from the shards underfoot. Still holding my flare (despite the risk of giving myself away) I negotiated the refuse heap. It sloped off, gently enough, until I was on solid ground, on ancient lifeless soil.

Now the atmosphere, to which I had paid little attention, began to weigh upon me. It was a familiar, vaporous air of streams and eddies. The darkness palpitated about me, longing to swallow my little light, and with the flare already fading I cast off. Where the Tower Gates lay, I knew not, nor how to open them. Nothing crossed my path. My only company was my breathing and my damaged body: the muscles and ligaments and beaten cells, for which I felt unspeakable sorrow.

Out of the whispering a mechanical sound, most like the squeal of ill-lubricated wheels, came into hearing. Needless to say, I pursued it, glad to have a purpose. Before I caught sight of anything, however, I found myself at a low wall. It was the well beside which Brother Nester had received me all those seeming centuries ago. Its ancient stones, arid of moss or lichens, glowed coldly in the flarelight. I crouched beneath it as the abrasion of metal on wood drew nearer.

It was a cart, a standard four-wheeler, in itself nothing remarkable. But in the feeble phosphorescence from my flare, I was able to discern its contents. It was loaded with corpses. Piled up like so much trash, they might have been made of paper. Occasionally a foot protruded from the tangle; here and there, a fist was raised in rigor mortis. The cart itself was drawn by a dozen naked slaves. Harnessed to yokes that seared cruel welts into their backs, these creatures, strain-humped, found their way, I fear, by taste, as though the air itself bore instructive odours. For they held, as they toiled, their tongues outstretched, as lizards do. The lack of light had blinded them. That is, in the course of their banishment they had lost the use of their eyes, which sat like ripening boils in their sockets and shrank from the soft interrogation of my flare.

Despite the hindrance of my light, the slaves laboured on. As ants negotiate an obstacle, they continued their chores by stepping around me. Several that had been pushing the cart from behind opened it at the back and began to haul its stiffening contents to the well. Once arrived at the well-mouth, they heaved the corpses, without ceremony, over the edge. There were hollow sounds of impact from the water below. It was more sound, perhaps, than ever the dead had made in the course of their lives: reverberating for an instant in the climb of the well, then lost for ever in the abysmal silence.

Back by the cart, among those carrion-ghosts, a form moved with purpose. I glimpsed it as one catches, at the edge of sight, what for an instant one fails to recognise as a shadow. It transfixed me with terror – a breathless and nauseating incredulity at the imminence of Death. I backed up to the well's edge until I was almost seated upon it. My flare dimmed and fizzled, as though sunk in water. And in a last, suspended second of visibility, I saw Brother Kay's henchman come at me with his scimitar. My hands caught his fists, I swallowed his hot breath, and I was blind. With the blade's point at my cheek, I dug my nails into his flesh until they were wet. When with a groan he relinquished his weapon, I felt how feeble the dwarf really was. It was like wrestling a child. I sought with my left hand his face and found an ear, of which I relieved him. The dwarf's screams inspired me with murderous fervour: I jerked my torso sideways (forever straining my lumbar) with the design of hurling him into the well. But the dwarf's grip was firm – perhaps I threw myself off balance – and together we plunged into cold, frantic waters.

Down we sank, clasping one another like suicidal lovers. Had I fallen alone, without my enemy, I would surely have drowned. That is, I would not have summoned, for something so paltry as my own life, the will to resurface. No, what saved me – if you will pardon the expression – was a fierce lust for the life of the Manservant. I mean, for his death. Doubly blind, with the rush of water thundering in my head, I fumbled to find his belly, the soft trigger to his drowning. With all my might, though slowed by the element, I punched him there, two or three times. My face above his felt the rush of bubbles that contained his life. I heard the shocked lungs swallow water. The dwarf's grip tightened, in spasm, at its extremities, but behind those fingertips no strength remained. His nails clutched my cloak like burrs. I brushed them off. And my heart exulted as I felt his body sink beneath me, sucked deep by hungry currents.

Electrified, my body was clever: it kicked and shook, burning for air, until of a sudden I burst, gasping, through the deadly membrane.

What can I say of that subterranean river, to you who have endured nothing similar, unless in the fathoms of nightmare? I could see nothing, as you know. Nor could I hear anything above the battle of the water with the

rock that contained it. I was buffeted by soft, anonymous matter that bore no contemplating. The stench
was unendurable. Only a vestigial fastidiousness kept
me from diving back under: drowning is one thing, but
drowning in effluent is another entirely. Eventually, as I
paddled to assist the flow, I encountered a wooden
plank (I assume it was a plank) and hugged it for
buoyancy. Clinging thus to my midget's raft, and fearing an encounter with the rock walls, I left behind my
first life on earth – the Tower, my parents, any assump-
tion that I had ever shared with my fellow men.

Ahead of me there was light: a speck at first, it grew
to resemble the *coelum empyreum*, the flaming heaven,
to which some say the dead ascend after lives of righteousness. Yet my earthly tunnel ended in a confluence
of polluted and salt waters. The brine was harsh on my
cuts. Salt air raked my Tower-adapted lungs. I was
sucked under, held there, then delivered, newborn, into
the spill of the sea.

I do not know how I came to the shore. Perhaps the
sea (which will swallow so much) drew the line at my
bones and brought them up whole on the grey shingle.
For a time I lay senseless: sans name, sans tongue, free.
It was the herring-gull that returned me to my so-called
senses. Having optimistically pecked my scalp, it at-
tacked me outright at my first sign of life. As though to
compensate the bird for its disappointment, I vomited
green matter, which it beaked greedily out from under
me. Thus emptied of my unmentionable ingestion, I felt
better, a little better, and was able, by rolling myself on

to my back, as the seal does, to see the great grey tent of the sky.

Something unwanted, vestigial within me, sent my hand into the heavy wet folds of my gown. My fingers found a corner of the scroll and cautiously extracted it. But seawater and sewage had rendered that delicate lettering illegible. Yes, brine and blood and shit had made their irrefutable contributions to the Master's paper. Indomitable disputants, they had dissolved the bonds of the wood paste, tearing the scroll to shreds when I exposed it to the salt, indifferent wind.

Empty handed, I lay in the lapping surf. There would be time, later, to stand and walk; to forage; to speak of nothing more momentous than the weather or the price of beer. There would be time, yes, to travel the world and seek out its Great Places, to piss in. Later, when dusk fell, with its cold assertions. *You can never go Home. No refuge for you, in the Tower's shadow.* Sprawled on the beach, I could not guess that it would never lift, that looming presence. Can't you see it, sitting upon me? I'm all in goose-pimples, look. Chilled to the bone, which I try to warm with fire-water. Shivering, I long for sleep. Asleep, I long to wake. Otherwise, I have no wants nor great desires. Only this. To find some sparse and underpeopled place; a bean-row isle, with a cabin and hives, where I might nurture waking dreams, untroubled by the Widow, Truth.

Explicit fabula alta

The Fool's Prologue

The Penitent Drunkard has finished. His audience lies snoring at his feet. Only the Fool looks attentive – though he too had nodded off in places.

Penitent Drunkard. I don't blame them. It's a tiring business, listening. A tougher trick than rhetoric. (*He grips his belly which, gargling, is rearing its so-to-speak head*.) What did you think, Fool?

Fool. Fanciful garbage. Did you really escape through the sewer?

Penitent Drunkard. You don't think I mixed my metaphors? (*The Fool tuts*.) Perhaps it lacked visual detail? (*The Fool shrugs, master of the ambiguous gesture*.) Oh God, they just hated it!

It is a subtler emetic than alcohol which sends our artist reeling to the stern. Seizing his opportunity, the Fool scampers halfway up the rigging (he knows a thing or two about staging) and shakes his stick for attention. Sleepy headed, the crew is unlikely to resist him.

'Brother Kay,' he begins, 'was on a hiding to nothing . . .'

The Fool's Tale

Ambition, my masters, is Fate's wanton. Picture her, if you will, as a maiden of great beauty luring men over a cliff's edge. 'Come up to this higher ground,' she beckons, 'where you shall win eternal fame.' And so, to escape oblivion, men rush into oblivion.

In the court of King Buvard there served a page by the name of Fly. Fly was all the name he had, for he was of lowly birth and so possessed little, not even a second syllable. Fly was born into service. His father, the court jester, had paid for his talents with his head (laughter is a fine sport but in excess it is as lethal as any poison). Raised by his scullery-maid mother, Fly soon learned to keep his head inclined at a serviceable angle. His eyes turned forever to the floor, he became a child of the tunnels and passageways. And yet, somewhere deep within that flyweight frame, ambition pulsed like a subterranean stream, its course uncharted and mysterious. Such waters can run forever undetected: it takes freak conditions (forty days of rain, a mighty earthquake) for them to flow to the surface.

Just such a calamity, my masters, took the form of Prince Wanton, the heir apparent.

'Boy,' said the Prince one morning as Fly (with thirty

other servants) attended the royal levee. 'You, the skinny one.' Fly was nudged by his colleagues to the edge of Prince Wanton's bed. 'What's your name?'

'. . .'

'Speak up.'

'Fff.'

Prince Wanton's powdered face cracked into a smile. 'What, boy, are you mute or are you stupid?'

'*Fly*, your Majesty.'

The Prince was startled for an instant, thinking himself in danger (his was not the closest of extended families). But when his composure returned, he laughed. 'I have noticed you, Fly. You're as servile and retiring as they come. I like you. Come, drop that ruff. We shall be friends from this day forth.'

The days that followed felt, to Fly, like waking inside a dream. He never knew what action of his had provoked the Prince's declaration of friendship, and it never seemed polite to ask. Every morning a page awoke him, powdered his body from wig to toe (how the perruque tickled his scalp!) and dressed him in silks. Then he would be summoned into the Prince's arms and kissed, with brotherly ardour, on both cheeks.

'Do not blush, my pal, my buddy,' said the Prince. 'Lift up your eyes: I am more appealing than the floor. What's wrong with your neck?' And with that the Prince would shadow-box Fly's arm and flick his regal fingers across Fly's occiput.

Learning was a slow process to begin with, since Fly was stiff with formality. 'Be more familiar with me,'

Prince Wanton would say as they refought his father's battles in the toy room. 'Yes, your Highness.' 'Stop bowing and scraping,' he would demand as they pulled the wings off insects in the garden. 'Of course, your Majesty.' 'And don't call me your Majesty,' as they tortured mice in the storehouse. 'Absolutely, my liege.'

After a fortnight of thigh slaps and vulgar puns, the strength of Fly's position dawned on him. He was privileged, one of the select. The friendly bruises ripening on his arm were the Prince's seal of approval. Never before had it occurred to him that he might amount to more than a cog in an unnoticed mechanism. It was, after all, a servant's purpose to pass unnoticed by his masters. Many in the royal family, if questioned, would have been unable to explain how food came to their plates, how their stools escaped from under tapestries, or why the gardens seemed so much neater than the thorny wildwood. In King Buvard's kingdom, alchemists still sought the Philosopher's Stone but apothecaries pursued a more enticing grail yet: a potion of Complete Invisibility. It was rumoured that a ransom still stood for the inventor, although the monarch who had proposed the sum now mouldered, forgotten, deep within the castle vaults.

'With you, Fly, I fart at tradition,' Prince Wanton boasted. 'For God's Anointed to befriend a servant? I am original, I think.'

Sure enough, the well born of the Court looked unfavourably on the Prince's innovation. Historians searched in vain for a precedent. Lords and ladies muttered darkly, affronted by the breach of etiquette. Expendable tykes like Fly had died for less in the past, they reasoned – yet as the heir's companion he was untouchable. Only the King could take matters into his hands – and there seemed little likelihood of that, with King Buvard neglecting even to comment on the outrage. Blithely he overlooked the Prince's refusal to go hunting; breezily he ignored his son's parody of swordsmanship, those noisy yawns at jousts. And slowly (as water wears away a stone, as ice prizes rock from rock) his ennoblement went to Fly's head. His deportment improved; a nervous flame burned behind his eyes; he learned to walk in noble fashion and how best to show his parts when bowing. In his new, turret-top chambers, Fly accepted his luxuries as grass accepts the dew. The back-stairs world faded out of his vision. He left his waste to fend for itself.

'One of these days,' he told his looking-glass double, 'you and I shall be friend to a king. Then we'll be rich and all the maids of Christendom shall dream of us a-nights.'

Many luxurious weeks passed. Eager Spring pushed through to Summer and still the boys played, leaving behind them a trail of limping cats and flightless birds. As the months passed, Fly forgot to pity the animals he helped to cripple; for Prince Wanton's quicksilver wit enchanted him, and the new words that he learned – not all of them edifying, my masters – easily compensated for the occasional discomfort of blood-letting. Fly never doubted the love of his prince; and who can blame a boy for choosing to be happy?

One midsummer's day, the King commissioned his craftsmen to build a model kingdom for his wayward son. Many noble families had to quit their apartments to make room for the boy's amusements; when it was finished, the miniature realm took up most of the castle's west wing.

'You care little for hunting and jousting, my son,' the King conceded one morning at breakfast. 'Perhaps you shall enjoy your toy realm better.'

Bringing the Prince to the model's border, King Buvard beamed and gripped his boy's shoulders with powerful fingers. 'All of this is in your power,' he said. 'Before you govern a flesh-and-mud kingdom, you shall rule one of wood and cloth.'

If His Majesty had hoped to distract his son from his friendship with Fly, he was soon disappointed. For Prince Wanton shrugged at the tiny wonders stretched out at his feet. Yawning and toying with a dagger, he permitted Fly to play at being king. Fly wandered, a happy giant, through castle keeps and sylvan valleys, christening the creatures like Adam in Paradise.

'I have a talent for this,' Fly mused aloud. Later, as they dressed for the garden, he felt the Prince's gaze sit too heavily upon him. 'Without me,' said the Prince softly, 'you would not exist.'

Autumn came and brought with it a new initiative from His Majesty. The wayward Prince was to be excused his musty, fustian tutors and given free rein of the royal library. To Fly it was a treasure-trove, its walls laden with gold-spined books. But Prince Wanton scowled at the shelves and at the dusty grey librarian hunched in a corner like a discarded glove puppet.

'In this library,' said the King, paternally pinching his son's earlobes, 'you will find all the knowledge of the world. Every man that is born for power longs for understanding. When you have read every book as I have, you will be ready to rule, my son.'

With that, the royal train withdrew. The librarian cramped his body into an officious bow and disappeared behind a tor of books. Prince Wanton fell into a chair and folded his arms about a scowl.

Many hours passed in stubborn stillness. Fly, who could not read, passed the time sifting for illustrations. He was a landlocked child peering for the first time into a rock pool: its wonders, nameless, were closed like clams to his curiosity.

'Wanton,' said Fly at last, 'now that I carry myself royally, isn't it time you gave me a scholar's education? I can do the walk but I'm empty within.'

Suddenly, as though bitten, Prince Wanton jumped to his feet. His eyes narrowed to bright black seams. 'I am not the King's subject,' he whispered. 'I am me, neither to be moulded nor invented.' Fly nodded, understanding nothing. 'I *will* myself into being,' the Prince continued. 'To prove which, I shall burn this library.'

Poor Fly swallowed a gasp and almost choked; his face turned a regal crimson. Through swimming eyes he saw the Prince's defiant grin gleam like a scimitar. Could he steer his royal friend away from rebellion? Should he alert the librarian? For he suffered to think of so many books curling into flame. And yet what comfort he enjoyed in Prince Wanton's favour. His father the King was incapable of anger, it seemed; and what rewards Fly hoped for when the son gained the crown! Gently, then, he bit his tongue.

The plan did not come into immediate effect. Stealth and strategy were called for. From his initial moodiness, Prince Wanton drifted publicly into enthusiasm for the bookish life. He petitioned the King to let him have a bed made in the library, so that he might never leave off reading. Could he not have his meals there, also? And candles, hundreds of candles to light his reading?

'No, don't trouble the librarian, Father, to supervise me – poor old fellow with his ruined back.'

His Majesty, laughing with delight, agreed to his son's every request. So that, before he knew it, Fly was locked in the library with burning tapers in his fists.

'First of all, the histories,' said the Prince. 'Lives of the generals, lives of the emperors. God rot their bones.'

Together they heaved books on to a smoking pyre, and Fly watched as Prince Wanton set light to the crumpled papers. Soon flames were peeping out of the kindling; they gnawed nervously at the books for a time. Then, losing its fear, the fire grew greedy. It snapped and lashed out like a chameleon. It zigzagged up a tapestry. In its excitement it tugged at the hem of a curtain; the curtain danced, ablaze, then dripped in shreds to the smoking floor. Prince Wanton cried out for help, as a map of the world rehearsed the Apocalypse behind his head.

Tried beyond a certain point, my masters, the most indulgent of fathers will beat his offspring senseless. Yet the methods of everyday men (the birch, the slipper and the palm) are as nothing compared to the chiding of kings.

'For this final disobedience,' said His Majesty, when the fire had been extinguished, 'and for your deception, I sentence you to sixty lashes of the cane.'

The Prince rocked on his knees. Wheezing in the custodial embrace of a soldier, Fly suffered to see his friend suffer.

'As for your companion,' King Buvard continued, 'let him be sent back below-stairs whence he came.'

Fly shut his eyes on the horror of it all. But the Prince was eloquent in his pleading. 'Father,' he said, 'the offence is mine – as were the idea and its execution. Fly was there only out of love for me. To see him suffer for my ill deeds would hurt me more than any flesh wound. Therefore, I beg you, let him take the beating in my stead, that I may pay the highest price for my disobedience.'

A low murmur ran through the throne-room. Fly gulped thin air.

'Very well,' said the King, standing taller than Fly remembered him. 'I pronounce that Flea the servant shall, in accordance with royal custom, be made the Prince's whipping-boy, to suffer eighty lashes for my son's edification.'

Alas, how drab now Fly's gilded wings. They hauled him into the dungeons. In the tunnels and passageways his howls of grief buzzed at the servants' ears – who swatted them away like gnats.

On the day of the beating, the dungeon chaplain was admitted into a cell. Lifting his cassock, like a girl in a stream, this ghostly father picked his way to the spot where Fly lay. '*Benedicite*,' he said, blessing Fly's filthy rump – for it was dark as death down there. 'Today you must face the cane, my son. You are expected to live so I need not trouble myself with your soul . . .'

'What?' said Fly.

'In this kingdom, my son, God's hierarchy is policy, not principle. As we know from Solomon, a king is more godly than his subjects. Since it is improper, in the eyes of the Almighty, to strike the fleshy seat of His Anointed, your intercession as whipping-boy happily reconciles discipline with Christian virtue.'

Fly said, 'What?'

'Princes learn by empathy, though lesser men like you must endure the whip in person. How else can one train a dog?'

'But I'm not a dog,' Fly whimpered.

'Royalty feels for its people as only natural rulers can. They experience pain vicariously – which is why the Prince nominated you for his punishment.'

So it was. Life for a prince is a series of lessons printed on the flesh of his subjects.

A day shall pass without description: you see, my masters, I am mindful of your stomachs. Travel with me instead to the bowels of the castle, into the oubliettes, whose cold oblivion even the invisible servants dread. In the dankest, most forgotten cell of all, a surgeon smears oil into Fly's raw and seeping back. The boy has lost much blood since the beating but those are scars that will heal. More gravely for our hero, he has lost his wits into the bargain. The agony which he endured (thrice he fainted, was tenderly revived, then flogged afresh) has dislodged something in his brain. Now, striped pink and purple, Fly drools like a teething baby. The surgeon looks at him and sees only a miscarriage, a thing aborted and nameless.

'Poor Prince,' he sighs, 'it's so hard on the boy.'

But Prince Wanton makes a miraculous recovery. At the feast in honour of his birthday he is happy to be clapped back into line, for he thinks himself his own master. Only King Buvard knows that, all the time he misbehaved, the Prince was slipping into a mould. The first and second tests of his character had served as mere preambles to the third; by which, with the selfless delegation of his punishment, he has proved himself truly his father's son.

And what of Fly after his wounds close? Not for him a return to servitude. He spends the last forty years of his life in a cage. Soiled straw is his bedding; he shares his meals with rats. The nuns who work there fear him as the Devil's own, for daily he will seize his buttock-cheeks to soothe the burning of a remembered cane, crying aloud: 'Loo, loo! My hams exist, by blood. Tom's a-happy to hurt!'

For such outbursts, Fly becomes a popular attraction

with the wealthy citizens of the town, who tip his gaolers handsomely for the sport. Most days Fly will seem not to notice his admirers. But sometimes he may declare, 'Methinks me thought you up, sir. Bless thy wits, I unthink you now.' To be addressed in this manner is considered a great privilege by Society. Women dine off their anecdotes for weeks, while in the taverns the wags drink toasts to the health of the Mad Metaphysician.

So it is that Fly – servant, whipping-boy, lunatic – achieves a certain fame in his lifetime, and dies notorious, the figment of a king's imagination, eaten whole by his bedsores.

> And so goes my story, quick as a snap;
> Take it or leave it, I don't care a crap.

Explicit liber Fly furioso.

The Monk's Prologue

For some time after the story, the audience sits unspeaking. The Fool listens to the brains as they cog and clunk. They are forgetting. In seconds they have lost the names of the main characters; then the plot fizzles; followed, at last, by all vestige of engagement. It is the Monk who fills the unravelling silence.

Monk. An irreverent story, Fool.

Fool. Thank you.

Monk. God spare us your frippery. It has no bearing on our lives and teaches us nothing.

(The Fool is silent. The face on the end of his stick does the smiling for him.)

Monk. I shall tell a story now, which I think you'll find—

Choristers. Stow it, slaphead! Keep your Morals to yourself.

Monk. High Culture, sirs, is what we need. For which, pray heed the following. You might even, though I doubt it, learn something.

The Monk claps his hands in prayer: 'Heavenly Muse, sharpen these travellers' wits, that my narrative be not stillborn in the childbeds of their minds.'

The Choristers snigger. But the Monk, well pleased with his metaphor, pulls tight his habit and begins to speak.

The Monk's Tale

Instatiate gluttonous Time, rein in your appetite a while, that I may bring my memories back to grandiloquent life. When we fall prey to the esurient gourmand – he that prefers before all repasts the impure heart – grant that we may pass safely through those bowels of judgement[1].

There subsisted once, in Flanders, a Minstrel. He strummed and scraped a living among the rich burghers of Gent, of Antwerp and of Bruges. His patrons thought highly of being thought of highly, but the Minstrel's music fell on insensitive ears. And yet his playing would have turned the head of Orpheus, or saved Marsyas, perhaps, from the whetted knife.[2]

It was my curious fortune to meet this fellow at the

---

[1] An allusion to the *Chronographia* of Gervase van Ursberg – a speculative history which depicts the world's end. Drawing heavily from the Book of Revelation, van Ursberg introduces the terrifying figure of the Cosmic Glutton, Colostamus, devouring the still-beating hearts of penitents and sinners alike. Sinners' hearts are digestible and therefore the possibility of physical resurrection is forever denied them, whereas the hearts of the penitent pass undamaged through the Glutton's digestive system, signifying the promise of the life to come. See Myrna Pullet, *Deism and Diet in Late Medieval Europe* (Kentucky, 1971).

[2] Marsyas the satyr, who challenged Apollo to a musical duel and lost. He was flayed for his effrontery.

height of his powers. I had come to Bruges to make use of the famous library (my Abbot granted me – oh – many sabbaticals) and I was close to completing my theological treatise, *Pudendae Angelorum*[3], when I was distracted from my study by the sound of music coming from without. My fellow scribes ignored what they dismissed as the caterwaulings of vagrant actors. I, however, who am blessed with perfect pitch, recognised a touch of Euterpa[4] in the melody. I set aside my books and hurried out into the Market Place.

The Minstrel's face was hidden beneath a blue cloak akin to the Moorish djellaba. In order to satisfy myself

---

[3] The Monk's book may well owe a debt to Sergius Maurus, twelfth-century mystic and Abbot of Capua. In his seminal text on the physical dimensions of supernatural beings, the *Anatomy of Angels*, Maurus argued that the heavenly host were hermaphrodites and that they reproduced, not sexually, but by counting backwards from the number infinity to zero. The theory caused immediate controversy, with the Angelic Materialists (led by Balthus of Avignon) demanding Maurus's excommunication as a heretic; for the implication of his teachings was that any angel wishing to reproduce would have to devote every moment of eternity to the task, thus distracting it from the Magnification of God. Pope Boniface III called a convention to solve the problem, in which Dandolo Fortunatus succesfully argued that angels need not count from infinity itself, rather from 'any number long enough to cover five acres of parchment'. Fortunatus speculated that 'although this counting will take a long time in *earthly* terms, on a *cosmic* scale it need not distract an angel for much longer than a fortnight'. The controversy is discussed at length in Jacques Roitelet's 'Le sexe controversé des anges', *Études Médiévales* 23 (1982).

[4] Muse of lyrical poetry and music in Greek mythology; cf. Guillaume de Machaut, 'Ballade Musagète':

> *Mais des IX fines dames qui donnent bonnour,*
> *Mon cuer Euterpe la tient en ardour.*

that this was no Immortal Being gone a-begging among us, I contrived to lose my sandal; whereupon I fell to one knee and, fumbling with the strap, surreptitiously observed the man's face. In accordance with the laws of perspective, my eye was drawn to the prominence of his nose. Were it endowed with capillaries and a mind for rivalry, the great sundial in the Alhambra[5] would have blushed to apprehend the chronometrical possibilities of that proboscis. Admiring it, I imagined a lifetime's frustration – for who can revel in beauty in the face of so unignorable an appendage? The Minstrel's other features recoiled in horror from it: the eyes shrinking into the cave of their sockets, the chin, a cleft cherry, taking refuge in the folds of the neck. Yes, the Minstrel's face had 'character', that supreme ugliness so particular to the truly gifted. For God, in His Wisdom, counterbalances our talents with our disasters.

'Good sir,' said I to those quivering nostrils, 'may I say, before this growing crowd, what a joy it is to discover, amidst Commerce, the perseverance of Art.'

The Minstrel lifted his head to my advantage – and I saw a soul wearied by the coarseness of its supposed

---

[5] Sultan Muhammad El-Ahmar, the palace's founder, was much obsessed with Time. 'I keep a close eye on my enemy,' he once observed (Alberto Zumaya, *Guida Turística*, Madrid, 1927) 'lest Time give me the slip and leave me frozen for ever in Granada.' Vexed by the sundial's redundancy at night, he ordered servants to travel slowly around it holding torches.

superiors. Nonetheless, the face was strong still, reminding me of St Erasmus when they spooled his innards on a windlass.[6] I hardly need tell you how a spirit of kinship was kindled between us. Adopting a divine's prerogative, I berated the plebeians for their insensitivity to sweet music. The tradesmen made belittling and unrepeatable allusions to clothed parts of my anatomy. Some fool menaced what he called my sacristy with a root vegetable.

'Fear nothing,' said I, for the Minstrel, sensing danger, threatened to depart. 'We must be steadfast like St Catherine.'[7] I clapped a hand to his shoulder and the hood flopped back, exposing his face.

Immediately, the vegetable pelting began. As St Sebastian suffered for his faith, so we endured many hateful projectiles.[8] Mopping up a fetid plum, I sought my bearings and saw the Minstrel hightailing it, full tilt, from the Market Place. 'Wait for me!' I cried above the blasphemies. With the mob staggering in my pursuit, I chased that lanky, ill-articulated figure.

[6] For the manner of his martyrdom, St Erasmus is invoked against cramps (Patrick Scoter, *Saints and Their Uses*, Dublin, 1956).

[7] After refusing to marry the Emperor Maxentius, the pulchritudinous Catherine of Alexandria was rescued from punishment – grinding between hooked and bladed wheels – by miraculous lightning. She was then beheaded (ibid.).

[8] An army captain under the Emperor Diocletian, St Sebastian was shot full of arrows and left for dead. After St Irene nursed him back to health, he returned to military service, whereupon he was clubbed to death (ibid.).

The Minstrel's stamina was as remarkable as his music. Lute and all, he fled at such a speed, without once slowing or looking back, that for all my efforts I feared I would lose him. Like a kettle tied to a dog's tail, I was dragged helter-skelter down streets stinking of slops. Happily, my resolve was stronger than that of our antagonists, and when it became clear that they had abandoned the pursuit I informed the Minstrel of danger's passing. Before I could catch up with him, however, he darted like a hare down the steps of a cellar.

'I say,' I said, 'what's the matter now?'

The Minstrel scrabbled behind a crate loaded with cheeses and crouched in its shadow. Seeing me watching him from above, he tried with a wave to shoo me. 'Get lost!' he hissed. 'Don't you see, they're out for blood. If they find me they'll kill me. And you too, for aiding and abetting.'

To this I could only reply that I was insured against such an eventuality by my churchman's garb, and what the devil did he mean, 'aiding and abetting'?

Before the Minstrel could elucidate, I heard, in the distance, angry voices and the clink of metal. It made my blood congeal.[9]

'Now do you believe me?' croaked the Minstrel.

My first thought was of flight. I summoned my legs to the purpose. But before I could run, a malapertness of

[9] A fashionable medical theory of the period; see Bohumil Dabčik, *Theoria Medica* (1506). Rigor mortis was sometimes explained as death by fear, hence the expression 'scared stiff'.

pedlars heaved into view at the far end of the street.[10]
They were armed with sticks, clubs and cleavers; many
brandished firebrands; others swung lengths of lynch-
ing rope. Without excogitation, I leapt into the cellar.

Long seconds passed. We heard the angry mob con-
verge, scuffle and separate. I thanked God for the
pestilential breath exhaled by those cheeses: it masked
our scent from the enemies' hounds.

With the danger gone, the Minstrel and I sat savouring our survival. We tried to ignore the miasma of our
hiding-place. At last I dared to speak. Out of me
poured every question conceivable. Who was he?
Why was he so hated? How had he offended? The
Minstrel nodded, and the calming effect of his nose as
it travelled up and down restored me to my usual
decorum. 'For this terrible fury,' he said sadly, 'you
deserve an explanation. My story cannot be told in a
couplet. Yet since we cannot break our cover until
nightfall . . .'

(Nightfall! Oh my nose! My toes!)

'. . . the telling may help us pass the time.'

And so, in our mephitic bolthole, the hunted Minstrel
told me his story.

You will recall – he commenced – the plague that
ravaged this region not two years ago? It was my ill

[10] Fifteenth-century 'proper term' that has not survived to this day. This
and similar fabrications can be found in the *Book of St Albans* attributed to
Juliana Barnes (1486).

fortune to find myself on the road when the earliest bubo burst. Yes, I was in Knocke when I heard the first death-rattle. Or was it Gent? No, it was Blankenberghe, I could smell sea wrack and guano. Pah! the details escape me, I have no head for facts. The point is, I was down on my luck already, having lost my benefactor, one Sebastian Brant, some two weeks earlier. I had been like the mythical bird in his service, you see, my gift pining for finer sensibilities.[11] At last, hearing the discordance of my bondage, Brant had set me loose, leaving me shelterless and unpatronised, happy for a time in the dream that I was free. But hunger is a cruel serfdom. When the plague began to bite I resigned myself to Fortune and, empty bellied, enlisted in the army. I say enlisted for brevity's sake. To speak more accurately, I acknowledged the physical rights of a press gang over my person. No, that too is a distortion. I was beaten and dragged screaming into service. I am not, as you may surmise, the military type. All attempts to make me proficient in the sharper arts of war met with failure. But there was such a need for soldiers in the region that my faults were tolerated. New recruits, you see, fooled the merchants into believing that something could be done against the plague. And so we were drummed into line, if not into shape, by four, then

---

[11] An allusion to 'L'Oiseau Vers', from the *Colloque des Bêtes*. Dr Fulmar Sanderling writes: 'This narrative poem tells of a fabulous bird that sings in alexandrines. The Verse Bird is captured by an ambitious but struggling young poet. The bird pines away in captivity until it barely manages *vers libre*, at which point the youth sets it free.'

three, then two training officers, who took in their depletion to marching with cinnamon-stuffed oranges hanging from their helmets. The captain and his adjutants went one step farther, inspecting our manoeuvres from behind long, herb-filled beaks.[12] When the common soldiery demanded, without success, equal protection from pox fumes, riots broke out and those armoured birds were hanged, squawking, from trees. Discipline evaporated, as an army groomed to defend Flanders from the Flemish grew hungry. We took to the fields, plundering what, as keepers of the peace, we felt to be our due. Eventually, a second army of better-fed conscripts marched north from Brussels to disband our plundering divisions. Both sides camped out in untended fields. And at dawn, half choked by the smoke of campfires, I bugled the opening salvos of the Battle of the Rye.[13] We give our skirmishes such grandiose names. But wars that change borders and chase folk from their homes are not the work of Olympians. The world is carved up by fat men poring over maps in farm-

[12] Methods used to escape infection. Since breathing apparatus of the sort described were hard to come by, death from apnoea was not uncommon. See G.G. Lammergeier, *The Medieval Way of Death*, vol. i (Cambridge, 1930), p. 34.

[13] 'An order-restoring army, dispatched from Brussels, defeated the rebellious units, who were weakened by St Anthony's Fire [blood disease contracted from rye-dwelling fungus]. Unpaid after the battle, the victorious troops plundered farmland, until their defeat by an order-restoring army dispatched from Brussels.' (Peregrine Longford, *The Spanish Netherlands*, Oxford, 1974, p. 89.)

houses. As for our own so-called battle, we hadn't even the consolation of pageantry. Bloody slaughter it was, unaccompanied by fanfare or *Te Deum*. It's not the valour one remembers, nor the rousing speeches. No. The soldier tramps home with the weeping of boys in his ears, he recalls with great particularity the fragmentation of his neighbour's jaw and the yearning of the dying for their mothers. I was in the fore, with my fellow musicians. Armed only with tabor and fife, we fell before the first cavalry charge. I forget how, the specifics don't matter, let's just say I lived, I gathered myself together as a man cleans up after a storm, I burrowed beneath corpses and played dead. As the fighting dissipated into vague pockets of distant slaughter, I drifted in and out of consciousness, reviving finally beneath a limpid, bird-swimming sky. I writhed and squirmed until the dead eased their stiffening grips on my clothes. Then, rolling on to my belly like a serpent, I pulled my cowl over my eyes to escape the sight of that pastoral shambles. Blinkered thus, I slithered through the ravaged crop. Sometimes hand or eye settled on weaponry, or worse. I concentrated then on the innocent minutiae of clod and pebble. A fieldmouse scurried under my nose and ascended a stalk. I stopped for a minute or an hour perhaps to watch a ladybird negotiate the fingers of my left hand. Mostly, however, I concentrated on the practicalities of retreat, hauling myself along slowly in what I took to be a straight line. Brambles halted my serpentine crawl, I mean my vermicular creep, each inch gained being a victory over exhaustion. I had reached the forest, in a posture and condition somewhat less than human. But what of the forest? What forest? I don't know, a forest, same as any other. I sniffed the damp rich soil, working up to my next effort. Painfully, my bleeding palms turned to the heavens, I hobbled to a sitting position and slumped against a tree stump. My sleep was deep and dreamless, easeful oblivion, and when it rained I wept bitterly to be woken. But Life is a hard habit to break. Famished, I chewed mushrooms in small, nervous bites. Strawberries laced with fox piss I polished with my meagre spittle. The fragile fruits crumbled to powder or smudged to fragrant nothing between my fingers. What little I saved I devoured, like Albrecht in the allegory.[14] When all had vanished I sat, unsated, and tried to reason. I determined to lie low in the forest until reprisals petered out. Could I keep Mind and Body together on so little nourishment? The two have always been so eager to part, I was reluctant to offer them an opportunity. Crawl on, a voice told me. Face to the earth, crawl forward, see what awaits you. I saw no need to fret about wolves, they were glutted already, no doubt, on carrion. And so, stooping like a hunchback

[14] An allusion to a story from Hans Vögel's much-imitated *Conference of Fowls*. First published by Johann Bergmann in Basle in 1494, the book's popularity owed more to Dürer's bawdy woodcuts than to the rather sententious narrative. The wild strawberry, more delicate and subtly fragranced than its hardy modern counterpart, was in medieval art a symbol of the exquisite but evanescent delights of the flesh; cf. Ute Krähe, 'Bosch's *Garden of Earthly Delights*: a new analysis', *Narragonia Review*, LXXI, 1968, pp. 49–95.

under bracken, I sank into the forest. Where I hobbled I know not. My back, forever bent, ached unrelentingly. You can imagine what a relief it was to straighten up one afternoon and reassume my humanity. But I stumble ahead of myself. I should say where, I should say how I rejoined my kind. One morning after rain, my eye picked out a patch of bright green through the trees. Imploring my scabby legs to carry me thither, I emerged from dark forest into a garden of Elysian beauty. My brain stirred from its animal torpor, until it deciphered an ordered world of topiary and rose beds. The geometrical precision with which the Garden was laid out banished the sylvan gloom of unknowing. I rose painfully from my stoop and, like one wrecked on an uncharted island, traced the Garden's contours until I had determined its proportions. The clearing itself was a perfect circle. At intervals of thirty yards along the circumference seven paths spoked off into a medial maze. The maze's box-hedge walls reached no higher than my knees. Seven entrances into the maze converged, after circuitous negotiation, into one exit, thence to the doorway of a two-storey house. I sweated my way through the maze and knocked at the front door. The house was freshly abandoned. I tried the latch and found it unlocked. I walked through an entrance hall into a vaulting, circular chamber. This, the core of the structure, rose to oak-beamed rafters. A stone staircase spiralled along its inner wall. On each floor the central chamber had six doors, equidistant. All but the one I had passed through were locked fast, impenetrable.[15] What fascinated me most, however, was not the singular architecture but a manuscript open at a lectern in the dead centre of the chamber. It was, I discovered, a logbook detailing the Garden's foundation, evolution and maintenance, replete with maps and sketches and inventories of shrubs and flowers.[16] The

[15] Nothing is incidental in this garden; it is constructed according to very deliberate numerological principles.

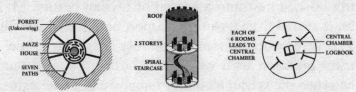

The five concentric circles (the most valued geometric form: perfect and unending) may represent the five chivalric virtues, as the pentangle symbolises the five wounds of the crucified Christ. The garden also has strong cosmological connotations. Plato's *Timaeus* describes how God created the body of the world as a perfect sphere; St Augustine incorporated the Platonic Geometer into Christian theology, invoking the Apocryphal Book of Wisdom, 'Thou hast ordered all things, in measure and number and weight' (11:20). The forest of 'unknowing', then, is the Chaos that reigned before Time. The seven paths divide the garden into seven sections, each representing different days of the Creation. (The paths may also represent the Seven Liberal Arts of the medieval curriculum.) The maze represents the human imagination: subject to blindness, doubt and error. Its seven entrances, leading to a single exit, indicate that wisdom can be sought from different sources, since all lead to one Truth. The house itself is the *fief du génie*, its twelve rooms suggesting the tribes of Israel, or the number of Christ's disciples, or the signs of the zodiac. The logbook in the central chamber is the omphalic hub of the entire structure. To learn more about numerology, see Griffin Teal's excellent *The Divine Geometer: Enquiries into Medieval Cosmology* (Brisbane, 1983) and *L'Univers Enantiomorphique: Mondes et Mots Divins* by Marguerite Gallinule (Paris, 1991).

[16] The logbook alludes to the idea that numerology enables one to 'read' both of God's books: the Book of Works (the universe) and the Book of Words (the Bible). Each, of course, contains the other.

Garden was designed to flourish, in parts, throughout the year. There was an orchard, apples and pears in the main, pertly ripening though unready. There was a rose garden where the air sang with scent. In a water garden blinking rills purled from pond to pond, the mossy earth plashed underfoot and unhoped-for kingfishers gashed the eye. Bridge-crossed the ponds sat, waterlilied and flax-thick, their still waters shadowed with slow fish. In the neighbouring grove stood blossom trees, ornamental so fruitless. Next came a part entirely given over to repose. Lime tree bowered, for love or lucubration its turf-topped benches were sentinelled by torches. A shaded, yellow-candelabra'd laburnum tunnel guided the eye to a love-seat balanced in a foam of woodbine, where stone philosophers stood in lichenous meditation. Close by, the coloured banks of a heather garden murmured with the commerce of industrious bees. Finally there was the herb garden, whose plants, amounting to every known medicinal, were labelled as in a graveyard whence Death has been banished. I cherished, you can imagine, these priceless treasures. Yes, Garden and Book became my reasons to endure. I had little need of food, instead I cut a strip of leather from my belt and sucked it. When on occasion this failed to satisfy, I took to the orchard, whose bitter green buds sat heavily on my stomach. But I never relented, for I had not forgotten my dissolution in the forest. With time, you see, wilderness grows over the mind like a vine. As though fleshless, the skull is overgrown with weeds, its walls crumble under the subtle kisses of creepers. Only in the Garden could the Mind save itself. I was Nature's master, taming Her as a husband cultivates the charms of his wife by curbing her frivolity. By studying the logbook, I learned to root away the weeds which drained the soil's fertility. I pruned the fruit trees, lopping superfluous branches so that bearing boughs might live. In this fashion I established even government, both Without and Within. Plague and plunder seemed as distant as Sodom did from Eden. Ah, but you have read stories of men made incautious by temporary good fortune. I entered the orchard one morning to find three pear trees stripped of their fruit. I was familiar by now with pests that blight tuber, leaf and root. Apothecary to plants, I could purge ailing species of mildew, gall or gangrene. But neither maggot nor codling-moth caterpillar could have done such damage. I shuddered with disgust, for I knew at once that men had found my sanctuary. The Garden, to these scavengers, was not what it was to me. As though we had eaten of the nave's mushroom, where I saw Beauty they saw a chance to cram their bellies.[17] I slept that night as though on splinters, and emerged at dawn to catch two marauders snapping my apple boughs. I shouted and scared them off, helped perhaps by my

[17] *Navis stultifera*; an edible mushroom famed for its ambiguous taste. Pliny wrote that it 'alters in flavour according to the palate of the eater. For one of sour temperament, it tastes equally to his disposition; to another of sweeter nature, it delights like ambrosia' (*Historia Naturalis*, XII). *Navis stultifera* (so named because of the ship's-hull concavity of the cap) continues to provoke disagreements, with gastronomic opinions as to its value ranging from hostility to grandiloquence.

appearance, which has, I confess, that effect on the unprepared. My rage that day absorbed me wholly. I could think, during my labours, of nothing but the vandals. That is to say, of nothing but their filth and their rags, their rickets, lesions and suppurations. So preoccupying were these details that I was distracted, so to speak, from one important particularity. Their, to be precise, youth. How, as it were, *young* they were. Because although those startled faces had looked from a distance ancient and haggard, the bodies had moved in a childlike fashion. I mean with a certain litheness, unweighted by self. The matter occurred to me only later when, bolstered by more of their kind, the scavengers hollered threats from the tree line. My enemies were mere urchins. Their voices were brittle and their menaces puerile. I let them shout, it seemed to please them. More serious was the escalation of their pilfering. Whatever plant was edible, either whole or in part, suffered depletion. Bream, rudd and tench began to tire of the *vita aquatica*, vanishing in puffs of smoke that wafted odoriferously from the forest. Confined as I was to indigestible leather, the smell of cooking made me salivate, an intolerable weakness on my part. With every day the number of urchins increased. I could do little to chase them. I would turn from some assaulted branch in the orchard to see the little gluttons making off with herbs from the herb garden. In desperation I scoured the logbook for some practical advice, but social breakdown was not listed. Then one day a delegation came to the house. I watched the gang of urchins through my spyhole. Instead of thinking their way through the maze, would you believe it, they cheated! Yes, quite without shame, they stepped over the box-hedge walls. What do you want? I said from behind the bolted door. With both hands I gripped the ashwood cane I had fashioned myself for support. I was growing, if that's the word, physically weak, and the stick kept me upright, as sticks will. We need to grow crops, said one of the boys. Then do so, I said, but elsewhere. There is nowhere else, said the boy, the forest is too dense and the plain too dangerous. This was followed by a whining chorus of lamentation. Minabilist savages, they found themselves in Paradise and saw instead a cabbage patch![18] This is private property, I said, leave my land at once before you destroy anything else. As they departed I opened the door and, taking care not to reveal my frailty, insisted without success that they observe the rules of the maze. Pointedly, they did not. This petty defiance presaged worse to come. For within minutes of their banishment, the little monsters began laying waste to the Garden. The ponds turned urinous, their tributaries clogged up with muck. Roses lost their petals, heather shrivelled into flames, flayed yews sap-bled to death. Unable to leave the house for fear of what they might do to the logbook, I watched

---

[18] Jordanus Scotus's *Cosmographia* offers a detailed description of the world, placing its centre, the Omphalos, not at Delphi but in uncharted Africa, among a mythical people called the *Minabiles*. They fail to understand the importance of the omphalos stone and use it to do their clothes-washing.

in despair the beheading of statues, the dismantling of the love-seat and the felling of the laburnum tunnel. As for the herb garden, oh, neatest of ironies, the devils destroyed the very means by which they might have soothed their bloated bellies or repaired their pustulous faces. Compared to this wanton devastation, I almost preferred their pilfering, which had at least some purpose. I had no choice but to change tactic. Like Don Amado's pyrrhic victory over Emeticus, my policy was a last resort, a bid to save what little remained by sacrificing that which was ruined already.[19] I called the marauders over. By the time they had assembled I was safely indoors, eyes and voice only through my spyhole. In view, I said, of the privations which beset us all, I propose to grant you an allotment. To grow crops in, as you see fit. I opened the door and revealed myself in the full glory of my collapse. Vulnerable, ataxic I. Trembling on my cane, I lashed them with my halitosis. Follow me, I said. Debilitated, defenceless, I dragged myself through the maze. Dumb with disgust, the marauders followed. Have you a leader, I enquired as I hauled my bones into the herb garden. The urchins argued among themselves. I am the leader, a starveling

---

[19] Don Miguel Carasco ('Emeticus'), Court Surgeon to King Pedro III of Aragon, pre-empted Modino di Liucci's *Anatomia* in his defence of human dissection. He is said to have taken an interest in an aged courtier, Don Lope Amado, seeking permission to dissect his corpse, 'that I may discover how life can be supported by so decrepit a frame'. Don Lope refused consent, concerned for his bodily resurrection. Eventually, to avoid disassembly, he swallowed a bag of gravel and leapt into the sea off Barcelona. See María Grajo's *Mitos Durables de Cataluña* (Barcelona, 1967).

said, quelling protest with a raised fist. I fixed his face in my memory. This area, I said, and the heather garden adjoining you may cultivate. All I ask in return is that you bring me the plants that you uproot. Do you understand me now? Yes, sir. You will not fail me? No, sir. Have you seeds enough? Yes, sir. And so I returned, hindered only by my quaking, to my keep. Hypocrisy, you say? Surrender? Remember how weak I was, I mean physically. The blind man boasts better hearing than the sighted. In the same way, I had to use my wits. Retreating in order to advance. The trade-off saved what survived of the five remaining gardens. Very soon, what had remained of my uprooted herb garden was being placed, as requested, at my door. It was the leader who made the deliveries, cheating of course in the maze. No matter, I gathered up the plants, rescuing seeds where seeds there were, one eye, the working one, on posterity. At last, the specimens that I sought arrived. The urchins could not discriminate open culture from isolated research, they brought the plants without regarding the bell-jars that had enclosed them. To be certain of what I was holding, I checked with the logbook. Spotted, withered leaves. Fetid fungal aromas. With a scalpel I scraped samples on to paper. *Aplanobacter brassici. Sclerotina sclerotorium. Nectria leguminosa.* I'll spare you the pharmacological details. Suffice to say that, after my labours, my only hurdle before final victory was that of distribution. Through my spyhole I watched the bent-backed, bow-legged industry of my new tenants. They sang badly and dug their petty furrows. I opened the door and summoned their leader. When there is food, I said with plaintive humility, might I have some? I am hungry like you. I suffer like you. All about the improvised farm, urchins downed their tools to listen. I have in my house, I said, some powder. To make your fields more fertile. And I patted the cavity beneath my ribs in a gesture of hungry anticipation. I must have looked a sight, because my etiolated, skeletal travesty of Gluttony raised laughter. Dusty faces all about me cracked into mirth. The leader took this merriment in, he nodded and smiled. The smile was directed at me, meaning assent. Nobody, after all, distrusts a buffoon. When I returned with my samples, smiling faces greeted me. I was helped through the maze, I was kept upright by patient hands as I tipped the fungal dust into the open soil. Later, to celebrate, I accepted a prime cut of squirrel brought steaming to my door. I gnawed it slowly, that pink flesh. It was a rare solid to pass my lips. And that, sir, is the kernel of my story. What remains is elementary, unnoteworthy, a formality that demands no special eloquence. The urchins' crops sprouted and grew. Nourished by my fertiliser, they wilted, rotted and died in the dust. Dismay among the urchins fed upon itself until, dehydrated, it thirsted for revenge. The mob gathered for blood. I doubt they would have squeezed much out of me. I could barely move, sucking my leather was beyond me, my saliva had gone the way of all spit. Knowing nothing of my recumbency, however, the mob trampled my maze, a final degradation, it pounded at my door until the bolts buckled. I reached up for the logbook but my fingers were blades of grass trying to shift a stone. I had time to see their leader, the filthy starveling, slump to the floor, crossbow bolt lodged in his cerebellum, when I blacked out. Happy oblivion! Its only disadvantage is that one cannot savour it. When I came to there was no choir celestial. Seraphim and cherubim were absent without leave, the pearly gates had been dismantled for repairs. In short, I was still earthbound. My back ached to greet me, and I realised that the agonising softness beneath me was a bed. I was in a room. I did not know the room, nor how I had come to be there. I tried to sleep again but I was clean slept out. In order to occupy myself, I studied in detail the handsome leather boots that stood beside the bed. My eyes ascended the boots' tawny uppers and settled on a pair of elegant, silk-embroidered pantaloons. When I had admired the patterning and fixed it in my swimming mind, I travelled higher, to a waistcoat of equal luxury, thence to an ermine gown, a chain of office, a studded collar. Who are you, the stranger asked, and what are you doing in my home? I said, I might very well ask the same question. The man looked offended. I wondered had I farted? This is *my* home, he said, I fled these premises with my household for fear of the plague. When the disease had burned itself out we returned to find the house besieged by children. We chased them off. There was blood in my doorway. And inside the Inner Sanctum, we discovered you, and a child's corpse. He blathered on for some time in this vein. Here are your belongings, he said. He dropped into my lap an ashwood cane, a cloak, a tuning-fork, the torn strap of a bugle, a crossbow, a tripwire, a leather bit and the gnawed femur of a squirrel. Is there any omission? he asked. I fingered my things. No, I said, no omissions. I felt his eyes scrutinising my face. His disgust was like slime on my skin. This is not, I said, how it looks. I am an artist. Providence sent me here to save your Garden from wrack and. The franklin, for such he was, emitted a shrill blast of derision. Have you seen, he said, the state of my grounds? I endeavoured to explain. My first attempt at an account emerged in parts, haltingly, punctuated by lapses of consciousness and the pouring of gruel through a funnel into my throat. Throughout, the franklin interjected. But what did I? Why had I? To what purpose all the? In the time that has elapsed since, I have given much thought to these questions. You, pious Monk, what drew you to the contemplative life? Not, I fancy, the wine or the dancing, nor its amorous possibilities. You prize the poetry of difficult things above the prosody of uncloistered life. The great menageries of Art, the multifoliate flowers of Philosophy are for you more consoling than the bear pit and the cathouse. And I share, good sir, your desire to turn away from the beastly *vita activa*, your longing for Beauty. What else was the Garden if not a refuge? And yet in defending it I was plunged once more into Action. I fought tooth and nail to save it from the mob. And to what advantage? To be cast out, without thanks, on to the disordered roads. Of course, it is the artist's lot in life to wander the wastes, unthanked for his work. That prim franklin stood before me and, without a moment's good conscience, banished me from his land. I protested, Give me a lute and I'll play for you. Give me a trowel and I'll dig for you. But the franklin made a sour face, as though I spat lemon juice. He turned to go. I clung like a clown to his pantaloons, sobbing at the prospect of my exile. In the end it took two servants to pull me, like a leech, from his legs. I was issued with bread, water and a little coin. I wish I could say I made a noble exit, that I cut a dashing figure as I limped into the forest gloom. But there is no man on earth less given to hyperbole than I. Quite simply, I went. Head bowed, eyes trained on soil and stone, as once in a field after battle. The world was all before me, licking its chops. And ever since, wherever I ply my unwanted trade, Rumour precedes me, strewing my path with thorns. Some of the urchins must have made it home. They can hardly be trusted for impartiality. To hear folk talk, you'd think I was the Restless Wanderer and Flanders the land of Nod.[20] I dare not show my face, it has, as you so capably demonstrated, a certain unmistakable quality. This great conk, this blot that pursues me, sits in my vision like a stump. Every waking hour, under my hood, I see its greasy opalescence. Once I used to be able to look beyond it. In the Garden I gave thanks for its enormity, yes, divine aromas wafted into its sensitive receptacles. All I smell now is shit. And all I hear when I play is the chatter of tradesmen who would kill me if they knew who I was. That, sir

---

[20] '. . . the land of Nod, on the east of Eden' (Genesis 4:16).

Monk, is why I bless you. Because you alone heard the essential. Not the dross, this life. You recognised my music. Your heart-strings trembled to it. And for such attention, much thanks.

Mnemosyne, mother of the Muses![21] how artless you are, to let slip from our heads much Learning but not our cruellest recollections. No sooner had the Minstrel finished his story – which filled me with great sadness for him and anger – than we were startled by voices. Men were approaching from the street. The Minstrel covered himself to the nose-tip with his hood; I likewise with mine. We huddled together behind the cheese crate.

Imagine our horror when the voices grew louder and four pairs of legs began to descend the cellar steps! There was a cramped recess by the cellar door: it was darker there, and we shuffled into it on our hams. Four burly labourers stopped only inches from us. They stood about the crate with their fingers to their noses, joking about the stink. We too held our breaths, though accustomed to the cheeses.

'Heave-ho, lads,' said one of the four. And daylight flooded over us as they hoisted the crate up the stairs.

It was I – it was the Minstrel – I forget who broke our cover, which was no cover at all. Gibbering and gnarled with cramp, we rose from the mud like the enshrouded dead. At which twin apparition, the labourers quite forgot their task. The crate teetered and toppled, it

---

[21] Mnemosyne, mother of the Muses.

upended, sending fat tomes of cheese cascading towards us. Despite the thick blood in my limbs[22], I caught my fingers on the cellar's ledge and hauled myself on to the street. The Minstrel, alas, barely had time to pass me his lute before the malodorous landslide overwhelmed him.

For several seconds, all parties were immobile. The labourers stood frozen to the steps, their hands still gripping the ghost of a crate. They looked at me. I looked at them. They looked at the Minstrel. 'It's him!' they exclaimed. 'The child-killer!'

At this point, for want of a better idea, I made the sign of the cross. And perhaps the blessing saved me, for immediately I sensed myself become invisible. I was free to watch, unimplicated, the scene playing out at my feet, as the labourers shook off their indecision and waded towards the Minstrel.

Helpless to intervene in a story from which I was suddenly excluded, I hoisted my habit and ran away. The streets filled with cries and the rumour of vengeance. Somewhere along the way the lute fell from my hands; I cannot recall letting it go, it disappeared as one loses the details of a dream upon waking. Yes, as I fought against the current of the crowd it seemed to me that I was returning to Reality. In my mind's eye I saw only the treatise that awaited me in the mute civility of the library.

---

[22] Cramp was thought to signify the coagulation of the blood for lack of oxygen. According to Dabčik, the stiffening of any part of the anatomy has the same cause. Hence (in reference to male arousal and its consequences) the euphemism *la petite mort*. See footnote 9.

Sure enough, the manuscript was exactly as I had left it, surrounded on all sides by the harvests of like minds. Still panting, I sat at the bench and eyed my fellow scholars. Here and there they sat, hunched in meditation or scratching at books with their sharp goose-quills. Slowly my breathing eased. The quiet of contemplation soothed my pounding heart. Judging it best to stay put for a time, I dipped my pen in ink and leaned over my labours. The library's walls were thick, its shelves well padded with books. I got up to close the window, and pulled the shutters to.

Explicit liber Godwottery

The Choristers' Prologue

'Well done,' says the Fool, soiling the Monk's quietus, 'you really distinguished yourself there.'

Monk. I was young and innocent.

First Chorister. Did you see the Minstrel's head on a spike?

Second Chorister. His corpse on a rope?

Third Chorister. Did you finish your tract?

Second Chorister. Your treatise?

Third Chorister. Your tract?

Monk. Er – my *Pudendae*?

Fool. Please! A little decorum, gentlemen, there are ladies present.

The Drinking Woman farts and guffaws. The Nun, resigned to suffering, lifts her eyes to Heaven and hopes for thunderbolts. It is the Swimmer (remember him?) who furthers the assault.

Swimmer. Brother Monk, I'm curious. Where *is* the famous library in Bruges?

Monk. The . . . library – ? It's in the . . . city.

Swimmer. Only I've lived there most of my life, and must confess I never found it.

Monk. Well, it's . . . before your time, I suppose.

The Monk sees creases of suspicion in the faces about

him. Beads of perspiration speckle his pate. 'I hope nobody questions the integrity of my story,' he blusters. 'If so, let him speak. Every word I said was true.'

Fool. Words are always true. It's the order you put them in that matters.

Choristers. Right, it's all relative.

Monk. No it isn't.

Choristers. It's subjective.

Monk & Nun. It is not!

A new challenge, it seems, has been set. The Choristers huddle, whispering, like conspirators. The Monk's innards flutter and he grips, with white knuckles, the edge of his table.

Choristers. Listen up. It's our turn.

The Choristers' Tale

Many years ago, in the town of Worms, there lived a physician by the name of Hans.

> *The man's name was Horatio. He was a surgeon. He lived in Wittenberg.*

>> *Hieronymo was a quack; and what's worse, a redhead. He scraped a living in the city of Worms, turning his wits on folk who had none.*

A scholar with a good local name, he was decent in his dealings.

> *His mind, over-educated, was not godly.*

>> *When his wealthy wife died he had her buried in the paupers' plot.*

Whenever illness struck,

> *if the humours were unbalanced,*

>> *or someone's ballocks ached,*

Hans put his skill to good purpose. He knew the properties of every herb. Cordials he made from liquor of couch grass, from comfrey, feverfew and celandine. He understood the workings of the body.

> *He was versed in the ways of the flesh.*

>> *and specialised in ailments of the codpiece.*

He could read both Latin and Greek. He knew Hippocras and Pliny and Plutarch.

➤ *The pagan writers of the south corrupted his head with heathenish notions.*

➤ *He knew a hundred drinking songs, like 'Frydeswyde the Frigger' and 'Gunda Get Your Jugs Out'.*

It seemed to Hans, from his learning, that God meant mankind to heal his body as well as his soul. For why else were there remedies locked in roots and leaves?

➤ *As a surgeon Horatio fought those ills that are sent to test us. Had he lived in the land of Uz he would no doubt have treated Job, glad to get in God's way.*

➤ *Hieronymo's methods were unorthodox but sometimes worked a treat. He knew, for instance, a potent cure for infertility. Before baldness and the pox stole his looks, he wintered one year in Weimar and did the childless wives there much service. In April he fled south to Worms – and wisely, for the autumn bore a harvest of red-haired babies.*

One evening Hans was shaken from his studies by the sound of heavy knocking. Taking his candle to light his way, he opened the door.

➤ *A monk stood in the street, huffing and puffing. His cassock was muddy, his face all marbled like a side of beef.*

'Sir doctor,' said the monk, 'your skills are needed. I have run this way to find you.'

➤ 'I've come straight from the monastery of St Simoniac. One of our brethren is ill, we fear possessed.'

➤ 'No!' said Hieronymo. 'A monk? Possessed? Here? In Worms?'

'Alas, you have been misdirected,' said Hans. 'I cannot perform exorcisms.' But the monk was adamant. 'Our abbot is away!' he said. 'We must fight Satan, if Satan it be. To be sure of our enemy, we seek a layman's diagnosis.'

➤ Horatio laughed. 'Possessed, is he? By a flagon of ale, I'll wager.'

➤ 'Yes, demons are rife this time of year. Only last week I chased a succubus from a summoner in Wimpfen. I'll just get my bag and we'll go fight the good fight together.'

Hans considered deeply. He was certainly curious to see the case; and the monk's words were like a challenge to his talent.

➤ Thinking highly of himself, Horatio agreed to follow, swearing all the way that Science would find the cure.

When they arrived the monastery was frantic with excitement. Hans walked through the cloisters.

➤ A crowd of monks gathered in his wake, like a plague of brown rats.

➤ They came to a cell near the chapel. The stench was terrible – Hieronymo recognised it immediately.

The cell was full of monks cowering and muttering prayers.

➤ *Horatio stood, proud and sceptical.*

➤➤ *A curtain was pulled back, revealing a fat monk strapped to a chair.*

The poor fellow – Brother Lempick was his name – stared wildly about him. His hair was unkempt, his tonsure neglected. Across his skin warts and boils festered. 'We dare not approach him,' said one of the monks. 'He fears the razor and abominates water. A sure sign of the Beast.'

➤ *Brother Lambert was his name. Demons had no dominion over him: he was an instrument of God.*

➤➤ *Brother Lubbert sat, bound and gagged, in the restraining chair. Hieronymo shot him a glance which no one else saw: it spoke of conspiracy. For on holy days Brother Lubbert was Lubbert the actor. In debt to Hieronymo, he had taken the role of the mad monk. So he drooled and snorted, growling like a badger and groaning like a bear. Whenever a monk drew near he spoke gibberish, or filled the air with hellish vapours from his arse. Sometimes he started and stared at phantoms, addressing them by their names: 'Abadon' and 'Astaroth', 'Mammon' and 'Mephisto'!*

Carefully, Hans examined his patient. He had heard terrible things of the monk's behaviour – how he spoke the Lord's Prayer backwards and crawled like a crab, how he bled from the eyes and flayed himself with his fingernails. But Hans spoke kindly and this seemed to calm Brother Lempick down.

➤ *It is the fate of God's favourites to be hated by the falsely righteous. The monks of St Simoniac beheld the aura that shone round Brother Lambert like the sun behind a cloud. They saw the love he bore God's creatures and how fervently he prayed – and for these things they hated him.*

➤ **Watching Brother Lubbert belch, fart and spit, Hieronymo had to admire the performance. 'Speak, you fiend!' he cried. 'What do you want with this man?' Brother Lubbert's eyes rolled like marbles in a basket. 'Shite! Fart! Death! I'll eat your head and shit down your neck!'**

'See, friends,' said Hans to the monks. 'Kindness with the sick always prevails.'

➤ *'Not with that fiend,' the monks replied, their faces crammed with slander. 'See how he stares and spits.' But Horatio could see nothing more than a white-haired monk, bound and gagged, lifting his eyes to the heavens.*

➤ *'I'll bugger your cattle! I'll batter your wife! Puke! Piss! Kill!'*

➤ *Then Horatio said, 'I see nothing wrong with this man.' 'He's putting it on,' shrieked the monks. 'Only an hour ago he was puking pea soup.'*

➤ *'Yup. It's devils all right. Whole squadron, I'd say. Exorcism's no good, it'd only inflame the lower dorsal hypotenuse. So, then. Pass the chisel.'*

*　　*　　*

'This man can be cured of his madness,' said Hans, easing the hair back from Brother Lempick's forehead. The captive monk looked at him imploringly, as meek as a lamb. 'I need three men to hold him.'

᙮ *Eight volunteers rushed to Horatio's aid.*

᙮ *To a man, the monks lost the use of their legs.*

After some trouble, three monks were volunteered. Hans, out of compassion, took the gag from Brother Lempick's mouth.

᙮ *'Keep the gag,' said the monks.*

᙮ *'I'll keep the gag,' said Hieronymo.*

'I shall make a small incision here,' said Hans. 'The distempered blood will flow from the brain and restore your brother to himself.'

᙮ *Fine: if an intervention was what they sought, Horatio would give them an intervention. 'It's a simple operation,' he said, 'quick and fairly painless. The science of man is on the move, gentlemen. No mumbo-jumbo can slow it.'*

᙮ *'Now, you've all heard of cutting for the stone of folly. This procedure looks the same, but it's radically different. You see, by opening the skull the air pressure inside the brain increases until it pushes the demons out. It's effective for devils as big as hedgehogs and as small as gnats. Survival rate is high enough. It is a messy business – but then someone's got to do it.'*

Hans unfolded a leather pouch.

⚘ *He took out his trepanning chisel and placed it on Brother Lambert's forehead.*

⚘ *Staring up, cross-eyed, at the blade, Brother Lubbert moaned for real fear. Violently he shook and foamed at the mouth . But the more he struggled the more convincing was the performance. He yelled through the gag: 'Stop! Stop! I'm an actor!' But the sounds made no sense and the press-ganged assistants slapped him down.*

Hans made swift measurements of Brother Lempick's head. The patient watched his movements with quiet, dog-like interest.

⚘ *Horatio hesitated. The volunteers, for all their keenness, had no cause to hold Brother Lambert down, for the old monk offered no resistance. His eyes were shut, as though trained on a better world on the inside of his eyelids.*

⚘ *Hieronymo grinned and sucked his tongue. Fat Lubbert had lazed about too long in his debt: it was time he learned his lesson.*

⚘ *The crowd leered in anticipation. Horatio began to sweat. He could not admit, even to himself, what his own eyes told him: that Brother Lambert's head was bathed in amber light.*

Hans put his lips by Brother Lempick's ear and whispered: 'This will save you, my friend.' He found the spot for the chisel. Then he rested the sharp edge on the skin and pressed it sharply down. Brother Lempick's skull collapsed like an egg. His brow frittered – the eyeballs burst like water blisters, and Hans paddled in the hot swamp of Brother Lempick's brain. The chisel snagged on something and was sinking down the monk's neck. Gasping and spattered, Hans struggled to pull the instrument free, but a claw emerged from the bubbling gore to snatch it back. 'Satan!' the monks cried. 'Satan is among us!' Brother Lempick's flesh crawled and puffed. Thick black fumes purled from open sores. There were slithering sounds, insidious and leathery. And demons burst, like spiders, from his belly.

~ *No, that's not it! You're corrupting the story.*

~~ ***Put a sock in it. You're* both *wrong. What happens is:***

~ *Horatio, in his pride—*

~~ *Hieronymo, the sly sod—*

~ *Horatio, in his pride, measured Brother Lambert's haloed head and found the place where he would dig.* You don't *dig* in trepanning!

~ *He found the place where he would dig and made an incision. The monks cheered as Brother Lambert's blood sprayed across the curtain. Horatio pressed the blade against the bone. One more push and the operation would be complete. He put his elbow into it and the bone made a satisfying 'crunch'. Bright red blood burst from Brother Lambert's wound. It poured in cataracts over the ground and stained the paving-stones. For all his skill, Horatio could not staunch the flow. Brother Lambert was dying. Horrified, Horatio watched the monks as they fell to*

*their knees in penitent rapture. His assistants, who,
moments earlier, had grinned like apes to see Brother
Lambert suffer, began to weep. 'God damn it!' said
Horatio. 'Can't you see this man is bleeding to
death?' But the monks were watching a saint's martyrdom. 'Angels!' they gasped. 'Heavenly Host!
Praise be to God!'*

*≈ Hieronymo squinted, took aim and stabbed
Lubbert in the nut. Lubbert screamed blue murder, but what came through the gag sounded like
'AAARGH! OOO UGGY AAG!' The monks squit
into their sandals, thinking they were set upon by
demons. 'Gentlemen,' said Hieronymo. 'This is all
part of the healing process.' But the monks were
praying in terror. Lubbert kicked and fell backwards, he farted and swore hellishly, his blood
spattering. 'It's a great success,' whispered Hieronymo. But he was making his way already to the
exit. The impressionable monks were seeing
things: imps and monsters, cooked up in their
heads, had broken loose, intent on devastation.
'I'll be off, then,' said Hieronymo. Nobody paid
him the least attention. Nobody, that is, but Lubbert, who in his rage had somehow snapped his
bonds and was getting to his feet. 'Easy,' said
Hieronymo – who took to his heels and fled.*

Hans cowered in his bedroom, clutching a psalter, as
demons laid waste to Worms. The night was bloated

with devilish music. Hymns and psalms were sung backwards; madrigals were groaned in gibberish, to the shrill agony of fife and flute. Hans covered his ears but the screams of the citizens pierced his head like daggers.

➳ *The city was transfigured. Paradise had taken root in the stones and cobbles. Birds of unthinkable beauty flew through the blossoming spires, making rich and wonderful song. In the streets, unicorns grazed where once curs and cats had scavenged. Yet the most wondrous change of all was in Wittenberg's citizens. Beaming with inner light, they sat and spoke with angels.*

➳ *'Lubbert, old pal, let's discuss this like rational adults.'*

'What have I done?' Hans wailed.

➳ *'What have I done?' Horatio moaned. Slumped to the floor in his library, he tore up his atheist books. 'I've killed a saint. Holy blood is on my hands and I can never wash them clean.'*

➳ *Hieronymo turned in the street. He could hear the monastery in the distance crash and holler. 'I'm sorry,' he said, as Lubbert rolled back his sleeves. 'It was all part of the illusion. Just listen to that crowd! You were sensational!' But Hieronymo couldn't talk himself out of this hole. 'I'm gonna eat your head,' said Lubbert, 'and shit down your neck.'*

Hans crawled to the shuttered window and peeped out. The night sky glowed orange from a thousand hellish fires. The street was a carnival of tree-hags and mice-men, of pig-boys and fish-girls. Something landed on the window ledge: an ugly bald bird, it laid an egg and greedily swallowed the hatchling.

Horatio swiped the air about his head. Something was buzzing in his ears.

'Help!' said Hieronymo, as Lubbert's fist landed in his crotch.

Hans lay curled up on the floor. This was the cruellest of griefs, for the madness that had burned in that devil's head was now the norm outside – and sanity survived (only just) in the head of Hans the guilty.

It is easier for an atheist to believe in Lucifer than in the grace of God. No wonder, then, that in his grief Horatio imagined himself plagued by monsters.

Before Lubbert's boot could make contact with Hieronymo's teeth, the ground trembled beneath his foot. The monks were running for the city centre, shouting their horrible news.

Worms had grown new towers. Dragons basked on the ramparts, their wings reflected, like charred branches, in the black surface of a moat.

Horatio had fled the city of angels, bringing his demons with him. The blessed miracles that flowed from Brother Lambert's blood were hidden from his eyes by clouds of angry beasts. They buzzed about his head. They crawled like lice through his hair. They sucked his blood with straws.

Hans saw these things from a distance as he struggled to catch his breath. Hundreds of demonic creatures had followed him as far as the city gates, tripping him up or throwing themselves under his feet, where their plump bodies burst like may bugs. Hans wiped the glue from his soles on the withered grass.

⁓ Horatio slapped at his face to destroy his imagined tormentors. But the pain of his blows drove him to a greater pitch of despair.

As Hans watched the suffering city, it occurred to him that the madness might be *his*. He knew from the pain that he was not dreaming – yet the swarm of demons was too awful to be true. Perhaps they were the surfeit of his over-nourished fancy?

⁓ Horatio looked back at Wittenberg. Where there was beauty, he saw only the Beast; where there were angels, he saw fiends. 'I shall be damned,' he said. 'I'll spend eternity in the fires of Hell, suffering with the evil dead.'

'If these scenes are my own doing,' Hans reasoned, 'then physician, heal thyself.'

⁓ Horatio scrabbled through his belongings and un-wrapped his tool kit. He sat down on a mound and lifted the trepanning chisel to his head.

With his other hand Hans readied a wooden hammer. He had never seen the operation turned on the self, but the thought of martyred Worms steeled him to the task.

⁓ Horatio brought the hammer square on to the butt of the chisel.

There was an instant of terrible pain—

⁓ —bone cracked like a shell—

—the sound seemed a long way off—

⁓ —it blasted like thunder.

Hans fell back on to the grass. His eyes were two mirrors of the sky.

⁓ As the life-blood oozed from his body, the despairing Horatio beheld Wittenberg in all its blessed glory. Words of praise formed like vapour in his mind. But he had passed up all hope of salvation.

'Lord, let my death bring an end to this dream.'

⁓ 'Damn it. Wrong diagnosis.'

Worms in the distance, like a meadow washed by a rainstorm, returned to its former self. A million demons, like mayfly on the flood, spilled into the River Neckar. They dragged the physician's body with them; but his soul ascended, clapping its hands, to Heaven.

⁓ Wittenberg's miracles outlasted the summer. The old found new vigour, the young found old wisdom. Fields yielded bumper harvests, slums were knocked down, churches built and the university founded. When the citizens found Horatio's corpse, they knew it for a suicide and buried it at a crossroads. What befell his spirit, only the Devil knows.

⁓ Very edifying, I don't think. If you're still interested, here're the facts. The people of Worms, being a gullible lot with too much time on their hands, spooked themselves into a frenzy. Hieronymo and Lubbert, sensing the danger, went into hiding. 'Revenge!' a crowd chanted, hurling stones at Hieronymo's house. 'He made this pla-

gue of monsters. Grab! Kill! Lynch!' Lubbert, still smarting from the cut to his head, sat up in thought. This made Hieronymo doubly nervous. ''Ere,' said Lubbert. 'It's you they're after, not me.' Hieronymo pulled a parchment from a drawer and quickly redrafted his will. 'In recognition of your friendship, Lubbert, I'm writing you in for ten per cent of my worldly goods.' The lynch mob battered down the front door. 'You've told your last fib,' said Lubbert as the first axe crashed through the wall. 'You ain't got no worldly goods.' Which was true in a trice, unless you think a halter and a stiffy much to boast of. And there's a moral, if you must—

Gentles, beware of the tales that you tell:
There's nothing so risky as fibbing too well.

Explicit liber Pandaemoniam

The Sleeping Drunkard's Prologue

Yes, you've noticed: we're running out of storytellers. All eyes turn to the Sleeping Drunkard dozing at the prow. Not a word is spoken, of consensus, so I couldn't say whose foot meets his ribs. The sharp jab jolts the sleeper, and one of his eyes peeps open.

All. A story we need a story give us a story . . . !

The sleeper groans. That other world claims him: he wades still in its self-forgetful waters.

Sleeping Drunkard. Can't give you a story – I don't know any.

'Oh, come', chides the Nun, 'we've all done our bit to pass the time.'

Sleeping Drunkard. We have?

Penitent Drunkard (*gleefully despondent*). He's not been listening.

The sleeper's eye, like a snail peering from its shell, retreats beneath its lid. The Drinking Woman, with fingers like pincers, prises open those shutters of flesh. The eyeballs roll, exposed, the pupils trying to shelter in the sockets.

Drinking Woman. We need something to keep us going!

Choristers. A song.

Nun. A psalm.

But the sleeper, still pinioned by the Drinking Woman (whose boozy breath stings his peepers), has nothing, nothing whatsoever, to offer. The rest of the crew pitches towards desperation.

Sleeping Drunkard. Perhaps there is one thing! If you'd let go of my eyes! (*Blinking and weeping.*) I have a recurring dream. It's not very racy. Probably it'll evaporate in the telling. (*He yawns, scummy-tongued.*) It will bore you.

All. Nonotatallquicklypleasetellit.

Sleeping Drunkard. They're only sorts of things in my head. No plot. No meaning, as far as I can tell. It'll most likely send you to sleep. (*A yawping stretch.*) Here's hoping, anyway.

The Sleeping Drunkard's Tale

Picture a room, a narrow room, with a sloping ceiling. Its walls are pale orange, though you can't much see them under paintings and books. Picture papers & pamphlets strewn across the white coverlet of a bed. Through the window you see the boughs of a chestnut tree – a small garden of holly and laurel – houses & trees beyond. This is the setting, that never varies. Now picture a desk, with a lectern & strange implements arranged upon it. These include: two lamps that burn no fuel, musical cabinets that require no winding, & a white bean with a grey tuber that sits on velvet & squirms to the touch. Hunched at this desk, a young man sits. He is tangle haired, pink cheeked. He wears a three-day beard. He scribbles inscrutably on scraps of paper.

That, more or less, is it. Though fancy bred, the vision is mundane. You'll get no strange entrances or metamorphoses, & only very little magic. The young man does not float weightlessly about the room, or talk to my dead relatives. There's just me, dreaming, & him, my dream.

Others in this eventless fantasy? His mother, his father. A cleaning woman, whose chatter he gracelessly avoids. Sometimes his cat, a languid beast with a black snout and sagging paunch, will jump on to the desk. It slumps on his work, & chews the corners of his books, & will not be moved. *Prlrhr-prlrhr*, the cat says. He gives up, quite readily, & scratches its head. He receives no friends. Nor, despite obvious reveries, does he enjoy the charms of women. For company, when he requires it, a black chest inlaid with glowing numbers fills the air with voices. He never engages these spirits in conversation, though at times he may abuse those with whom he disagrees. From this same chest – whose drawer slips out, like a tongue to receive the Communion wafer – he solicits music – some of it sublime, much impossibly grating – to which he tries, unsuccessfully, to write.

But to concentrate on his *work*, the cryptic scrawling – Sometimes, for amusement, he will crouch on his chair &, wiggling his toes, spin clockwise. When he tires of this, he paddles back again anticlockwise. He can alternate thus for long periods. Then you might find him slumped to the floor, picking flecks off the carpet or staring out of the window at the chestnut tree. Oh, my dream-figment is the dullest dream-figment in the history of sleep. I can't stomach him. Yet there he is, pottering *in perpetuum* in his cell.

He seems obsessed with a bleached bone. It sits behind him on the bed. When the bone wails he picks it up & soothes it with his voice. Later, he puts it down and returns reluctantly to his work. Or rather, his books. Have I mentioned his books? His compulsion for collecting & possessing them, the promiscuity of his reading, which sends him flitting from volume to volume without finishing anything. Now I'm just a humble conjuror, what do I know about learning? Enough to compare his bookishness to a hunter's zeal for trophies. He is as proud of those sheaves as a real man should be of his children.

But sticking to the point – Often he will break off for a nap. You've seen a cat turning fussily about itself to settle. He's worse. After battling with the coverlet & duffing his pillow, he dozes fitfully – a terrible snorer – which may explain his solitude. When sleep eludes him, he will exit & I hear voices, remote, from the next room. There is music, too, & shuffling. But I never hear his voice alongside the others. And not one of those neighbours calls round to visit.

Isolated thus – save when his mother comes with advice & socks, which are folded & tucked & arranged for him in a drawer.

Isolated thus – excluding the cat & his cheerful brisk father – my young figment – for what is he, if not the phantom of my heated conjuror's brain? – my figment, I tell you, come evening, clings to his scribbling as to a rock in a perilous ocean.

Let me describe his occupation – his preoccupation – anyway, his method – if that isn't too strong a word. First he scrawls, in a cramped, illegible hand, on scraps of paper, using the backs of bills, fished from a basket & pressed flat with the side of his fist. When he has dirtied, to his satisfaction, all the white spaces, he pins the scrap to a lectern & transcribes it, with alterations, in a green ledger.

The green ledger version, when completed – every inch filled, with blottings mostly & crossings-out – he transcribes, with alterations, into a small blue book. Cribbing from the small blue book, he thrums on lettered ivory keys. A white box sighs – *pffvwiiizsssjjioouuw* – on to printed quarto – which he corrects with red ink – whereupon he thrums on ivory keys – & the box sighs quarto print – which he corrects with blue ink – whereupon he thrums on ivory keys – & the box sighs quarto print – & so on, until he cannot possibly take it any longer.

The words, by the way, are all Greek to me.

As time passes – if you'll pardon the expression – & I grow weary of my charge – depriving myself of sleep's supposed balm – as time passes, I say, *he* wakes up. Night falls & there's so-to-speak life in the fellow. He works with gawking open mouth & shallow breath into the small hours. When at last he winds things up, he goes through rituals. Counting his books. Arranging his slippers. Checking for spiders under the bed. Once his cell is in order – with papers piled & the spirits put to rest – my figment reaches beneath the desk. This is where the contraption purrs. He reaches beneath the desk, where I have no vision, for the purring to stop. And I wake up.

I am almost sorry to do so. For without my dreaming him, he has gone out, snap, like a candle. So I head back there, when I can, to give him more life. After all, I conjured him up. The dreary lumpen fellow owes me everything. He is my punishment. For humbly I confess, all my life I have been the most wretched sinner. I have conned, hoodwinked & bamboozled the credulous with my sleights of hand. Moneys, jewels, whole family wages I have magicked from innocents' pockets into my own. To hear me speak, in my trickster prime, of kabbalistic lore & devilish pacts, while at the rapt crowd's back my assistant picked the people's purses, you would expect a dreamscape of strangeness and resonance. But no. Having done good to no living thing, I must endure my boredom as penance. *He* is the dependant, my disappointing child.

And yet – sometimes I get an inkling – *yuah* – an intimation that I might be mistaken. Perhaps I am *not* the father, refined from his creation. When he is away too long, my eyes fill up with fishes. A shark glides from left to right – a moray eel peeps from a rock – air rises, in precisely recurring patterns, from blinking limpets. There is a washy sound of the deep, punctuated by bubbles – *flfo-fflofvl-blovf* – & a dreadful calm. Until he returns & I am rescued from the sea.

You know – *orr* – how the gorge – *wuah* excuse me – how the gorge sometimes rises? Well, that's – *wooaah* dear – how it feels, when the dread takes me. The dream is like a whirlpool. I can get no deeper into the spout of it.

Lately, lastly, my dream youth is hard work personified. No longer dallying or ineffectual, he wears a fixed expression. He has a gleam in his eyes. There is murder in them . . .

'IN GOD'S NAME (the listeners howl), SOMEBODY SHUT HIM UP!'

The Glutton's Prologue

Collectively, the Choristers with their fists and the Drinking Woman with her flagon and the Nun with her lute and the Monk with his sandals cudgel and kick their torturer. Curling up, the Sleeping Drunkard suffers their blows until the frenzy subsides; lying there, the reprimanded conjuror could almost be asleep.

Choristers. A new story, come!

The crew searches for the Glutton. All that they find, behind the bush-mast, is a leathery bag. It twitches and growls; it grumbles; foul-smelling gases escape from its lining.

'Where is he?' asks the Nun, pinching her nose.

'In there,' says the Fool, pointing his staff at the noxious sack.

Monk. It looks like a chicken.

Drinking Woman. A wineskin.

Fool. It's his stomach.

Without a tale to contribute, and maddened by the foul-arsed bird, the Glutton has devoured himself. Nobody in the fracas of the last narrator's beating heard his sounds of pained delight, such as a man might make between the chaps of a damsel, or when tasting spices in quick, tearful bites.

The flatulent sack says—

The Glutton's Tale

Fff. Oo. Pprrpffrrppfff.

Epilogue

The stench is not that of your usual gas but redolent of
the entire Glutton. It's as though a whole life has been
broken down and expelled as vapour. One catches the
honeyed fetor of baby turd; a mother's sweet milk; and
the oniony tang of growing bone. The crew of the boat
gags at chemical miasmas of lust and ambition, and at
disappointment, which reeks of rancid cheese. There is
no escaping this olfactory chronicle: it passes through
fingers into the nose, as a shout, for all that one covers
one's ears, will penetrate the skull.

Nauseated, the Fool vomits from his vantage aft,
drenching the Penitent Drunkard and setting off the
delicate Monk. The Nun, finding herself spattered with
belly-beer, brings up cherry stew over the table; which
sends the Drinking Woman puking into her flagon;
which, overflowing, drips on to the Sleeping Drunkard;
who fills the stern with a quart of home-brew. The
Choristers, caught in the crossfire, scramble to their side
of the boat and evacuate, in time-honoured fashion, the
contents of their stomachs into the sea.

Last to spasm (once the Swimmer has contributed his
modest pint) is the Penitent Drunkard. You might imagine that, after all this time, the fellow has nothing left to

surrender; and you'd be right. It's like watching a starved bird attempting to regurgitate. The hard lump that plips into the water looks no bigger than a hazelnut. Yet it is, I have no doubt, the cause of all that follows.

Squinting at this hard-crusted phlegm, the Penitent Drunkard is startled to see something wriggle up at him from the depths. A funnel-shaped worm, the colour of tripe, opens a pink orifice and gobbles the floater. Quietly horrified, the Penitent Drunkard takes hold of the boat's ladle and – in an attempt to kill the scavenger – slaps the water. But the worm is neither destroyed nor frightened. It catches, in what can only be called its mouth, the neck of the ladle and tugs it from the Drunkard's hands.

'That's our bloody rudder!' shrieks the Monk. 'How are we supposed to navigate now?'

There is no time for an answer. The boat from frame to mast begins to tremble, shaken by fierce displacement of water. The sea, only yards away, explodes. A quivering mass, twice the width of the vessel, surfaces. It looks at first like a net winched heaving with fish. I cannot, for all my frightened efforts, assemble the parts into an animal whole. Sickly opalescent bodies twitch within its ambit, exposing the supposed worm as the tip of an appendage.

'I can't believe it,' protests the Penitent Drunkard. As though in proof, a monstrous, barnacled claw catches him by the throat. The wretch is hauled, jerking and wheezing, from the boat. Nobody makes a move to save him. And the monster sinks beneath the waves, dragging its quarry with it.

The response one might expect, from witnesses to such horror, does not materialise. No screaming or wrenching of hair. The survivors keep acidly still, mastering even their eyelashes, as though the flicker of a film of skin might be enough to attract similar disaster to them. Of the Penitent Drunkard there is no sign; only a few bubbles, of uncertain origin, breaking disconsolately on the surface.

In this stillness the Swimmer, conscious of the inhabited fathoms below his naked legs, attempts to scrabble on board. 'For God's sake man,' someone above hisses, 'hold *still*.' It is the tactic of the rabbit faced with implacable dread. The Swimmer, however, responds like a fish, thrashing about in panic and drawing the deep's attention.

How shall I describe the final assault? You will have experienced, strolling beside a lake, the eye-snagging leap of a fish: that sloppy, sleek body arching out of strangeness into burning air. Now magnify, if you can, that predator one hundredfold. It is such a fish that bursts from the sea, swallows the dangling ball of dough and snaps the line. Most people on board have the sense quickly to avoid the descending fin – which slaps one of the Choristers square on the back. Propelled unconscious into the sea, the poor fellow begins to take on water, as a wafer soaks up wine.

'Save him – oh, save him!' his kinsmen cry. But they too must undergo transformation. A second Chorister glazes over with sweat the consistency of honey. He licks his lips and finds his tongue sticking to his chops.

His eyelids glued together, his hair pasted to his scalp, he must not see the swarm approaching. It falls out of nowhere: a deafening, humming cloud from which the others cower. Bees the size of starlings mob the man, ramming themselves avidly into his mouth, until he tumbles backwards out of the boat.

His neighbour, meanwhile, finds his index finger growing – elongating into a hollow tube the length of a reed. Too long to fit within the boat, it hovers above the water, until something hidden bites the straw and begins to suck. We watch in despair as the third Chorister blanches, his skin emptying, and he is lugged over the side.

Now general mayhem is unleashed. The Drinking Woman bickers with a tentacle until (cunningly stealing her flagon) it lures her into its element; where she is clapped inside an oyster shell with only her feet emerging.

Praying for deliverance, the Nun finds herself assaulted by her own wimple. It stretches like a membrane across her face until, blinded, she steps into the rump of her lute and topples overboard.

Not that the boat itself is a place of safety: scaly brutes with unmentionable tusks gash its wooden flanks.

Now, on my left, the Sleeping Drunkard weeps and sinks, gripping his glassware flagon. To my right, the Fool is imprisoned in the maw of a devilish whale. As the water rises to its palate-roof, he clings to the gaol-mouth's bars. 'At last!' the Fool shouts, quaking with rapture. 'At last!'

Above me the Monk – attempting to escape the rising bilge – clambers feebly up the mast. But he slips on chicken grease, and his habit ravels up to expose stark pitted buttocks. With a squeal, he ditches in the unwholesome soup. A slow, lugubrious creature, with eyes of unblinking anthracite, swallows the Monk's watery cries, which re-emerge, excreted as whispers, from a dark, mysterious rectum.

Something clammy, like poultry skin, brushes against my feet. I read sickness and dread in the Swimmer's face. His tapering fingers slip wetly from mine. Sharp pain travels up my arm as the creature burrows into him. Our eyes meet across the chasm. My mouth, I know, is incapable of speech, and I bid the Swimmer no farewell as he slips, lifeless, out of my reach.

For a long time (it seems) I wait in the desolate open. The mast sinks at my back. Its boughs sigh, drowning, each leaf growing a fur of bubbles. I picture the Swimmer nearing the sea floor, arms mildly floating above his head, his eyes closed, a world locked in behind the lids. All that he'd wanted was an open ear – and I would have listened, yes, in spite of his conceit. Gladly I'd have trudged, all puckered, in the wash, kept afloat by his discourse, had it only been new, always renewed I mean.

Now that he has sunk, I must come to the surface.

The Second Swimmer is me.

Recalling how it all began (this chronicle, I mean), I cannot fail to notice an oversight in my prologue – a clue to my existence, which I'd hoped to conceal. I alluded, did I not, at the outset, to a begging-bowl but never assigned it a beggar, placing it in nobody's hands? Of course, the begging-bowl is mine. I had filled it with seawater. Quite intentionally, for the others to take note. 'Drink, dream and be merry, friends: to this brine you must sink.'

Exactly why they must drown I never know. Is it punishment or cleansing? For sins venial or mortal? If either, why the Fool? The fate of the others – with their carnality, their pride and despair, their sloth and gluttony – I could perhaps account for. But licensed fools should be reprieved: their satirical calling ensures them immunity. Perhaps the sea covets his motley skills, jesters being servants, chattels of a kind? Or does Fortune weary of those that know Her game? The Fool was, after all, so sure of himself, defined by dress and custom.

No such certainty for me, the Mute. I am like an echoing chamber.

Is it not telling that I should forget the fundamentals (of my life, I mean) when I cannot purge myself of the meanest syllable that they uttered? I should be glad, no doubt, of those tired old fables for company. Instead I rage at their voices, which circle about me like gnats at sundown. I imagine them all, becoming argil on the seabed, such as potters use or vintners sometimes to bung their bottles. But *alive*, what was their purpose? What *use* were they put to?

They bore witness. However clumsily, however fancifully. Where there was absence, they added to Creation. Now that I have recalled their loss, and repeated their tales, surely like them I deserve release? It is my ever rekindled hope. That in this act of retelling I too – being watched over and suffered for – will be permitted to forget.

I picture them caught among banners of kelp. Fishes pick at their bones. Their lives unravel like spools of wool. They are forgetting, undreaming their lives.

Now the last sprigs of the mast go under. Robbed of its lookout, the green owl spreads its wings. Breasting the water, it lifts sharply and fires a pellet at my head. I rinse, as best I can, my black cap in the sea, and watch the bird flap in the direction of what I like to call the horizon. Briefly I see myself from its perspective. A struggling worm I must seem; the Glutton's stomach a beech nut.

That gruesome sack floats by. I clap my hands to my ears, not to hear the whimpers, the gibbering, of the Glutton's particular hell. I strike out against it, pounding and kicking the filthy water. In my progress (you'll forgive the expression) my knuckles knock a floating object.

It is the begging-bowl.

I take it between my teeth, leaving my arms free for swimming.

Far ahead, the owl dives, as though ditching itself in the sea. But the owl never drowns. That is not its function. It settles, in fact, in the top branches of a tree. The tree seems, at first, to grow out of the water, as though this were land not long ago flooded. Something dark, like the undercase of a walnut, and colourfully occupied, sits beneath the boughs. No voices carry on the timid breeze; yet I imagine well enough the banter and the bawling. That old familiar sickness squats in the quag of my belly. I swim towards the ship, which is, rather, a boat.

Let me describe it to you.

Acknowledgements

Thanks to Isobel Dixon, Helen Garnons-Williams, Natalie and Simon Lindsay, Antony Peter, Jill Shepherd and Major W.A. Spowers.

Much of this book was written during my stay as writer-in-residence at Wellington College, Berkshire. Thanks are due to C.J. Driver and to his successor as Master, Hugh Munro, for their invaluable support.